SOUL INTENTIONS

MICHAEL CANTWELL

Soul Intentions is fiction. Names, characters and incidents are the product of the author's imagination or used fictitiously.

DEDICATION

This is dedicated to everyone who has read my stories. Thank you. I am humbled. I would also like to give special thanks to all of you, who inspire me to create characters and continue to write stories.

For what shall it profit a man, if he gain the whole world, and suffer the loss of his soul?

Jesus Christ

MOR3 T!TL3S

A Beautiful Song
Three Long Days
Soul Directive
Fortunate Soul
Presidential Shadows
Presidential Whispers
Presidential Blues
True Justice

michaelcantwellbooks.com

For 10 free short stories visit:
www.michaelcantwellbooks.com/story

CHAPT3R OИ3

The granite steps were damp and cold from the drizzling rain falling on an early British afternoon. The time had come for me to return what was never mine. My subject sat with his hands covering his face, his shirt torn at the sleeve, his breaking point near. I cautiously sat on the same steps to his right knowing the time was now or never. It took nearly five minutes before Dylan James reacted to my presence.

"Your face seems familiar to me," he said. "People assume because I meet hundreds from around the world and I'm generally surrounded by bright lights and cameras, I wouldn't notice when someone is following me. I do. Who are you? Are you a fan looking for an autograph? Or do you want to sit here and pity me like so many others do now?"

"It is not important for you to know who I am, but only that you focus on what you believe is lost in your life. If you don't, it will be impossible for me to give you back what you seek."

My subject had been without his soul far too long. I do not know for sure what it must feel like to lose something so valuable, yet in watching my human targets struggle without them for several decades, it is not a feeling I want to know firsthand.

His tired face and frail body slumped even more at the shoulders. However, for the first time in months, I knew he was ready for me to restore his soul. He stared down into the cold grey steps where we were sitting.

"I know I'm lost," the rock and roll legend said. "My wife left me far too young. My ability to do the only thing in life I have ever loved was destroyed, yet you sit here, a total stranger and I feel like you know all this without me telling you, and I don't know why. Did you do this to me? Did you take my most precious of gifts from me? If you are the one who is punishing me, please stop. My daughters need me. My band needs me. I need me. Please, I know you've been following me for several months and I don't know why. But if you can help me, I beg you to release me from my misery!"

Maybe I did pity him to some degree. Here was someone who had everything most humans seek, yet because of one mishap in his life, he threw it all away.

"You did this to yourself fool, but I will try to repair the damage you have done. However, I cannot repair what is broken until you open your mind and body. Allow yourself to understand what it is you have lost. It is imperative you admit to yourself what you have done to your life."

Dylan frowned. I could tell he was still a non-believer, but I continued.

"Stop blaming your ills on everyone else and admit you are the one responsible, not me, not your family, and not your band mates. It will be in a single moment, a simple frame in your life, where I can offer back what was stolen from you because you stopped appreciating all which was given to you."

He lifted his head. Our eyes met. I focused on his face and hit the shutter release. Mission complete. I noticed one small tear leaking from the corner of his left eye as he asked, "How long was I without it?"

The Council forbid me to be doing any of this, but I felt obligated to tell him. It seemed I had broken so many ancient laws already, what was one more? Choking back my own emotions, I could only respond, "Longer than I had anticipated, but let us both take comfort in knowing you are whole again." After delivering my final remark, I could only hope he had found his long lost hopes and dreams and my Elders would not send me back on another mission to again steal what I had just returned.

Myself, I felt drained of life, yet somehow relieved. My subject was given a reprieve, something I had never before attempted. My body reacted in the opposite way to what it felt when I stole all the souls in my past. To return one was new to me, and expressly forbidden by the laws of our High Council.

A young woman, who recognized my subject, now sat to his left. She spoke to both of us, but with my senses dulled, I could barely speak. I was not sure I could stand and walk away, but I knew I had to try. My legs wobbled as I hobbled down the many steps of The Royal Albert Hall. For a few moments, I was not sure I would survive my last snap of the camera shutter. It was not until a tall stranger, clean-shaven and pale skinned with long flowing white hair, whispered for me to lean on him. When I did, instantly my abilities to function became normal.

Some cultures believe someone can steal your soul if you take their photograph or they see themselves in a mirror. Others believe you can lose part of your soul with the click of a shutter release and still others have no desire to seek the truth. Those who believe that such a force exists know the truth. How can I be so certain in my words?

I am one of the few remaining, who roam this earth, and are responsible for collecting broken souls. They are the damaged souls, ones in which my Elders have deemed far too ruined to deserve to remain within their earthly bodies. However, the time had come when my Elders had lost their way for not hearing my pleas. Anytime I talked of exploring it my way, I was branded a heretic and shame was brought to my family name.

"Caeles our mission is clear and concise, the longer you deny our truths the more you damage all of our kind," I would hear from the leader of the High Council on a regular basis.

In Latin, they call it "anima furtim," to steal one's soul. However, over time I began to develop my own plan, my own system. Unfortunately, my first attempt made me weak and disoriented. The system needed work before I would try again. Despite my Elders objections and threats, there will be a next time.

Many of my superiors had lost faith in my judgments. I was now being tracked in the same manner I would track my own subjects. Once word spread I had returned a soul, the Elders were furious with me. What else was new? I had again over stepped my limits and used my powers with little regard for our laws. The Elders were furious that I restored a soul years after I had stolen it from the original owner.

"We ordered you before our Council yet again because our powers are to take, never to return," Elder Orcus said with a puffy red face. "Our mission is not to offer hope to the hopeless or restore what has been deemed forever broken. These people we send to you as subjects, they don't deserve to keep their most precious of all gifts and you know this Caeles. You've been taught this since you could barely read and write, yet you insist on disobeying us, even with our most sacred law! Have you nothing to say to defend your actions?"

What could I say? It was true in all my years of reading the ancient scrolls, nowhere did it read where our kind could or should restore souls our kind had already stolen. Our mission on earth has always been to steal from humans, who no longer appreciated their blessings on earth.

Yet as I stood before the six dying men, who comprised our highest Council, the Elders who would decide my fate, I felt confused. I recognized our powers grew stronger the more we stole. This was not my opinion or a lesson taught to me. It was physical. I could feel all my senses explode with energy every time I ripped a soul from my intended target.

4

I could feel it when others of our kind stole as well. I knew it was very important for our own survival to continue to steal. However, after I restored my first soul, and discovered respite on another's shoulder, I felt a moment of peace in my own soul, never realized in my past.

"No, Elder Orcus, I cannot defend my actions before the High Council," I said staring at all six men on the dais. "I only beg that before you hand down your ruling you seek to understand the power of healing can be a powerful source of energy, possibly more than destruction."

"Damn you Caeles. Have you not listened to a word I've told you today, or the last time you stood before this Council? We've shown you mercy in the past, yet you continue to develop powers not permitted by our laws. Do you not realize I have the power to destroy your soul as you stand in front of me?"

My powers grew stronger each day. I peered at the three hundred year old men deciding my fate. Any one of them could have removed my soul with a flick of a finger. However, I refused to believe that I had to answer to any one of them for my actions.

"Caeles, I can see into your soul as I can anyone else's here on earth," Orcus said. "I see confusion and murkiness that was not there the last time you stood before this Council. Our entire survival depends on thieves like you to be strong and vigilant. As you are aware, our numbers have diminished in recent years. We once numbered in the thousands across the globe with the power to steal. Now we are but a small number who still possess the sacred power granted centuries ago."

I stood defiantly listening as he rambled.

"If you insist on returning souls, I don't know what will become of our kind. You must know all of us felt the same weakness when you restored that pitiful man's soul. That includes your own family. This Council cannot and will not tolerate your reckless behavior in restoring what is broken and jeopardizing our people's existence here on earth. Rules have been in place for centuries and will exist long after your time on earth has expired."

As Charon Orcus, the highest of our Elders, sat staring down at me with his piercing black eyes and long grey hair, again scolding me for my actions, I knew I was at a point of no return. My previous penalty for disobedience disallowed me stealing souls for a year. That might seem like a holiday for many, but for every year we cannot steal, we lose years from our time here on earth.

Our powers thrive from thieving. He understood by denying me the right to steal, it not only weakened my body, but also disoriented my mind to the point of permanent dementia. However, the longer he kept me from thievery, the longer there was one less on earth collecting broken souls. We cannot survive as a species without collecting and feeding off broken souls.

Orcus conferred with the others, before announcing, "This Council will no longer tolerate you developing new powers. Do not dare to believe that your newfound skills can save you should you attempt your foolishness again. I can assure you the Council of Elders will have no mercy on you. Your punishment will be harsh, swift, but just. You cannot continue to behave so poorly by ignoring our decrees and customs. Should you break any law or attempt to take another soul before my ruling; your fate will be death. Now retire to your home and await your punishment."

With his decree, I knew of only three words, which would allow me to leave with my soul and possibly my life, "Yes, Elder Orcus."

The Council placed themselves with a difficult decision. Remove me from the ranks of the few remaining soul stealers and slowly watch our kind suffer, or go beyond their archaic beliefs and listen to my plea that healing souls can nourish us as well. I held out little optimism they would hear my plea.

CHAPT3R TWO

Magister Verax lectured me as a child. He not only taught me the basic skills and subjects expected from someone residing on earth, but also about our history. A curious learner from an early age, I would constantly request information about who we were and why we seemed different.

"Magister, why all the secrecy and how did we develop our special skills in the first place?"

"These are not developed skills," the bulky two hundred and ten year old man explained. "They were granted from the heavens above. After Jesus Christ hung on the cross, the Lord of Life wanted to punish man for his evil deeds. Our kind was created to remove the souls of everyone who could no longer see the gifts bestowed upon them. In return for devoting our lives to stealing damaged souls, the better we did, the longer we could endure on earth. Comprised of fifty men, fifty women, all about the same age, and all from what is now present day Western Europe, they became the original disciples of the Lord of Life."

"How were all these men and women chosen Magister?"

"The first chosen were a direct descendant of our leader, Charon Orcus. Charon's ancestor was given the task of finding another ninety-nine humans to follow the laws given to us. They would learn to thieve damaged souls. The Lord of Life gave the initial one hundred the amazing responsibility and power to see into a soul and steal it if necessary. A power we are never to exploit."

"Magister, over time we have moved around the world, how do we know who belongs to our kind and who does not? After all, we do seem alike on the outside. And another question, why can't we all see into souls or steal if we are all from the original one hundred as you imply?"

Veras smirked. "Caeles, our bloodlines have been a guarded secret and stored on the island of Crete throughout the generations. Because some in our history have comingled lives with pure human form as lovers, once they did, none of their offspring have been known to develop the ability to see into another's soul. Taking a pure human as a partner is not forbidden, but it is not encouraged either. It has drawbacks since our secrets are then exposed to a wider audience. But then again try telling Mrs. Jones next door your husband will live nearly three hundred years and might remove your soul and get her reaction. If you get close enough to form a bond with our kind, you are not likely to advertise it. It is also one theory as to why our species is now struggling to survive here on earth."

He continued on, "Eventually we all die dear boy, as will our Elders, but careful attention is paid to making sure our Elder's bloodlines have remained pure throughout our history. It is one reason why they are the Elders and you and I will never carry that honor. No Elder through all the generations has ever mated with a pure human after the Lord of Life bestowed upon the original one hundred, the gift. It is carefully regulated how many of the purest of lines procreate. Your family has a history of taking humans as partners, the most recent being a grandfather on your mother's side of the family tree. Even though you may develop the power to steal as you age, you will never develop the ability to see into another's soul. Only the purest of the bloodlines ever develop that power. This is not theory, but proven history."

I remained confused. "Magister, am I to understand that even though I may develop the power to steal, I will never develop the power to see into another's soul? This is because my family has mated with pure human form thus interrupting the bloodlines?

And only if I can see into another's soul will I have the right to sit on the Council?"

Not sure of being totally committed to his response, he softly said, "That is correct Caeles, only the purest of bloodlines will ever have the power to see and therefore have the right to sit on the Council. Despite our dwindling numbers, the purest of the pure are still kept to a minimum."

I must have muttered under my breather louder than I thought, "We will see about that," since I clearly remember getting a stern look as I returned to my lessons.

I grew up in typical suburban neighborhoods outside of London, England and Madison, New Jersey, as well as Rome, Italy. We moved quite a bit during my youth. One issue we have is since we live up to four times longer than full-blooded humans, our appearance changes slower than your typical person. It is an odd thing for someone, who looks like a child to humans, yet is nearly forty years in numerical age. That was me. Our family had to move every few years not to draw attention. When my mother passed her one hundredth birthday, she had the beauty of a twenty something woman. Not an easy thing to explain to nosy neighbors.

It was not an easy childhood, since when I appeared to be a ten-year-old boy I already had the knowledge of a thirty five year old man.

My mother would tell me, "Most thirty five year old human men act like ten year old boys, so you will fit right in." I assumed she was teasing me.

By the time I looked like your average teenager, I spoke several languages. I was well versed in the math and sciences as well as world history. I also had read many of the literary classics. It did have one big advantage. I was popular with local teen-age girls, who saw me as a genius. On the other side, some of the boys used me as a punching bag because of my perceived advanced brainpower. However, I kept a good journal of names, hoping I could pay them a return visit later in life, to rip their souls from their abusive bodies.

As well as my tutor, my father also explained to me that I was one in a long line of people given a special talent. One where I could possibly develop the ability to capture souls for the good of our own race's survival. Not everyone in our bloodlines, not him, or my mother ever developed the gift to steal or see into another soul. Not even the Elders could explain why some developed the power to steal, while others did not.

Some wanted to believe it had to do with the bloodlines. Others wanted to believe even though we were granted the right, it was still a skill that needed to be learned and developed. Like any skill, some beings happen to be better at one thing over another. For me, I am not so sure, since I watched my father work at developing the skill for years when I was a child. It was a great honor among our people to remove souls. Most, if not all, worked diligently to develop the precious skill.

My mother never worked at developing the power. She would tell me that her bloodlines were filtered with too many pure humans over the generations and in her opinion, "I never had the patience or desire to put forth the effort needed to learn."

In truth, I think she was happy to be a mother and support my father in making sure we had a peaceful home.

In numerical age, the number fifty remains important to our kind. It is the day the journey begins in learning how to steal souls. By that age, despite still looking like a young man of eighteen years, we have reached the age of "liberty." We are educated to steal by our fathers, even if our own fathers never developed the skill themselves. The lessons are knowledge that has passed through the generations. It is not important if you are male or female, at the age of fifty, it is the duty of a father to administer your training. Some give up quickly, like my mother told me she did, but most take it to the final stage.

Training for me was a series of physical and mental challenges all designed to get my mind, body and soul in top form. It ranged from becoming a top player in chess and poker, to yoga, to being lost in the woods and using the brightest stars to guide me. Our kind produced several grand masters in chess, along with winners of top poker tournaments around the globe. We almost felt guilty in taking the prize money, but we also had our bills to pay.

In chess, we learned patience, as well as to learn how to think steps ahead of our opponents. In poker, we learned to read our opponents thoughts. We watched for facial expressions, and learned how to bluff. Yoga and other physical routines were to keep our bodies in top condition. Our mothers closely monitored our nutrition from the time we were born.

For me, I knew I would develop the skills after left to defend myself in the northern sections of Australia. It was when I first felt one with nature. While there, I thought I was spying on a tribe of Aborigines, watching their every move, only to discover they had been watching me all along. I spent three months with the tribe learning about nature and their culture. The tribe leaders taught me how to value what grew from the ground and what lived in the local waterways.

It was the first time in my life that my conscience really got the better of me. Once the leader and I could communicate on a basic level, I knew he was suspicious why I was lost in his land. I knew I could not tell him anymore than I was attempting to "become one with the land."

It had others in the tribe weary of me as well. However, once they realized I meant no harm, it became easier to enjoy and even occasionally participate in their rituals. If you look hard enough, you will find a drawing of my visit on a large rock in their region drawn by one of the elders of the tribe.

I spent too much time away. I was ordered to justify myself in front of the Council. My time allocated was to be no more than thirty days. I was gone ninety-three. Lucky for me, once the Council realized my skills had taken great leaps while in Australia, I only a stern warning was issued.

Despite there not being a hard and fast time for the training, it generally lasted about five years. My father schooled me with the idea, "The number five has a special power of healing."

I never understood how learning to steal souls led to "healing" when I was younger, but possibly, I strived to understand. I always suspected my family had secrets they did not want me to fully understand until later in my life.

The hardest part of my training was when I expected to develop the power, knowing my father never would, and my mother forfeited her chance. I could see the envy in my father's eyes. Yet, other times I felt his joy. He always stood by with words of encouragement, like his father did for him. His father was a master thief. I never knew if my grandfather was disappointed in my father or not.

For me, I knew there was sadness behind my father's words when he spoke of never being able to achieve the skills. He did all he could to disguise it, but from time to time I could feel his emotions running deep inside me. Even though I could not see into his soul, I could sense more than I anticipated. I did not know exactly what the feeling was, but it became more evident the more I trained. My senses honed to others.

Before attempting the final stage of removing a soul, the last step in training was to become a salesman. It was so we would have to deal with society directly. It was a lesson in patience and empathy as well as attempting to understand what made humans tick. This was not my favorite part of training. I much preferred living in the back regions of Australia watching the stars. Humans can be rude, arrogant and insulting to people they perceive as weaker. It only showed me most times they were only masking their own insecurities, while attempting to act superior.

Little did any of them know, even though I looked to be a man in my early twenties, I had traveled the earth many times over, and my knowledge of the world was vastly superior to almost everyone I attempted to sell a car. Yet, I had to learn patience and not spill out my story. I will admit I came very close to attempting my first stolen soul with one incredibly rude ass of a man from New York. However, once again, I logged his credentials into my journal begging our paths would again cross.

My father made it to the same point I was at in my training years before me, but he never could complete the final task. I knew secretly he attempted the last test even at an advanced age, but he never succeeded. I wanted to believe deep down he was pleased with me, but he was also a proud man who never could accept the fact he failed at taking even the weakest of souls.

The final step was to remove the soul from a small animal. Even though our mission was to only take from humans, who had lost their ability to appreciate life, one exception was made to ensure we could succeed before investing time and energy on a much larger subject. Since we cannot sustain our kind on common animals, large or small, we limited our test to one success, on one small animal, generally a common rat.

"My son, even though the past few years have been difficult for you, this last step is the shortest in time to complete, yet only a small percentage of us complete the task at hand," Father said. "If you give it your total focus and desire, it will be over in a few minutes. Now, do something I was never able to do, feel the power of removing the soul from this rat. It will not give you the same sensation as a human. We do not feel it throughout our kind should you succeed like we do when we steal from a human. But you will feel the rush from removing a soul."

I wanted him to let me get on with it, but he refused to rush into anything.

13

I warn you," he said. "if you don't feel it, do not lie about it and continue the journey to the Council. If you tell them you're ready, but never felt what you should, you will fail without question on your first mission with humans. Should you fail, you will never be given a second chance. Don't lie about it. I don't have the experience to tell you how the sensation feels, but you will know if you succeed. I wanted so many times to believe I felt it, but I knew I was only attempting to convince myself of a lie. "

How was I supposed to know what it felt like if my father could not properly explain it to me? It did not matter. I had anticipated this moment for over fifty year. I shook inside, but careful not to let my father see the fear rooting deep inside me. He knew I was strong willed, but we both knew less than twenty percent of us now could remove even the smallest of souls.

We purchased a rat from a pet store, which was supposed to be snake food. I surrounded the brown rodent with my eyes and thoughts. I looked at the fear in his eyes as if somehow the creature knew what was about to happen.

I reached down and cupped him in the palm of my hand. I felt his fur. I felt the uneasiness in the rodent's body. I closed my eyes. I tried to connect as best I could with the rat. I could clearly hear my father's heart pound in his chest as he stood nearby. I could feel the breeze pick up as we stood in the open field. I could the smell the rain off in the distance. I felt and heard every movement in nature that surrounded me and the other living souls in my vicinity. I lowered the rat to a small patch of open dirt so that I could get a clear view, and snap, I took my first image as a soul stealer.

Instantly, a bolt of lightning touched the horizon in front of me. A surge went from my fingers up to my brain then down to my toes. It did not last long. I asked my father if he felt the ground shake or for a tiny instant feel the earth standstill. He did not. I knew my training had concluded.

Should I make my presence known to you, it could be as any name or occupation, though my given name is Caeles Novo. I will look to you as an ordinary person walking on the common streets across any section of the globe. Depending on how well I complete my mission, my life here on earth could extend close to three hundred years. Yet despite my unique aging process, my kind is very similar to the human species, with human emotions and human frailties. I am trained to take from you the one thing you should not ever want to lose. I am very, very good at my vocation. You might consider me an assassin. I was trained to believe I am doing society a favor by doing the work assigned from the heavens.

I've lost count at how many times I have taken a soul. In recent times, I fear my actions are not saving our existence, but damaging it. It is a painful transition when you question if your life has been a lie. Everything I taught to me now rushes through my brain on a daily basis. I question my mortality. I question if am truly doing the work I was destined to do. I am trapped in a world I spent more than fifty years of my life studying, yet I realize I know so little about who I am.

There are so many days I want to hide in a remote part on earth, never to be found. Yet, every time I succeed with a mission, my kind flourishes. I am recognized as a savior. I feel a rush inside me that ordinary humans only think they experience when they speak of a "rush" for winning a championship or doing something good for another.

I feel that same sensation, only it is magnified a thousand times over. The earth stops for me every time I steal a soul and for that instant in time, I am one with the world. I should feel gratitude that I am able to experience something that so few who have lived on earth could ever know, yet inside, I am broken.

From the time we can speak, we are taught to recite our mantra. We are lectured to do it the first moment we awake, and when we lie down for the evening. I have recently had too many sleepless nights with those short words radiating in my brain, no longer convinced I utter the truth.

"You, the ungrateful fool, who dare to destroy your soul. We are the keepers of all things pure and righteous. In taking your soul, we are destroying the evil you have so carelessly allowed to enter your most prized possession."

The High Council and Magister Verax have pounded this idea into my senses so deep, that I can't fathom how I could question something so ingrained in every fiber of my being. What could be wrong in me correcting a wrong? Why should I pity your irresponsible acts? If you can't take care of the perfect gift given to you at birth, then you don't deserve to keep it, right? It was all I knew for many decades of soul stealing. I was led to believe this was my purpose in life. Is my life all a lie, or am I destined to be the greatest soul stealer who ever walked the planet earth?

CHAPT3R THR33

Photography was one of the skills my father instilled in me during my five-year training period. "Caeles, photography is the study of light. How you manipulate that light to your advantage is what you must learn. Over time, you will learn how to be a better photographer and the many ways you can control light. For now, understand you can control it with the shutter speed, the aperture, the speed of the film and the speed of the lens. Your assignments will never be to take the perfect image, but to identify your subject on the emulsion of that small strip of plastic. After all, the Elders are the ones who dance in the shadows and the see whites and the blacks of your inner core. They are the ones responsible for decisions about whom we steal from since our victims cannot see the beauty in their world. They are the ones who decide who keeps a soul and who does not."

Photography was new to our kind. Over the generations, the methods of thievery have changed using different human senses. Originally, they used the sense of touch, and for a short time, the sense of smell. As technology developed so too did the Elders who adapted by changing the methods. For many years, it took two to steal, since they used a system of having the subject cross a path between two mirrors. When my father was assigned to teach me photography, in some ways, we learned the creative process as one. It was one way our relationship grew stronger.

Once, while photographing in New York City's Central Park, I found my way into a debate with an art student. He wanted to question if photography was an art form or a hobby. I played along until I got bored with his immature way of thinking and left him with, "It's a science that can artfully steal your soul."

The poor boy had no idea what I meant, but he did upset me. I do admit to losing my patience quickly with anyone who cannot see that photography is an art form as well as a science.

After having lived on earth for over fifty five years, it was time to be set free to do what I was trained to do. I was in top physical and mental health and appeared to humans as a man in his early twenties. Photo training was done using the first camera ever given to me, a Kodak Brownie #2. It had coarse leather like covering and used 120roll film. It was nothing like the current digital cameras, which have made my job in recent years much easier. Kodak once claimed, "You push the button and we do the rest."

Keeping it all in perspective, Kodak had no idea how little the camera did compared to what I was assigned to do.

My first mission using my new skill set was on a young rock and roll singer and piano player. His career began to take flight in the 1950's. My assignment was to take his photo while he was performing if possible, but from the start, my goal would not be that simple. I was still learning the limitations of working in low light. In the 1950's, getting an image on film with any solid values was not an easy proposition in a concert hall with bad lighting.

The light was poor and the Brownie camera and film could not compare with the speed with which you can capture an image these days. The limitation of the lens forced me close to the action on stage to make sure my subject was in the photograph. It was also the only way to get enough light to enrich my negative. Fighting a hoard of young screaming fans as well as security all the while keeping a steady hand was not going to be so simple. A blurry photo would only extend the task. Bodyguards surrounded my victim off stage. Getting him in a photo alone even in day light was not an easy proposition. I needed him in a photograph all to himself. No one else could be captured in the same image for fear they might lose their souls as well.

Since the Elders were still working out all the limitations of using a camera, I was given some leeway as far as the time given to complete my task. Even they were not convinced only the main subject would lose their soul if others could be identified with certainty in the frame. I told myself that was the reason why I would not take the photo quickly and assume mission accomplished. I recognized on my first assignment, it was not as simple as pushing down on the shutter release.

Johnny Joe Jackson was dynamite with a set of eighty-eight black and white keys at his fingertips. He played his piano as if it was on fire. Funny thing, I think it was the second time I watched Johnny Joe perform, he did in fact light his piano on fire. Along with his instrument, he almost set the entire convention hall a blaze while at the same time hammering away on his white baby grand as if no one else was in harm's way.

The last remaining sounds struggled to find their way from his instrument while he practiced his madness. "They call this the devil's music, well let's burn this house down since you are all in hell for coming here to see me tonight," he yelled during the encore.

Hardly a crime worthy of taking one's soul, but Johnny did have his demons. He was belligerent on and off the stage not only to his pianos, but to anyone who dared cross his disturbed path. I was told he didn't start out that way. By the time I met Johnny, he was destined to be a star in the music business. Later he enjoyed a string of number one hits to prove it. However, as good a musician as he had developed into, he had grown into even more of a despicable person.

Johnny Joe was born in Mississippi in 1934, the last of five children. His parents were lower middle-income people like many in his region, but proud hardworking decent folk. He was raised in a religious home. At a tender age Johnny Joe made it clear he was never going to be a weekly attendee at church, even though his parents begged him to go.

Since his family was not financially able to offer him more than one hot meal a day and a handful of hand me down clothes, he rebelled from the start. Early in life, Johnny's sins never equaled even a low-level criminal.

He never cheated, lied or hurt others intentionally, but every day he grew more distant from the world. His family did their best to get Johnny to appreciate his surroundings, but they failed on most counts. He never felt the warmth of a large family desperately wanting to offer him love. Even as a youngster, he saw himself as a loner wanting to spend time staring into space with no direction and little hope.

By his mid-teens, it was a chore to keep Johnny interested in school. He learned to lie about his daily whereabouts when expected to be sitting at his desk.

"I really was there Dad. Those lying teachers are trying to make me look bad," he would say. Johnny was a poor liar, though he did not care.

Shortly after turning fifteen, he would occasionally skip school the entire day and take long bike rides across town. It was there he heard a distant sound coming from a tired building in desperate need of some paint and new window.

Johnny peddled his bike closer to peek inside the half-broken window to hear what the unidentified sound was coming from the building. A fresh sound overtook his senses. He spied upon ten old men sitting on wooden chairs swaying back and forth to soulful beats and joyful rhythms. Johnny had heard music before in school, but this was different. At the other edge of the room were four dark skinned men with sweat pouring from their faces and smiles a mile long, obviously enjoying themselves.

Times were not easy for some in the Deep South of the United States since segregation was very much alive at that time. Johnny's skin was pale white. Like his mother, they each had a string of freckles down their arms and across the bridges of their nose. He had grown to be a boy of over six feet tall, like his father and his father before him.

At fifteen, Johnny's jet-black wavy hair matched his fathers. However, Johnny's foul mouth was something his father never tolerated. In this era, most children were raised with better manners and respect for their elders, not Johnny Joe Jackson. His parents did what they could, but Johnny was not one to take orders easily. No matter how hard as his parents tried to raise Johnny properly, never acquiesced.

As the music played on, joy pumped through Johnny's heart, a rare occurrence. He began to swivel on his bike seat to the beat of the music, until a hand wrenched his left arm.

"Hey boy, you got no business looking inside this window," a male sounding voice said. "And for sure you got no business on this street."

As Johnny turned to unhinge whomever it was who dared to grab him, he noticed a large colored man twice his own size in height and width. Johnny decided punching the larger man maybe wasn't his best option. The music stopped, as Johnny was dragged by the arm into the wooden building, with only a cracked wooden floor and a few thin walls between freedom and a group of strangers.

"Look here what I found listening outside dat window," Johnny's captured said. "Seems here this boy made a wrong turn and thought he could just wander up in here and listen to ya'll play."

There were now several men staring back in Johnny's direction, some smiling and others giving him a not so friendly stare. Silence struck for several moments, until the piano player

21

broke the silence, "Well next time you want to listen to some good music boy, don't stand outside no window, pick yourself a chair. Only we reserve the ones in the front for us colored folk. You sit that bony ass of yours in the back row if you wanna listen."

"I weren't looking for trouble Mister," Johnny said, "but I just never heard music like this. I wanted to see who was playing it. I didn't mean no disrespect, and I wasn't spying. I liked what I was hearing. That's all." Johnny stood partially terrified and partially defiant not knowing what else to do. His comments removed the tension from the room.

The piano player stood up and moved towards the center of the room within breathing distance of Johnny. They observed each other, neither side wanting to budge. Inside Johnny shook with a fear he had yet to experience in life.

Calmly, the man who appeared to be in his late thirties, walked completely around Johnny and the man still attached to Johnny's arm, two, maybe three times. The room was silent as he looked deep into Johnny's now ready to tear up eyes, and fired back, "Like I said boy, then you need to pull up a chair and listen to some good ole' fashion blues."

The stranger, who had Johnny's arm, shoved him towards the back door when Clive barked, "Let the boy git some learning in what the blues does to a man. Don't send him home to his mamma howling just yet."

Clive "Fingers" Johnson was the piano player in the band. He stood over six feet tall with a lean body and hands that seem to stretch half way across the set of black and white keys. His infectious personality instantly seemed larger than life to Johnny. Clive's smile filled the room as he returned to sit on his wooden stool in front of his instrument. The two guitar players wrapped the shoulders straps back around them as the drummer yelled out, "One, two, three." The room again filled with a sound Johnny Joe Jackson would never forget.

Johnny twitched nervously in his chair. His right foot no longer take commands from his brain. His foot furiously tapped the wooden floor following the heavy beat of the music. He noticed instantly how much passion Clive and the others had for making music. Clive's left hand zigged while the right hand zagged across the keys.

The taller guitar player, now completely covered in sweat closed his eyes when it was his turn to take the lead. He bent the strings on his Gibson flat top to make a sound that would make most wail with delight. The other guitarist soon followed the lead with his Epiphone Emperor, while the drums pounded out a rhythm surely never played in Johnny's neighborhood. If they did play these sounds, why had everyone kept this from him? Was this what he had been seeking every time he sat looking off into space during classroom lessons?

The smaller guitar player sang with a ragged voice chirping words about loss and despair that somehow Johnny thought he relate. However, these men lived the blues and played the blues. Johnny knew he had stumbled onto something unique in his small world.

The band was practicing for only the third time as a group. Clive was the oldest member of the band. He had searched some of the local bars and hangouts to form a band. He found Jackson "Pappa" Collins to play one guitar, Leon "Sly" Graham on the other, and Buddy Jones to pound the skins. One of the locals owned the partially burned out building and was letting the band use it to practice. The owner of the building asked the band to let any locals sit and listen in exchange for using the building. The band didn't mind, since they enjoyed an audience. They hoped to play in front of a larger group, but for now they were hidden away in a small rural neighborhood.

After listening to the band practice for more than an hour, dusk approached rapidly. Johnny knew it was time to head home. As he made his way a few feet to the exit, the band stopped again and Clive yelled out, "Hey boney ass white boy, we practice again on Saturday, maybe you should come back." Johnny smiled and waved as if to let them know he would return.

Upon returning home, his parents were upset he skipped out on school for the entire day. After all the yelling stopped ringing in his ear from his father, Johnny tried to explain where he had been and what he had seen.

"Dad, twas music like nobody plays round here. I wanna learn to play like them colored folk do."

Johnny's father didn't know if he should ground him for skipping school, or be happy that possibly he found something in his life that made him smile. Johnny kept yapping on and on until his father agreed Johnny wouldn't be grounded, but it was only if he promised not to skip school. If he went to school, he could go back to hear the band again on Saturday.

For one of the few times, Johnny kept his word with his father and went to school the remainder of the week. He couldn't wait until Saturday. He paid attention all week in class not wanting to upset any teachers and lose his chance to hear the band. Johnny's mother didn't want him to go back, since she didn't know the men or the area. She tried to get Johnny's father to tell him Johnny he couldn't return. However, Johnny's father knew he could use it to keep Johnny in school. Neither side wanted to go back on their word.

CHAPT3R FOUR

Johnny was the first person to arrive at the building. On an over cast Saturday afternoon, he sat out front for over two hours, watching a few crows fly overhead in search of a meal. Occasionally, a neighborhood kid walked past to inquire if Johnny was lost.

Clive finally arrived in his beat up truck. He jumped out from behind the wheel wearing a large smile and began to quiz Johnny. "I see your mamma let you come back, or didn't you tell her where'd you be heading? And don't lie to me boy, Clive don't take kindly to no liars, you hear?"

"I ain't gonna lie to nobody, and my mamma don't tell me where I go and don't."

Clive laughed at Johnny. "Yeah, sure smart mouth. I been round the world and if there's sumtin I know, mammas don't like it when their boys wander off to strange lands, especially with colored folk. Or did you forget to mention that to your mamma?"

"I told her and my daddy where'd I be going and what I'd be doing, and here I stand. Maybe you ought be worrying if your band's gonna show up and not bout my mamma."

Again Clive laughed. "Them boys will come round here soon enough. Why don't you come inside and tell me where you from. You might start with your name, boy."

They wandered into the building each sitting on one of the tired wooden stools again staring at each other almost daring the other to blink.

"Not much to tell, I suppose. My name is Johnny Joe Jackson. I don't got many friends, don't like school, my daddy likes to yells at me, my mamma cries at me, even when I ain't done nuttin wrong. Only thing I know is, I was counting days till I could hear y'all play."

Clive looked closer at Johnny, almost as if he was trying to see into his soul. He wiped the side of his unshaven face from just under his nose to below his chin, waiting for more words from Johnny, but they never came. This time Clive blinked.

"Well Johnny long name, mine's is Clive Johnson. My friends can call me Fingers, but right now, you ain't yet one of my friends. Maybe someday you will be, but not today. I don't make friends easy. You listen here. I got me some friends. I got em all round the world. You see, I used to play ball in the Negro league, but you ain't likely to know much bout that, now do ya?"

"No, my daddy never was much on traveling too many places, and I never played no ball."

"Well, I played all around parts of the south, all the way to Kansas City. One of my teammates was the greatest pitcher of them all, Satchel Paige. He's the one who gimme the name 'Fingers.' Most people suspect it's cause I play piana, but it ain't. Satchel looked at the way I gripped that baseball with my long fingers, and he never did call me nuttin else."

Johnny stopped Clive, "My daddy says Babe Ruth was the greatest of them all. He never told me bout no pitcher named Paige. But like I said, I don't play no ball."

Clive sat back in his chair, not surprised at Johnny's remarks, but he still gave him a reply with a stern tone behind it. "You take a good listen to Clive. You white folk, ya'll too scared to know the truth bout some things. For one, Mr. Paige woulda struck out that fat boy Ruth. And you can run home and tell your daddy I says so. I seen Mr. Paige up close. When he wanted to strike somebody out, he did. You know nuttin bout the world boy."

"I know enough to know I ain't going to be in Mississippi all my life. Don't know what I plan on doing yet, but I'ze be moving on from these parts."

"What you think you gonna find out there boy?" Clive asked. "I seen the world. I seen things that would make a silly ass fool like you run home pissing in his drawers to his mamma."

Before Clive could finish his thoughts, Johnny felt he needed to prove he was not afraid to see anything, and he was not going to be intimidated by Clive or anyone else. However, Clive was determined to finish what he had to say.

"I was playing ball one day and next, I was grabbed up for the United States Army, to chase Nazi's across Europe to kill Mr. Hitler. I'm telling you boy, I seen crows eat the eyes from dead soldiers, others with their guts hanging out, still alive begging for the doc. I seen people burned out of their homes. I seen kids left screaming in the streets. You think you know horror boy, but all you knows is your mamma mad cause' you don't do no chores. Don't come round here thinking you know shit, cause' you don't. Now, you want to sit up in here and listen to my band play music, that's all good by me. But you gotta mind your manners, if you do, maybe ole' Clive will teach you about life and how to play this here piana. But if you get all uppity with me or the other peoples that come round here, I won't pay no mind when they take you out back and kick your simple minded ass all the way back home. You feel me?"

Johnny wanted to fight back, but the urge to hear the music was greater than his urge to prove he was not scared of anyone or anything Clive had to tell him. "Damn, Mr. Clive, will you really teach me how to play the piano, really?"

"Oh, I see now I got your attention, eh Johnny long name? I don't do nuttin free, so you'ze have to find a way to pay me back. Maybe if you learn to tame that problem you got with staring at me, I'ze find my way to teaching you some simple songs to play."

The door cracked open. The other members of the group walked into the building and prepared for practice. They talked about being surprised to see Johnny had returned. Clive directed them about what he wanted to play and they all got started. During the three-hour jam session disguised as practice, some from the neighborhood wandered in and out.

Johnny listened to the entire session, watching every move each musician made. Before practice ended, he started to visualize himself as the leader of that band, only he was the one playing the piano, not Clive. It would be a large white baby grand, on the largest stages around the globe. The ladies would be falling at his feet and all the men would envy him.

In the coming days, Johnny spent more time with the band and in particular Clive. He started to offer Johnny a few lessons on the piano. Over time the band and the locals, who listened to the band, all took a liking to Johnny. Maybe it was because he was one of the few with skin the color of curdled milk, who treated them with respect, or maybe it was because he appreciated their music. Either way, they shared a kinship rarely seen in Mississippi in 1948.

If not for the relationship with the musicians and the older men, who would listen to them play, Johnny might have self-destructed in a fight amongst his peers long before he could reach maturity. He was not one to pick a fight, but he surely knew how to use his fists to end one.

Johnny begged his parents and school music teacher to offer him lessons on the piano. His music teacher began offering them twice a week after school, hoping to keep him coming back to school. However, as soon as Johnny would break into one of the early songs taught to him by Clive, he was informed it was, "the devils music."

Johnny's dad would warn him, "Son if we pay for lessons you have to learn to play what Mr. Joel wants you to play, not what you want to learn. If you will do that, I will find the money to pay for your lessons. But only if you do it the way you're instructed."

Johnny was so desperate to learn, he did it his father's way, for two more lessons. He was never going to be able to persuade anyone to allow him to sing and play the music he wanted to play, other than Clive. It frustrated Johnny to the point of finding one last reason not to finish school.

The idea Johnny could not express himself through music only fueled his anger against his parents and anyone else who could not see this was now his dream. When the men would ask Johnny why he was not in school, his response was always the same, "They don't let me go there no more." The men were smart enough to know it was not true but then again, Johnny was not their son and only Clive had finished high school out of the four in the group.

Clive showed Johnny patience no one else had in his lifetime. The lessons Clive offered were not structured lessons of masters in the past. They were lessons in two keys and twelve bars. Johnny Joe quickly allowed the piano to become an extension of both hands.

Clive could tell the boy had some talent and because he was an eager learner, he would offer Johnny lessons a few days a week before the band would play for the locals. Eventually, the band allowed Johnny to play one or two songs when they performed at the local hall, where they had dances on weekends.

Johnny was the only white skinned person in the church hall, but he paid no attention to it. The locals didn't seem to mind it much either, because if Johnny didn't care why should they. It was all about the music, not discrimination. Johnny and the band only cared about the music.

Over the next eighteen months, the band started to play for money on weekends in small halls around the state. It was to mostly colored audiences, since it was difficult for them to play in the white sections of town. Even if they did on rare occasions, the audiences did not show up in the same numbers that would in colored areas.

That was until Clive came up with the idea to put Johnny out front as the face of the band. He was now a handsome freshly minted seventeen year old, who could attract young females and a wider audience.

The band had Johnny sing lead on many songs and he would sit behind the piano for a few, although it was agreed that Clive would remain the bandleader and piano player. Johnny didn't care. He was out front of a band, which was now getting hired in halls with white audiences. Then, it all changed.

Arthur Amison was the heir to a British steam ship company that sent goods back and forth from England to India. He had no real desire to run the company day to day, but he did have a passion for music. He also had designs on finding the next Django Reinhardt. Arthur had seen Django play in Paris a few years earlier, and was now on a mission to create a record label and find hidden talent across Europe and the United States. He'd been looking aggressively in larger cities known for musical talent like New York, Chicago, New Orleans and Memphis in search of one undiscovered gem, before deciding to make a trip to smaller communities.

While driving through Mississippi, he stopped in a small town called Tupelo. He spied a sign with a young singer playing that evening. The Clive Five, featuring Johnny Joe Jackson, were about to become famous beyond anyone's dreams.

Arthur Amison stood over six feet tall, a very polished looking man of average weight, wearing a finely fitted suit. He exuded confidence with every move. Aurthur worked his way back stage after the show and asked with his very proper and British accent, "Who might be the leader of this soon to be famous ensemble?"

Clive always weary of strangers, politely stated back with the same amount of confidence in his Southern drawl, "Depends on who be asking, now don't it Mister?" Clive never could shake his habit of going nose to nose with strangers, especially when it came to people asking about his band. He moved into Arthur Amison's personal space daring him to back away.

"Right. Well, my name is Arthur Kevin Amison. I've been traveling your fine country looking for musicians and songwriters that can join me in creating a record label here in the States. I'm looking for something fresh and exciting. Your boy who sings, he has energy and the raw sound I've been driving myself mad seeking." Before he could say more, Clive spoke.

"Look here, Mister Am-I-sun, Johnny ain't my boy or your boy, and don't you go round thinking none of us ever will be. So, you can take your fancy clothes and that fancy tone in your voice and find yo-self the door."

"Well, we seemed to have gotten off on the wrong foot, what is your name, Sir?"

"My name don't be no concern of yours, and we doing just fine the way we is."

Over hearing the conversation between the two men, Leon the bass player, interrupted Clive before he scared Amison away for good.

"Clive, why don't you listen to what the man has to say for his self? You think we not good enough to be on a record album or something? Get yo brains out yo ass for a minute and listen to the man."

The others in the band also took notice and convinced Clive to listen to what Mr. Amison had to say for himself.

"Sorry Chaps, I do apologize for my sudden appearance, and I certainly didn't mean to be disrespectful by calling anyone boy. I'm from across the pond in England and well, at times even though we speak the same language, it seems we don't. I will only take ten minutes of your time, and you have nothing to lose. I've already signed up four other groups and one songwriter for my new record label. I intend to make it a smashing success. Give me ten minutes and then I will be on my way."

Within the hour, the band scribbled their names on a contract making adding them to the roster of the newly formed Checkers label. Clive remained hesitant to sign off on the deal suspecting bad things were about to happen, but the other band members could not wait to ink the contract. Clive relented.

"Alright then" Amison said. "My man Eric Lowell will contact you about getting some new suits and a proper shave. I will start working on getting you booked into some bigger venues. Who is the songwriter in this group?"

Clive showed he was not ready for any big changes. "Hold on Mister, we'd not agreed to wearing no suits, and we play the songs that's been round since I was knee high to my daddy. We still going to play what we play. You hearing me Mister?"

"Yes, yes of course you are Mr. Johnson. But if you're going to be recording musicians, you will need some original material and well your clothes, well, you need to look like successful performers. Let's try it my way for a few months. Shall we, Chaps? If after we try my way, you're unhappy with our success, you can tear up your contract. So tell me, who writes your songs?"

Johnny stepped up, "I do."

"Right, well then, it's settled. I want you to come with me to Chicago and meet with the songwriter I hired last month. Her name is Alexis Simpson. She's a pretty young lady and has written some simply fabulous numbers. I think they will be perfect for your band, but I want you to sit with her and well, make them your own. When we possess four numbers that sound positively smashing, we will put all of you in the recording studio."

Johnny Joe Jackson was off to Chicago leaving the others behind with puzzled looks and one sour attitude.

CHAPT3R F!V3

Chicago first impression hit Johnny harder than Joe Lewis right hook. This was a city where he could feel the energy the moment their Buick sedan hit the city limits. His previous existence revolved around rural Mississippi, with the highlight playing in front of four hundred adoring fans, not far from his hometown in Jackson. One busy street near Wrigley Field on game day had more people walking on it, than he had seen in one gathering place. It was a complete culture shock to him, but very pleasing.

Mr. Amison introduced Miss Alexis Simpson to Johnny and left them alone in a hotel room to, "Make me some smashing sounds that will make people, as you young Americans say, boogie in your seats." Amison was off to scour the streets of Chicago in search of another recording star.

Alexis Simpson was a shy eighteen year old in search of her identity. She had responded to an advertisement that Amison had put in the Chicago newspapers. He placed an ad stating, "Searching for someone with strong writing skills and a wonderful imagination to change the world through music."

Alexis contacted him the next day, picking her from the more than fifty others, who contacted him from the one-day advertisement. Despite her age, her parents refused to allow her to leave the Chicago area, until Amison could prove their daughter would be safe in his care.

Alexis had the looks of a beauty queen, but her woman's curves were always clothed in a conservative fashion. Her looks were always hidden while growing up. Her radiant jade colored eyes and long flowing lashes were the first thing Johnny noticed about her. Her soft innocent smile was second.

In return, Alexis couldn't take her eyes off his perfectly combed jet black hair and perfectly honed body. He was no longer the, "skinny assed white boy," found peeking in the window. He had developed a man's body with an immature eighteen-year old mind. Johnny may have been married to his music, but he instantly realized Alexis Simpson would be his mistress. Alexis was star struck with the teenager, who was not yet a star.

"They don't make girls like you where I come from, Miss Green Eyes," Johnny suggested in his very boyish and inexperienced way.

"Oh, then maybe you should tell me, how do they make girls where ever it is you come from John?"

Johnny stuttered, looking for the right comeback, but he had never been around a lady before. He had only met a few girls from school, but in those days, he paid them little attention. Besides, Alexis grew up in the big city. She had seen boys come and go, and attempting to garner some attention from her. None had success. She wasn't going to fall for his weak efforts in charming her.

After several back and forth words with Johnny stumbling badly, Alexis let him keep what was left of his dignity.

"Mr. Amison is paying me," she said. "I'm not sure about you, but he is paying me to write songs. I prefer to do that so I can retain my employment beyond today. If you can keep your mind on working for a few hours and stop staring at me, maybe I'll show you our beautiful city. But you have to promise me you'll focus on our work this afternoon."

The idea of Johnny being pushed around even slightly by this female was not sitting well at first, but as she batted her eyes and offered that soft smile with her pouty lips. He quickly relented to her charms.

"Yeah, he's gonna make me a star. My band's back home waiting on me to make some songs too, so I guess we should do some writing. But I think it best you do the writing part on the paper cause my spelling ain't so good."

Alexis gave him one last smile. "That's fine John. I'm the one with the pencil, so it only makes sense I do the writing."

She had previously written several songs on her own before meeting Amison. She and Johnny reviewed them for several hours. Johnny may have not finished high school, but he was quick to learn and had a well above average intelligence. Both were pleased with the results. After a few hours of hard work in updating them, to fit more of a blues style, and Johnny's voice, they were off to see the big city.

As promised, Alexis took Johnny on a tour of the lakefront, as well as parts of downtown Chicago. He knew he could never return to his roots in Mississippi, unless it was to lead the band in front of a large audience. One full day with a fine looking woman like Alexis, and in a big city only fueled Johnny's desire to be a star.

They worked as a team for several days until Mr. Amison had seen enough to know it was time to put the band in a studio and to start promoting them.

"The two of you are just splendid together," he said. "You have done amazing work. Now let's get the rest of the band here, Johnny. Oh, I am so pleased, so pleased. Johnny, I have someone who is going to take you around to watch some of the other performers in town. I want you to notice how they play to the audience. Watch what they do. Alexis, I have another band in town starting tomorrow. I want you to sit with them in the studio and help them finish a few numbers they have already started. They're more of a singing group, but I know you will do wonderful things with them."

"Ah, scuse me Mr. Amison, but I thought Alexis was my songwriting partner?"

"She is my dear soul, she is."

"Then why you going on having her work with some other group too?"

"Well, she works for my company, Mr. Jackson, same as you. I pay her. I pay you. When the day comes that you pay her, then you can tell her what to do, until that day, you will go see the singer across town tonight, and she will be up early working with the men I assign her to work with. Now, run along. Call your bandmates and have them drive to Chicago by the end of the week. I'd like the band recording no later than Monday of next week."

Johnny gave Amison a long stare, but realized there was not much he could do. Amison was going to make him a star, change his life forever. He needed to watch his temper. Without Clive around to keep Johnny in check, his temper came close to boiling over more than once.

"Hey Clive, good news. Tell the rest of the band to get on up here to Chicago right away. We got four songs to record and Amison says we can do some of the ones you like too. He wants us recording by Monday."

"The fella's is ready to go. I still don't have a good feeling about this whole thing, Johnny. What you find up there in Chicago?"

"Just get on up here, Clive. The place got people hopping all over. I'm going off to see some singer tonight and I met this fine lady who can write some pretty music. She got fancy words and a fine looking body too."

"You keep your mind on to your music boy. Don't be thinking you be up there to be doing nothing more than making music and getting out-a there. You pay good attention to ole' Clive. I keep telling you. I seen many places and many fine looking women. They want to take your soul from you if you not careful. You hearing me Johnny?"

"Don't you worry bout me, Clive. I got this going on now. You collect the fellas and get on up here. Not only do they have fancy ladies, they got food like I ain't never ate before. And the buildings so tall, I lose them in the sky. They got ball teams up here Clive. I seen some place they call Wrigley Field."

Clive laughed loudly over the phone, "I know all about the ball clubs up there, boy. I'ze be there in three days. You make sure Amison, he don't forget who the main man is, you hear?"

"You the boss Clive. I know. He knows. I'll see you in a few days."

Five days later, The Clive Five recorded what turned out to be their first hit played on commercial radio, 'Seeing In Your Dreams.' Songwriting credits were given to Alexis Simpson, Johnny Joe Jackson and Arthur K. Amison. The band was so excited to hear the song being played in front of Parker's Five and Dime on a new Philco radio. They didn't pay any attention to the song writing credits.

They had never read the contract's fine print either, where it stated that any songs recorded would list Amison as one of the songwriters. Within a few weeks, the second single was released, which played in the larger cities from New York to New Orleans.

Venues opened their doors to the Clive Five. Amison had it set up, where all of his acts would perform on the same stage, during the same evening. It didn't take long before The Clive Five were the headliners. It also wasn't long before the band's name changed to, 'The Clive Five, featuring Johnny Joe Jackson,' permanently. Clive was furious with Amison when the change was made, but Amison pointed out the fine print in the contract, where he had the right to change the name of the band.

The others, in particular Johnny, didn't care since they had money in their pockets and food in their bellies. They even had made enough to send a few dollars back home to support their families. Amison was shrewd, but he was smart enough to know to give them just enough cash in their pockets to make them feel satisfied. He also made sure they were performing six days a week, so they didn't have much time to really think about it. Amison had other chores to tend to rather than constantly be on the road with his recording acts.

Johnny quickly became a star. On nights in larger venues, two pianos sat on stage. One was out front, where Johnny played a handful of songs and the other was tucked off to the side of the stage, where Clive would be playing the majority of the piano parts. Johnny's was more for show, though he did learn to play four or five songs. After four months on the road performing, the bands were called back to Chicago to record more singles.

Johnny kept in touch with Alexis, sending her a letter almost daily, and on his off day each week, he would call her on the telephone. She had been following the band's progress through his letters. Johnny sent some Alexis some ideas for new songs.

Despite that Mr. Amison wasn't around often, he had his assistant Gabe Fisher Jr. run the operation. Gabe controlled studio time and band touring schedules. However, turmoil was bubbling around the band. Johnny refused to work in the studio without Alexis. Clive was growing more and more discontent with the band and how he believed his influence as bandleader was waning.

"Johnny, twas me who started this here band. I was the one taught you the piana, boy. Ain't nobody wanted to give you no mind to playing no music. That was me. Now, you the one they all come to see. No sir, they don't come no more to hear the band play, they all come see you shake your ass on stage. It aint' bout no music no more, son. It's all about young girls watching you. I swear we played some joints where they don't even hear the music and them girls be screaming like nobody's business."

"Clive, we doing just what Mr. Amison said he would do for us. And we making more money playing music than you could ever dream. Damn, Clive, can't you be happy?"

"No, boy. He doing what he say he do for you and it ain't bout no money. He ain't doing so much for the rest of us fella's, who don't get to stay in the fancy hotels and eating places with you."

"I'll talk with Mr. Amison next time I see him, Clive. I promise ya. Hey, why don't you sing one of the new songs and we make it a piano song. We'll make it real nice and pretty and when we play it in shows, you sing it. I'll have Alexis write a song for you."

"I don't need no girl to write me no love songs you hear? Surely I don't take your pity, boy. I can play the piana better than anyone on these stages. I don't need you treating me like I'ze your back up player. This band is called the Clive Five for a reason, and y'all need to be remembering on that fact."

Clive stormed out and recording was done for the day.

Tensions eased after the first single was released from the new recordings and the band's music played on the radio along with big stars like Perry Como, Patty Page and Tony Bennett. Only the sound from the Clive Five was unlike all the others. They had a raw sound, more upbeat that the young girls flocked to see.

It was enough to get them a one-week engagement at Radio City Music Hall in New York City. Johnny refused to go to New York unless Alexis could travel with the band. Amison had cleared it with her parents for Alexis to travel on a very limited schedule. She would meet them in New York after the band played in Detroit, Cleveland and Philadelphia. They would play shows in places larger than they had ever witnessed before. The band was now a success and Johnny Joe Jackson's photo was going to be featured on the cover of a national magazine.

When the band reached New York, all the shows were sold out at Radio City Music Hall. The band had a rare two days off, before they were to perform. Johnny made arrangements to pick up Alexis from Grand Central Station and planned on spending the rest of the day with her.

"Things is going to be great now, Alexis. The crowds is growing and Mr. Amison promised the band more money. I'll have money to buy you nice things now, Miss Green Eyes. You and me, we can make a go of it and get married real soon."

Alexis' stance became rigid as Johnny hailed a cab. "John, I don't want your money and I don't need fancy clothes or rings on my finger right now. I love writing music for you and all the others. Traveling around with bands is not a life for me. I always wanted to see New York and I love the idea that you wanted me here with you. But I am not ready to get married. I do love you, John. I want you in my life, but let's go slow and see how long we can keep a good thing going. Ok?"

"That's another thing. You ain't gonna be writing no more music for them other groups. I'm going to talk with Mr. Amison, and tell him that if he wants me to be singing for him, he's gonna have to see things my way now."

"Please, please don't do that, John. He'll never agree with that and truly, I do love writing songs with you, but I love to write all styles of music. The other groups have a different sound from you guys, so I get to write different styles. Please understand. I will always be your songwriting partner, but I do love staying busy, and I love working for Mr. Amison. It's the only job I've ever had. I can't imagine doing anything else with my life."

Johnny clenched his fist. "You're MY woman. I don't like sharing you with them other bands. You listen to me, Darling. I'm going to speak with Amison. I want you to be with me. I want good things for you now, and I want us both to be happy."

Alexis offered her soft smile. "I am happy, John. Please understand. Over time, who knows what will happen. But, for right now, I like being who I am. I'm being paid to do what I love. You are too. Let's have a nice few days here in New York before I have to go home. Please, John?"

Johnny took two steps back from Alexis and rubbed his hands through his greased back hair. He rubbed his forehead with both thumbs almost crushing his own skull. He closed his eyes attempting not to show his deep disappointment with Alexis, even if it was obvious to her.

The shows came off a rousing success with Johnny's name highlighted. The band's name was printed in smaller letters than Johnny's on the side of buses all over New York City. Other than Clive, the band members were impressed. In order to attempt to calm Clive, Amison booked the band at the Apollo theatre for two nights after the Radio City shows.

The band went in and played mostly the old blues songs they played when they started out. Clive sang lead on many of the songs until the crowd grew restless and starting to yell out Johnny's name and the names of the songs, for which they were now known. They ended with Johnny's songs much to the delight of the crowd. Clive realized it was no longer his band.

The band headed back to Chicago to record a new single that Alexis wrote while in New York. Amison promised them a two-week break, once they recorded the new single. After that, it would be back on the road, this time hitting the southern states from North Carolina to Louisiana. It was also going to be the band's first trip back to Mississippi since they had become household names across much of the nation. While on break, Johnny begged Alexis to join them on the road, or at least meet them in Atlanta or New Orleans.

"John, we've had this conversation so many times. My work is here in Chicago, in the offices of the record label. I love our times together, but you're a big star now, you have an obligation to your music and your fans. When this all slows down, I will be here waiting for you. We're so young, there is so much in front of us. My songs are all over the new ratings system. They're starting to write about our success in the newspapers and magazines. My name's been mentioned in one of them, and one newspaper wants to do a story on me. Me, John. This way I can have some recognition too, and I don't have to be in front of a crowd. You know me, John. I don't like crowds. I can please so many of them with my music. Please, John. I beg you to understand me. I need to create songs as much you need to sing them."

"But we can be married and you can still write your words, Miss Green Eyes."

"Give it a little more time, John. There is no one else in my life. I do love you."

"I'm hitching a ride back home for a week with Clive. We can talk about this when I get back to Chicago."

CHAPT3R S!X

The headline in the local section of the Chicago newspaper read, "Woman Found Dead in Home," the day after Johnny left for home. Martha Simpson, mother of songwriting sensation Alexis Simpson was found dead sitting in her favorite chair, with a book in her lap. The story went on to say how she was in good spirits before her husband left for work. Alexis discovered her mother's cold body when Alexis came home for dinner. There were no signs of forced entry and foul play wasn't originally suspected. However, detectives would investigate. There were some accounts of a serial killer in the area, but this case didn't fit the profile. Everyone was shocked.

Johnny was on the road driving back to see his family. Alexis was unable to let him know what had happened. When he arrived home, there was a massage from Alexis asking him to return her call. Johnny took the evening to spend time with his family before returning her call the following morning. He was still upset with her after she turned him down again to be his bride and was in mood to call her quickly.

"John, it's so terrible. Mother wasn't ill or anything. I just can't believe she died in her sleep. The police have been asking us all kinds of questions. They even took my father down to the station, but they released him after he could prove he was at work all day. I know my father would never harm my mother. The detective found a small feather in her mouth, and he's suggesting she was suffocated with a nearby pillow. Why would anyone want

44

to do something like that to my mother? In her whole life, she never harmed anyone, John. I want to believe she died in her sleep. I need you. Can you please come back to Chicago?"

"I just got back to Mississippi for some rest and some time with my mama, Green Eyes. She will be so unhappy if I leave now. But for you, gimme a day with my family, and I'll catch a train ride back to see you."

"Thank you, John. Please come as soon as you can make it. My entire family is falling apart."

Johnny let Clive know about the death. He also told him he was heading back to Chicago the next day. He would meet the band in North Carolina.

"You was quiet as a field mouse on our way home, boy," Clive said. "Plus you was two hours late to meeting me for the ride home. Don't imagine you know nuttin about the lady being dead now do you, Johnny?"

"Damn, Clive. The woman I love, her mamma turns up dead and you want to accuse me or sumtin? Why you got to have those thoughts in your head?"

"I ain't accusing you, boy. I'ze only saying that I seen men after they killed peoples in the war and you had that same look in your eyes that night. I didn't pay it no mind till now. Like I said, you was quiet as a field mouse all the way home and I'ze seen that stare before in the war. You take it anyways you want. Now you get on back to Chicago and take care of that woman of yours."

"Piss on you, Clive. I ain't had nothing to do with that woman dying. I was late catching the ride cause I fell asleep in my room. I told you that already."

"Yeah I know, Johnny, and the bellman told me he rung your room and no one answered. Now you best stop talking to me and go see Alexis."

As promised, Johnny took the train back to Chicago and arrived the day after the funeral. He went to Alexis's home and upon his arrival, he found Detective Elliot Nesstor asking probing questions.

"Mr. Jackson, I was told that you were in a car on the road to Mississippi at the time of Mrs. Simpson's death. Is that true, Sir?"

"I would not know exactly, since I do not know when she died. Why is that important to you?"

"The neighbor, a Mrs. Joan Lamson, claims she was looking out her kitchen window making meatballs when she saw someone fitting your description coming and going from the house all within a fifteen minute time period the afternoon Mrs. Simpson expired. Did you happen to come here that afternoon, Mr. Jackson?"

"No, I was in a car heading back to Mississippi early that afternoon with Clive, my bandmate. You can ask him. He'll tell you where I was."

"Yes, we have tried to contact Mr. Johnson, but have not been able to locate him. However, we will."

Alexis broke out in tears and reached for Johnny.

"John, tell me and Detective Nesstor that you had nothing to do with my mother's death. You're not the type of man that could hurt her."

"No, Green Eyes. I don't know nothing bout any man looking like me here that day. I was in a car riding back to see my mamma and daddy. I didn't have nothing to do with her being dead. You know baby. I was with you that day too, for lunch. I met Clive soon after I was with you."

A short, stout woman wearing an apron with hints of sauce entered the room after a knock on the front door. Joan Lamson had arrived.

"Mrs. Lamson, as you know, I am Detective Nesstor. I would like to introduce you to Johnny Jackson. Maybe you've met him before?"

Joan cocked her head slowly. She viewed Johnny. "No. I don't believe I've had the pleasure of meeting such a big star. My granddaughter loves you, Mr. Jackson. Alexis has told me so much about you."

"Thank you, Mrs. Lamson. It's nice to meet you too. Alexis has told me all about your fine cooking. I sure am looking forward to push up against your dinner table one day."

Nesstor frowned. "Ok, Mr. Jackson. We'll let you spend some time alone with the family, but where can I find you in case I have any more questions? Do you have a way of contacting, Mr. Clive Johnson?"

"Clive is staying with his family in Mississippi and they don't have no phone. Next time I see him we all will be in North Carolina, in bout a weeks time. I can have him call you then. Till then, I guess I'm staying at the place downtown where I been staying. Alexis knows the number, I aint' got it."

Nesstor shook Johnny's hand and looked him square. "Thank you for your time. We'll be in touch."

Things quieted down surrounding the death, but Alexis grew distant from Johnny. She asked him several times about the day her mother died, but he grew weary of their conversations. After three days, Johnny changed plans and left Chicago. He went back to Mississippi to meet the band and spend a couple more days with his family. When he arrived, he immediately met up with Clive at his home.

"Clive, that detective is going to be calling on you. You gotta tell him I was with you early that afternoon. No one wants to believe I was sleeping in my room when that lady died."

"Johnny, I ain't looking for no trouble with no policeman. I'ze not a perfect man, but I don't go round making trouble and I don't go round lying to the police. I know you rode back with me and all I can tell that man is that we left long before my suppertime. Course my suppertime ain't usually till after ten at night. That's all I can tell that man."

"Clive, that detective can make lots of trouble for me and that means the band too. We doing so good now. The other guys and you is paying your bills, and Mr. Amison says we got more money coming. Damn, Clive, you gotta tell that man I was with you that afternoon."

"I ain't gotta do much in this world, boy. Like I say, lying to that man, that's not something I plan on doing. Now, if you got some confessing here, maybe I can help you."

"I aint got no confessing to do, Clive, I was sleeping in that room."

"You best stop all this lying to me, boy. I know you lying to me now. I can see it in your face. It got lies written all over it. Now, you want my help in telling that man we left long before my suppertime when he comes calling on me, you best know it's time to tell me the truth."

Johnny scratched his face, looked away, walked a few paces then walked back with his head staring at the ground.

"I went to see her that day, but not to kill her. I liked that woman. I surely did. I had seen Alexis earlier in the day and asked her to marry me again. She said no, again. When I asked her why, she told me some reasons and one was cause her mamma and daddy tells her she is too young, and I ain't no marrying type. I went to her mamma's house to see if I could talk sense into the woman. When she refused to help me, I dunno. I got all angry and put some pillow that was in my lap up against her face till she promised to change her mind. She didn't seem to struggle a whole lot and when I took the pillow away, she didn't move no more. I didn't want to kill nobody Clive. I wanted that woman to listen to me. I wanted her to tell Alexis to marry me and next thing I know, she stopped her breathing. I put a book in her lap and traveled back to my room. I cried some tears for her. I wiped my face, then I come down to meet you. Now, you promised to help me, Clive. I had no plans on hurting that woman. It was an accident."

Clive let out a deep sigh, "Boy, you in a fine mess. I still ain't looking to lie to no police. They don't take too kindly to us colored lying to them, especially with a dead white woman, who don't harm nobody. I'll tell that man we left long before my suppertime but I won't say no mo. You right. We all making mo money now than we was before we met Mr. Amison. Me and the boys need that money to use for our kids to eat. But if that man gets close to finding out, I ain't gonna tell him you killed that woman, but I will tell him about the real time we left.

Clive was torn. If Johnny was locked away for murder, Clive could once again be the bandleader. But on the other side, the band would quickly return to playing small church halls in rural Mississippi with little money to show for it. Johnny was the star attraction, not Clive "Fingers" Johnson.

The next morning, the band was on their way to North Carolina. It was hard for Johnny to know if Clive had told anyone else or the other band members, since he sat up front on the train. Johnny sat in the front of the train, the rest of the band traveled in a separate car towards the back. Even though they were a band, this was still the south during segregation, so they did not travel in the same part of the train.

When they arrived in North Carolina, Johnny tried to call Alexis and make things right with her. She refused his first two calls. She called him back a day later.

"I don't feel right about something, John. I know you've told me over and over that you were with Clive, and I know you were with him later that night. I know it. But I can't help to think about how upset you were with me that afternoon. I want to believe that you would never harm anyone, especially my own mother. However, I've seen you lose your temper, John. Please tell me one more time that you didn't harm my mother. Tell me, John. I need to know today. It's important that I know today. Right now."

"Green Eyes, why would I want to harm that woman? Did she ever harm me? And I done told you over and over, but why do I have to tell you again and why right now?"

"Detective Nesstor never could track Clive down in Mississippi, but he called here the other day asking about all the places your band is playing this week. I think he intends to find Clive there and once he does, the truth will come out. It's important for me to know the man I loved would never harm me or my family. I need the truth, John."

"My beautiful Green Eyes, I done told you so many times. I would never want to harm you.

"But, John, I worry because I remember now on the day she died, I told you that my mother and father are against us being married and so is Mr. Amison."

"Stop right there. You never told me nothing about Amison talking all bad about me too."

"He didn't talk bad about you, John. He looks out for me. He only said that he thinks maybe someone better will come along one day."

"Damn, girl. I got all these people running their mouths against me. I ain't never harmed these people. What do they have against me?"

"Last chance, John. Tell me you were in that car when my mother died."

"For the last time, girl. I done told everyone I don't know when she died, but I was in that car after I seen you for lunch. I gotta go."

Johnny left his room to track down Clive. He knew Clive liked to find the local parks to sit on the benches and, "sniff the air round me." He found Clive sitting on a bench just after dark.

"Clive that detective is coming all the way from Chicago to talk with you. I need to know for sure what you're going to tell him."

"I done told you, boy. I'm going to tell him we done left on the road long before my suppertime. If he asks when my suppertime might be or something else, I will do what I can, but I aint going to lie to no police. I ain't going to take no beating from no police for lying. Maybe you need to pay for your sins, boy. I won't be the one putting them on you. That will be between you and your God and that policeman. But this here, this is your problem. This ain't mine."

"That's not right of you, Clive. You told me that if I confessed, you would help me. All I'm asking is that you tell him you don't remember the exact time. It was long before the sun set. That's all I am asking, Clive."

Clive laughed in Johnny's face. "I did help you, boy. I got you to tell your sins to your God out loud and stopped all your lying. Maybe that God will let you keep your soul and find your way to Heaven, but I can't promise you that, boy.

"Funny thing is, Clive. Without you, I wouldn't be famous. Nobody would be knowing Johnny Joe Jackson. I know that and you know that. I do want to thank you for all you have done for me and let you know in some way, I will always love you. But now, it is time for you to die."

CHAPT3R $3V3И

"Caeles as you are aware, we can't predict the future. Even if we believe we can change one's destiny, we're forbidden to try. Maybe it was your subject's destiny to be famous had you not been near him, so I cannot fault you for your methods. You have done well in getting close to him, but that has not stopped him from ruining everything he achieved. It's time for you to remove his soul. Go to him immediately, and do what is expected. He has forfeited the right to own a soul. The High Council demands it of you. Do your duty and report back."

"Yes Elder Orcus. I am on my way."

The next afternoon the band looked for Clive. He was never late for a sound check. No one had seen him since he went for a walk the previous evening.

"Johnny, you need to call the local police about Clive," one band member said. "They might act quicker coming from you than from one of us, if you know what I mean."

Johnny knew exactly where Clive was, but he didn't want to act like he knew. "Sure, Leon. I'll call the police and see if they can help find Clive. It's not like him to wander off this long."

"After you do that Johnny, Mr. Amison wants to see you at the ticket window out front of the building."

Johnny didn't bother to call the police before seeing Amison. He took his time to make sure he had his wits and composure before heading out front of the building.

"Johnny, I need to see you for a moment please," the sharply dressed Mr. Amison said. "I have decided it is time for the band to release a full record album with all the singles we have done so far, plus we will add a few new songs. Doesn't that sound like a simply wonderful idea to you?"

Johnny couldn't believe that this was what Amison wanted to see him about. A huge sigh of relief came rushing out of his body. He relaxed his shoulders and cracked his neck.

"Sounds like good news, Mr. Amison. Does that mean we all get more money now?"

"Oh, you are about to get it, Johnny. I need you to come over here in the light, so I might take your photograph. We'll need a good photo for the artist, who is designing the cover. He asked me to provide him with your photograph. I would like to take an image of you, possibly with that lake off in the distance as the backdrop. Please move over to the other side of the building."

Once I had Johnny exactly where I wanted him, and in perfect focus, I stole my first human soul. No more rats, no more practicing. I had done it. The only problem was I didn't expect it to be that powerful as the energy coursed throughout my body.

"Mr. Amison, are you ok? Maybe you should sit down for a moment. You don't look so good."

"I'm fine, Johnny. How do you feel?"

"Don't feel much different I suppose. Leon wants me to call the police cause we can't find Clive. What you think we should do? It's been less than a day since he was round here. What's you think Mr. Amison?"

"I think if you look inside yourself, you will know the truth. Now, I have to get back to Chicago and deliver this photograph. My time here is done. Good luck, John. I hope one day you will find what you are missing."

"I ain't missing a what Mr. Amison, I'm missing a Clive."

"You keep telling yourself that, John. Now I must go. Good luck with your future."

I stumbled down to the same park, where Johnny attacked Clive. His body then thrown into the lake to drown. A local passerby had seen the body floating on the surface and called the police. They were removing the body as I found my way to a bench to sit and regain my composure. I sat for about five minutes when approached by an old man wearing tattered clothes with long white hair, in need of a haircut and bath.

"Real shame what happened to that man eh, mister? I mean, I wonder if anyone even knows the poor man's name, or how he ended up in the water? Did you ever wonder what happens to someone's soul when they die? I know I wonder? Can you lose a soul before you are even dead?"

I was still shaking from stealing Johnny's soul and having a hard time focusing on the man's words. It did not occur to me he was searching for a deeper conversation, until he seemed to repeat exactly what he just said to me and attempted to hold my hand. I immediately jerked my hand back wondering why this stranger would attempt such an action or talk to me about souls. The stranger spoke again. "I can offer you comfort if you allow it Caeles. Take my hand and you will be restored."

"I don't need to be restored. I am as alive as I have ever been, but thank you, and how do you my name?"

"I know deep inside your soul you do believe what you speak, but I have seen the truth and what you believe, is not the truth. One day I will show you the truth."

The man got up from the bench and vanished.

My next stop was back to Chicago. I was about to sell the record company to Laurent Scheffler. He had recently moved to America from The Netherlands looking to get into the music industry. Our group had made a tidy profit, but my time as a record executive was complete. I had achieved my goal without having to fight the teenaged girls in the crowd to get an excellent image of Johnny Joe Jackson.

"Alexis, I have given you twenty percent of the stock of the record company. Sheffler will be purchasing the other eighty percent. We could not have been as successful as we have become without your songs. I appreciate all you have done, but now it is time for me to move on to my next project. There is one stipulation to you receiving the stock however. Should you ever marry or have a child with Johnny Jackson, the stock becomes the property of Mr. Sheffler or his assigns. You may not understand why I stipulated this as part of the arrangement, but I must. I hope you will understand."

"I think I understand Mr. Amison. I can't explain my feelings, but I've always felt like you were my guardian angel and this is again your way of protecting me. I've chosen not to be involved with John since my mother's death. I don't know why, but I feel like John knows more than he's telling me about that day. Now with Clive's death, he seems to have a dark cloud around him. Thank you for all you have done for me, Mr. Amison. I hope one day I can repay you."

With that last bit of business taken care of, I was off to stand before the High Council.

"Caeles the Council wants to salute you for your outstanding work with your first subject. Not only were you able to steal his soul, your record company idea paid for all the costs associated with it, plus a small profit. We were all able to gain power from your theft and you left with little trace. It was outstanding work on your part. I know you have already started on your next assignment, but you've earned a few weeks respite. Go home and spend some time with your family. After you rest, go back to Chicago and continue watching your next target. I believe she is a very dangerous woman, Caeles. I don't know why her soul is so dark. No one on the Council understands it. Even with the information you have brought back to us, it seems a mystery. It's why you need to continue to follow her to make certain we're not making an error when giving the command to remove her soul."

As anxious as I was to return to Chicago, I took a few days to visit with my parents. They were now living in West Palm Beach, Florida. My father worked as a contractor building expensive homes in Palm Beach. My mother worked in a clothing shop along Clematis Street. It was good to be home though, because I wanted to talk with my father about the man who sat next to me on the bench.

"Father, Elder Orcus tells me that after we steal a soul all our surroundings are not as they seem. I told him a tattered man came and sat next to me moments after I took Johnny's soul. He seemed to know my name and possibly my mission. I was told that we have illusions immediately following the removal of a soul, which can last for several hours. With me, I felt back to normal within the hour."

"My son, I have no experience as you know in removing another's soul. It's hard for me to be certain of our leader's words. I will say on his behalf however, that others have shared with me the same experience. They've had illusions, some even speaking of others telling them they will be healed if they take their hand. So your case is not uncommon."

I listened as my father told me of recounts of stories told to him over the years, but my experience seemed so real. The man did sit next to me. I could feel his hand touch mine. It was not an illusion as some are trying to explain away to me. However, one thing father said did stick with me.

"What is real to you may not be to others. What is real to them may not be to you. We only have our past to guide us in our future. Always seek what you believe to be true, Caeles, for if you follow the truth, no one can tell you it's an illusion."

I spent a few days watching the waves crash on the beach and getting filled up on my mother's cooking, but I knew my mission was to head back to Chicago. I had already started following my second subject, while I owned the record company. It was one reason I started the company where I did. Soon after assigning Johnny to me, Elder Orcus told me he was possibly getting false readings on a woman who lived in Chicago, and he asked me to keep an eye out for her. It made my job easier to set up base in the "Windy City." It didn't hurt that I was becoming a fan of baseball. My visits to Wrigley Field were a real treat.

Barbara Gifford was my second assignment. It took some extensive research to find out about her background and why the Council had her on their radar. Nothing seemed out of place, yet the Council and in particular, Elder Orcus saw darkness in her.

She was born Barbara Ann Daniels and raised in upstate New York. Her father immigrated from Ireland and her mother, a French Canadian. Her dad did very well in the textile business and they lived in an upscale home. Barbara was the youngest of three children, the other two being her brothers, Charles and Darby. Barbara was intelligent, and growing up was usually placed in classes with older students. She did so well, she graduated a year early from Cornell University in 1945.

Richard Anthony Gifford was studying business at Cornell when he met Barbara. He came from a poor upbringing and had to work during college to pay his debts for school. He was also very bright and earned a small amount in scholarship money during his time at Cornell. His father passed away when he was quite young and was raised mostly by his grandmother, while his mother worked. He was not a handsome man, and never stood out in a crowd. He was more than competent with his studies and wanted to own his own accounting firm in the future.

Neither Barbara nor Richard showed much emotion to others, but they did enjoy each other's company. They dated for two years in college and for one year after graduating from Cornell.

Richard didn't want to stay in the New York area, so he looked for employment elsewhere. Offered a position with an accounting firm in Chicago, he accepted. Barbara stayed behind in New York until Richard could settle into a small apartment. He missed having her at his side and soon proposed marriage. They were married two months later. Barbara took a position as a secretary in a prestigious Chicago law firm. She felt it was way beneath her abilities and she was right, but it was all she could find at the time.

"Richard, when are you going to start your own business?" she would ask. "We make a good team together. I can run the office and you can concentrate on your clients. I can handle all the marketing and paying the bills."

It was an almost nightly conversation around the dinner table. Barbara was never satisfied, but Richard was in no hurry to leave his secure paycheck. He never cared about wealth. He mostly wanted to do a good job and rest easy on weekends.

"Barbara my sweet, I have no doubt you would make a wonderful office manager, but I have a fantastic job. If I were to leave my position there would be no guarantees I could make it on my own. It could take years for me to build up a clientele to make the same income we have currently. As much as I would love to work for myself, it does not make economic sense at this time. Besides, if you were to leave your job, it would mean we lose your income as well. I don't see any benefit in making that move."

Barbara was the stronger willed of the two. Eventually she wore Richard down and talked him into starting his own tax and bookkeeping service. She agreed to stay at her job for one year or until it made financial sense for her to work with him full time. Richard didn't realize how much business his wife could send his way from her law firm clients. She had a way about her that could persuade people to do things without them even realizing it. Within a year, he was making the same income as he had working for his previous employer. It didn't take too much longer till Barbara talked her husband into leaving her job and joining him.

She excelled at marketing. Barbara increased her husband's business by more than enough to cover the loss of her salary and to hire a part time worker in the office for smaller accounts. She attracted business from over a ninety-mile radius through targeted advertising. With their growing business, they bought a nice home outside the city limits and lived a comfortable lifestyle. For Barbara, it was never enough.

Richard and Barbara were now both in their late twenties with Barbara only having their expanding business on her mind. She had developed into an attractive woman, but not one who would show off her looks. At just under six feet, she reminded some of a model with long auburn hair and a slender hourglass figure. She would occasionally spend some savings on fancy clothes, but it was never a priority. She knew how to find clients for the family business, which was her strength.

Eventually, Barbara found a niche market in small companies that needed someone to process their bills. She successfully directed much of her marketing efforts towards that type of client. They would send their bills to the office in the mail twice a month and the company now had another employee, who would handle those types of accounts. Barbara never met anyone in person. All transactions were done via mail. If someone had to deal with the clients in the office or on the telephone, it was Tim Walsh, who would take care of it. Tim was a young man fresh out of Loyola University with a background in accounting.

Despite her comfortable lifestyle with Richard, Barbara still sought more. After she gained the trust of clients, she created a few small companies of her own. Invoices would be sent to their client's offices for inventory or small services that would be easily overlooked by her clients. They would be packaged along with the other legitimate bills and would be paid by Tim. They each had their own mailing address, usually a post office box, which was not highly unusual, and didn't offer suspicion. The plan worked well until one day one of their clients called to ask about a charge to clean the company uniforms.

"Will you check to see why my company is being billed for this since my cousin does all the cleaning and never sends me an invoice? If he is charging me now, I'd like to know since we do all of his landscaping in return for the free cleaning."

Barbara told Tim to assure the client that she would handle it personally.

Carl Palaski owned a successful landscaping business that handled upscale homes not far from Richard and Barbara's suburban home. Richard insisted on doing his own yard work, so they never employed Carl's company. He would come to the office once a year to have his tax work finalized and that was the extent of his visits to Richard's office. He had never met Barbara before the call came in about the uniforms.

Barbara met Carl for lunch one day to make amends and make sure her small mistake didn't get noticed with other accounts. "I am so sorry for this, Carl. Somehow, those items were put in your account in error. Here's the cash for the invoice. It won't happen again."

"It was nice of you to come all this way to pay me back, Barbara, but you could have sent me a check."

"That's ok, Carl. It never should have happened and I wanted to apologize in person for our error. It's the first time anything like this has happened. By the way, have you ever considered growing your business? I don't know if you're aware, but I do all the marketing for my husband's company. I think I can help you grow your business as well. We can work on a commission where I get paid a small fee for each new client I bring to your company. That way it doesn't cost you anything out of pocket until your business grows. Will you think about it?"

"Sure, I'll think on it, but I'm pleased with the size of it now, Barbara. If I were to increase my sales, I'd have to add another truck and employees. It's not a matter of just paying you, there would be a lot of added costs even for a small jump in revenues."

"You sound just like my Richard, always worried about every last penny. I did very well growing his business and I have no doubt I can grow yours as well." With that she reached over, touched Carl's hand and looked deeply into his eyes. "I made it worthwhile it to him, I can make it worthwhile to you too, Carl. Think about it."

A few days later Carl made a trip into town and invited Barbara for lunch to discuss a mutual arrangement. Carl made it obvious that he wanted Barbara to do more than add revenue to his company. At first, she was a bit taken back, but inside Barbara's mind she started to imagine how she could get Carl to trust her and weave her way into his bank accounts. Carl didn't have a wife or close family. He had worked for many years developing his business and Barbara knew no one was really watching over Carl's money, but Carl. What Barbara didn't realize was that Carl had not built his success by being foolish with his money.

The two came to an agreement over how Barbara would be paid to bring in new business. Barbara pretended not to see or hear Carl's advances as much as Carl had wanted. However, they did agree to have lunch once a week for the next month to see how the business relationship was progressing.

After several lunches, Carl started to open up to Barbara about his past. His father once owned a successful company that manufactured tires for the auto industry. Before Carl was old enough to participate in working in his father's company, his parents were killed in an auto accident. The company was sold, with Carl as the sole beneficiary. He was moved to three different adoption homes, until he could live on his own at eighteen years of age. None of his grandparents were alive at the time of his parent's death, expect for his grandmother on his mother's side, but she lived in Hungary and Carl was not about to move there. When he turned eighteen, he was allowed to use some of his trust fund money to start his business. He had more than enough to pay his expenses. By the time he was twenty-five and allowed access to the remainder of his money, he let it sit in the bank. His own company was providing sufficient revenue to pay all his living expenses and for him to live a comfortable life. Since he had no family, he worked six days a week from before dawn till after dark. In the winters, he would do handy man work and remove snow from neighbor's sidewalks. He stayed busy year round. He never told Barbara exactly how much money he had in the bank, but the way he talked, he didn't have to work as hard as he did.

Barbara doubled Carl's accounts over the course of a few months. She talked him into buying another truck and employed more workers. His business was now spread over forty miles, whereas before it was confined within a ten-mile radius. Barbara and Carl began to have dinner together, and a love affair ensued.

CHAPT3R 3!GHT

"Carl, this cannot continue," said one afternoon at lunch. "Something needs to change and change quickly."

Carl smirked. "What do you mean, my Love? I thought everything was going so well?"

"What I mean is that you're adding businesses weekly, and you might even have to add another truck to keep up with it all. Yet, every time I ask about my percentage, you keep changing the subject. I know our relationship developed into something it was never supposed to be, and for that I will have to live with myself, but you do owe me."

"I owe you what?" I've wined and dined you in the best places in Chicago for months. I've showered you with new jewelry that is wrapped your pretty neck and wrist. I've taken very good care of you. I don't owe you a damn nickel. In fact, I'm pissed off you would now dare to ask me for more."

Barbara slammed her fork on the plate. "This wasn't our agreement, Carl. What you did to get me in bed has nothing to do with what you owe me with my marketing skills."

"Well maybe I assumed I was paying for your skills every time you rang up room service in the fancy hotel room, where you insisted we meet once a week."

"Are you now suggesting I'm a whore, Carl?"

"I'm suggesting you sure didn't mind me spending my hard earned dough to please you for the small amount of net income your so called skills provided me. Now stop asking me for more than you already have, or your dim witted husband is going to find out where you have been spending your weekly meetings, and it wasn't to get him new business."

"Do not dare threaten me you ignorant little man. I will get what's owed to me."

Barbara threw her napkin the on the table and stormed back to the office. Her flush face and short temper caught the attention of her husband. He walked into her office and asked if everything was alright.

"I know I've not paid you much attention lately, sweetie," Richard said. It was tax season, and with all the extra clients you brought in this year, I guess I should have been more prepared and hired extra staff, but I didn't. I'm sorry I've not been the best of husbands lately. How would you like it if we book a vacation for a couple of weeks? Would you like that?"

"Yes, I would Richard. I have a feeling it will be best if we both leave town."

After cooling off for a few days, Barbara called Carl and asked him if she could come over and cook dinner for him and apologize. Richard was attending a seminar out of town for the weekend. Carl didn't accept the invitation right away, but Barbara insisted her apology was sincere. She could stay the evening with him, something they had never done.

Barbara's meal would be something out of the ordinary. She had remembered reading about a type of fish she wanted to serve, though it wasn't easy for her to obtain on short notice. She searched a few Japanese restaurants in the area until she finally found the fish not already gutted and cooked. She had to pay off the owner of the restaurant a large sum of cash to obtain the entire fish.

Upon arriving at Carl's suburban home and sharing an extended kiss, Barbara said, "Thanks so much for accepting my apology, Carl, and allowing me to make you dinner. I know how much you enjoy a nice fish dinner. I found the perfect one for you."

She cooked it up as close as she could remember from the book, she read many years earlier. She prided herself on being a well-read person as well as a good cook.

Soon after eating a few mouthfuls, she noticed Carl was starting to lose the ability to move his arms or move in his chair. His face refused to twitch. Barbara knew not to eat her portion of fish and only eat her salad.

Barbara's face took on a sinister look with a raised eyebrow. "What's wrong, Carl? Oh, wait you didn't really eat any of the fish did you? I guess I didn't tell you. You're eating the Japanese Fugu fish. It emits a deadly toxin. This one happens to be called tetrodotoxin, it slowly paralyzes you to where you can no longer breathe."

Carl's eyes widened.

She continued. "The beauty of it is most western doctors can't detect it. It will look like you died of natural causes here at the table and maybe in a few days when people start to notice you've not been to work, your body will be found. However, that won't be until at least Monday, my dearest when you will be long dead. Lucky for you, I have a potion that will stop all this nastiness, but you need to sign a paper for me. All this will then go away. But you do need to act quickly because you don't look so good."

With the assistance of Barbara, Carl signed his Last Will and Testament granting ninety percent of Carl's money to a charity already set up by Barbara. His company would go to his assistant because after all, Barbara had no use for it. She really didn't want any attention heading her way after his death.

She sat and watched Carl inhale his last struggling attempt at life. She could see the fear in his eyes, but never once did she offer a tear. She never had a potion, only a small vile of water she brought with her for show.

After Carl exhaled for the last time, she cleaned up all the remains of the fish and dinner. She made him a peanut butter and jelly sandwich, tore off part of it as if he had eaten some of it and made sure she never touched his body, other than put a dab of peanut butter on his lip.

She put the newly signed Will in an envelope with his other work papers in his desk. She had made sure the paper was notarized. While working for the law firm, she would collect papers that were to be shredded.

One time a new attorney in her office, who was a notary, was testing his new seal. She was ordered to destroy the tests, but she kept a few for safekeeping. She used her typewriter in the office and typed a perfectly looking legitimate Last Will and Testament dated and signed from a few years previous to that fateful evening.

Barbara meticulously cleaned up any traces of herself ever having been inside Carl's home. She even wiped the oven and kitchen clean of any wandering fingerprint of hers. She wore gloves when touching the envelope and around Carl's desk, careful not to leave any clues. She later put Carl's fingerprints on the Will and the envelope after he was paralyzed and couldn't stop her. She was home before nine o'clock and called her husband's hotel room from their home to show she was home in the evening.

It was about that time when Elder Orcus asked me to start to follow Barbara. It seemed she had masked her own emotions so well that even a master of reading souls was not sure of her guilt or innocence. Since we do not have any special powers to read minds or see where people are on maps or any special talent other than to see and steal souls, the Elders did not know of her now appetite to kill. They only knew they had to be more accurate before removing her soul. When I was given the assignment to follow Barbara, I had no idea she had committed a murder or the detailed extent she had gone to cover her tracks. It didn't make it any easier that I was also running a budding record company with a singer, who was registering off the charts as being a bad soul. Johnny was my main target at the time of Barbara's first murder.

A few days later, the news arrived that Carl Palaski had been found dead in his apartment. The case fell on Detective Elliot Nesstor's desk. Richard and Barbara both attended the small memorial service. It wasn't until weeks later, when Carl's attorney and the landlord were cleaning out his belongings, that they found the Last Will and Testament. Carl's attorney wasn't convinced of its authenticity.

It took months, before the funds were released into the account Barbara had set up, because her company documents with the state showed the company was only a few months old when Carl died, yet his Last Will and Testaments was dated almost two years earlier. An attorney representing the newly formed company testified that the charity had been set up for years. However, the formal filings with the State of Illinois were not done until recently since the company had no funds.

That little trick cost Barbara a lot money to get the attorney to lie to a judge. Since Carl had no family and no one other than Carl's attorney protesting the will, the judge ordered the funds released. Barbara's fake charity bank account instantly swelled with over five hundred thousand dollars.

Barbara didn't stop there. It almost seemed too easy for her to kill and steal money. Detective Nesstor looked into the death of Carl Palaski and found little to continue an investigation. Barbara was extremely thorough in covering her trail.

Since I wasn't trained as a spy or detective, following Barbara full time and running a record company, was becoming increasingly difficult to do. I knew she was meeting with a new man from time to time, but there was little evidence that she was a person capable of committing murder. From a short distance, I could see that she would go home every evening after office hours to have dinner with her husband.

She rarely strayed far from home on weekends, and the few times I could follow her during office hours, she seemed to be meeting with clients in crowded restaurants. There wasn't much I could report to the Council that warranted stealing her soul.

I wasn't close enough to her to understand how manipulative and calculating she was as a person. Ordered to keep my distance, I followed her as much as possible. I was, at that time, still required to keep an eye on Johnny and the record company. It was a good thing I didn't have my own family to attend to, since my days and evenings were filled with working, spying or attending performances by various groups or artists. I also had to keep a close eye on the relationship between Johnny and Alexis, since I knew it was very likely he would be losing his soul.

A second person associated with Barbara was found dead in their home. He was also a single man with only a few relatives, who lived many miles away from her downtown office. A Last Will and Testament was found shortly after he was found dead.

An amount was left to a single charity, though compared to Carl's death it was a smaller amount. The elderly man was self-made through the stock market. He lived and worked alone and had few friends. Not well known to his neighbors, no one noticed if he had visitors. However, there were now two people connected to Barbara and Richard's company, who had turned up dead within a year.

Detective Nesstor again investigated, but nothing suspicious was discovered during his investigation. This man was found dead in bed several days after the coroner's office believed time of death occurred. There were no traces of foul play, nor did anyone see anyone coming or leaving the home. I had seen Barbara have lunch with the man one time, but never anything more. If she was involved with his murder, she acted quickly.

Soon after the second death associated with Barbara, my work with the record company was complete. I had taken my first soul. While visiting my parents in Florida, a third body turned up cold in the Chicago suburbs.

This time there was no connection to the accounting firm. I had never seen Barbara with the man. The only connection was that he was a single man and money was donated to a recently formed charity. My assignment was to now follow Barbara full time.

Mario Espendari responded to one of Barbara's advertisements for bookkeeping work. His family was rich in land used for wine making, as well as some commercial buildings in Rome. Wine making had been the family business for many generations. He was the sole heir to the company and family fortune. Mario came to the United States looking for potential new outlets for his wine business and possibly investing in Chicago real estate. He didn't really need much bookkeeping help as much as he was looking for tax advice from Richard Gifford.

While in the office, Barbara spied Mario in his fine Italian suit. Mario didn't have looks that would be mistaken for a magazine model, but he was not unattractive either. Barbara saw him as a man just over six feet in height, slender, but not thin, nothing that really stood out. However, she did notice his very expensive suit, his well-groomed hair, and polished fingernails. She assumed he was a wealthy man and appeared to be her same age. After learning from Richard that Mario was looking for tax advice, Barbara insisted on meeting the man.

"Mr. Espendari, thank you so much for reaching out to our firm. Possibly one day next week we could have lunch, and I can tell you all about the other services we provide?"

"That's very kind of you Ma'am, but Mr. Gifford did a fine job of explaining what I needed to know."

"Yes, I am sure he did. He's a very detailed man, but did he explain to you that on special occasions, I offer marketing services to exceptional clients, like yourself? Possibly we can have lunch and I can speak to you on those terms?"

"And what gives you the impression I am exceptional or would need marketing help?"

"Well Mr. Espendari, I hate to admit it, but my office is next to Richard's and I wasn't attempting to pry, but I did overhear some of your conversation. I do believe it's possible we can assist you with more than tax services. All I am asking is an hour of your time with some polite conversation. I'm sure I can make it worth your time."

"Why do I have this feeling that you are not going to give up until I agree, Miss, Mrs.?"

"Oh, I apologize for my lack of a proper introduction. I'm Barbara, Barbara Gifford, yes Richard is my husband."

"I see, well I am not one who has often dines with other men's wives, so I thank you for the kind offer, but I think I must kindly decline."

"Sir, I think you are misunderstanding my offer. I work here as the office manager, but I also have my own business of marketing for others as well. Richard and I agreed to this when I first came to work with him. Please, it is nothing more than a friendly lunch where I can discuss what I do with my marketing expertise."

"Well, if nothing else, you are persistent. If you are half as good at marketing as you are in talking people into doing things they are a little uneasy about, then maybe we can work together. Here is the number where I am staying, let me know when it is convenient to meet."

It only took Barbara one day to call Mario. She saw potential opportunity in him and didn't want him to slip out of town before she explored if he fit her profile.

Barbara greeted him inside the lobby at the Grumpy Grouper. "Thank you for agreeing to meet me Mr. Espendari."

"Thank you for the invitation Mrs. Gifford."

After sitting and ordering wine, they clicked wine glasses. They exchanged brief exchanges about their day before Barbara announced, "Please, no reason for all this formality, call me Barbara."

"Ok Barbara, by all means call me Mr. Espendari. Well maybe not, we Italians are known for our warmth and hospitality so please, Mario it is." He leaned back and offered a wide smile that Barbara quickly returned.

"Now then, Barbara, tell me why the lunch, what is it that you think you can do for me that I cannot or have not done for myself?"

"Mario what is the rush to talk about business?" I'm a woman who needs information. I need to see if you're a proper candidate for my services before they can be offered." She offered another smile with a small lift on the right side of her mouth.

"Oh, and just what is it you are seeking, my lady, only information?"

Barbara leaned forward slightly in her chair and looked Mario directly in his eyes. "The more I know about you, the easier it will be for the both of us, Mario. Start with telling me about your family and all your businesses and why have you come to our beautiful town. It is hardly a place to grow wine, but I'm sure you don't need me to tell you about your business."

"I have not come here to make wine. That much is certain. However, a potential distributor of wine does have headquarters here in your city. There may be an opportunity for me to expand my business. I also have considered buying some property in the United States, so while I am here, I thought I would investigate potential sites. My finance people in Italy did a fine job of explaining your tax code to me, but one can never be too careful. I saw one of your advertisements and gave your husband a call to get his advice as well. Your marketing worked to find me, so why not offer you a chance to explain what you can do for me."

"Trust me, Mario. If you allow me the opportunity. there is so much I can do for you. But again, tell me about your wife and your children, your family. I need to know all I can about you because that helps me, in making decisions about how to assist you."

"I realize more than you think I do, that is to say, in why you want my information, Barbara. After all, I did not become successful at such a young age, and be stupid with my resources. Do not mistake me for an easy mark, or you will be sorely disappointed in where our relationship will end."

"I was in no way attempting to insult you, Mario. I apologize if my words were upsetting to you. I have a way of being too aggressive at times, and most men frankly, can't handle my aggression. Some might even suggest; it can be deadly at times." She leaned back and giggled, but never took her eyes off Mario, hoping for a reaction she could use for future reference.

"To answer your question, I am a single man, I'm afraid. I have no wife, no children, only my business. My employees, they are my family now. I worked the wine business with mio padre until his passing last year. Since then, I am slowly taking control and making some changes I wanted to do before, but mio padre would not allow. He was not one who wanted to deal with strangers in strange lands. He never ventured past Rome or our winery. He would only go to Rome one day a month to attend to his business, only to return the next day. He had his routines and rarely swayed far from them. Me, I want to see the world. I want to experience all the things I could not when he was alive. I am free to run the company as I see fit since I have no brothers or sisters. Mia madre passed away a few years ago and it has been only mio padre and I since she died."

"How sad, Mario, but now you can experience things you never thought possible. Possibly you can even do some good in helping the less fortunate along the way."

"Do not feel sorry for me. I have wanted for little in my life. I have seen more than you might think. I will warn you. I am very well educated. Speaking several languages has made it easy for me to travel the world. It has only been in recent years, that my travel stopped. Now, I am hoping to see what is good in you Barbara, in marketing terms of course."

"Of Course, what else could you possibly be speaking about, Mario?"

After an hour or so, it was agreed that Barbara would work up a marketing plan for selling Mario's family wine in the United States. Mario told Barbara he would keep his meeting with the Chicago distributor, but he wanted to hear what she could offer.

Two weeks later, they met for lunch again. Barbara had indeed worked up a very good marketing plan. It started supplying small quantities using small distributors in the larger cities along the northeast coast like Boston, New York, Philadelphia and the Baltimore areas. They would then introduce it to the Chicago area, and later the west coast of the United States. She would arrange for press releases and interviews for Mario.

He was impressed with her work, but he wasn't sure he could handle the supply needed to start in too many places at once. Barbara asked about where the fields were exactly in Italy. She asked if she could visit, since she had talked about a vacation with Richard to Italy for several years.

"Oh, we are not really set up for visitors, and it is not easy to find on a map, but if you ever do get there, I would be happy to show you around."

Not the reaction Barbara was expecting.

CHAPTER NINE

Several weeks passed with Mario spending time with Barbara on a regular basis. She can be a very sweet person at times, but just as manipulative as sweet. She insisted on knowing why Mario never married or had children. Family seemed to be important to her.

I had to admit it was becoming more difficult to remove myself as Mario and concentrate on my job of discovering if she had a soul worth stealing. My emotions for her were starting to cloud my judgment. With Johnny, it was easy. I never connected with Johnny on an emotional level like I had with Barbara. I considered Johnny a lost soul from day one of my assignment. He was lost in society, doing all he could to make a name for himself.

Ultimately, he allowed his affections for Alexis get the better of him and paid the price with his soul. Maybe it was because I felt I needed to protect Alexis, removing Johnny's soul was an easier task. Barbara could be quite charming. This was making me question my belief, should a soul ever be taken?

The Council asked me to return to our compound. "Caeles, the High Council wants a current report about your latest subject. Why have you asked for delays in meeting with us?"

"Elder Orcus, with all due respect to you and the Council, you have admitted even you have issues in seeing my subject's true soul. I too am struggling to find her true spirit. One time we meet she is sensitive, warm and the most giving person you will find on earth. The next she can appear cold and calculating with little to no soul. I cannot stand before this Council and tell you with certainty she deserves to lose her soul."

"Caeles, the Council recognizes the goodness in your soul. We consider that when we send you on assignments. However, your mission is not one of rehabilitation, but one of information gathering and if commanded, theft. Do not fight direct orders from this High Council. I would strongly suggest that you not deviate with any of your well intentioned, yet wrongheaded ideas. Our mission will never be to restore or rehabilitate. Our sole mission on earth is one of taking from those who have lost their way. Now, has your subject lost her way? We demand your thoughts on that one question. Any other thoughts you may have are inconsequential to me, or anyone else on this Council."

"I cannot say with any certainty. I beg that you offer me more time. I know you want an accurate and concise answer, but I am afraid I do not have one to offer."

"At times even some of our most experienced of stealers run across a difficult task. They possibly become too close to their subjects, and when the time to strike occurs, they can't and I must assign someone else. Other times they take the soul, but do so with a heavy heart. Do you want to continue this mission?"

I knew I had to continue. I refused to have her soul removed in error. Standing strong in front of the Council was essential.

"I will continue with the blessings of the Council. I understand my mission. I only ask that before heading back to Chicago, I can spend a few days with my family. I think some time with them will clear my mind."

"Time granted," Elder Orcus said. "However, you will return to us thirty days from today and the Council will make its final ruling. I now see darkness in her that was not as evident in the past. Should you feel the time is right to steal, you don't have to return to the Council. Take the soul."

Once home, it was my mother, who offered words of wisdom and insight I had not previously considered.

"Caeles, my dear child, you suffer because you are my son. There are days I believe your father could never learn the art of stealing because he loved me too much. Once that is in your heart, I'm not sure you can take another's soul. I know the Council has shown great patience with you, as you are new to our ways."

I nodded and continued to listen.

Your great grandfather was one of the best soul stealers to ever live, until he met your great grandmother. Then he lost the ability. A woman has the ability to change a man and most times, the man is not aware. I will never know if I'm correct about your father, but I don't regret his love for me."

Her best advice followed.

Be who you are in life. Don't allow others rule you, and don't allow others to tell you when something is right when you know it's wrong in your heart. One day, I will tell you more about your family's past, but for now, go find your way in this world. If this woman is evil, then do what you must to make it right. Have no regrets, Caeles, I don't. I made my choices many years ago."

After a long weekend with my mother and father, I took the plane ride back to Chicago. Before Mario returned to Barbara, Mr. Amison paid a short visit to check on Alexis.

"How is everything going with your new boss and song writing Alexis?"

"Mr. Sheffler is a very kind and generous man. He went back to his home country for a few weeks so the office has been quiet. He signed two new acts and in case you didn't notice, one of my songs was in the top ten on the charts for four whole weeks. I'm so excited."

"How's Johnny been doing since I left?"

"I can't explain it, Mr. Amison. It's like he was castrated or something. He has no energy, little desire to sing and without Clive, the band is falling apart. Mr. Sheffler is working to find a new bandleader and has spoken with John many times, but he's lifeless now. I don't know if he misses Clive or if he had anything to do with Clive's murder, but the time I saw him, he was muttering over and over how much he missed Clive and wanted a do over. I asked him what he meant and he would only tell me that everyone gets a second chance and he wished he could have his. He said it with such a scary blank stare. I went to their show here in town last week and John was not himself. I would never marry him, but I sure wish he could find the old John. At times, he was a joy to be with."

"Miracles happen every day, Alexis. Maybe one day it will be Johnny's turn to find his miracle and have his soul returned."

"Wow, that's exactly right, Mr. Amsion. I couldn't put it into words until now, but John lost his soul. I pray that one day he finds it."

"Like I said my sweet, Alexis, miracles do happen."

After a brief visit with Alexis, Mario returned. I was a bit out of practice with my British accent, but returning to my Italian one was even harder. Staying in character at times becomes an issue when I speak quickly. My accents at times overlap, so normally I chalk it up to having spent time all around Europe. Barbara questioned me on it one time. She is not nearly as easy to fool as Johnny or even Alexis. I was constantly on guard with Barbara.

Three days after Mario returned; he received a call from Barbara. She offered to make him lunch at her home. Richard was away at a high school reunion. She had missed his company and wanted to ask him a question. Mario, well, I, accepted.

"Mario, even though our relationship to this point has been about business I do think our friendship has grown to the point where I can ask you a question, don't you?"

"Si, ask away."

"Tell me one last time why you don't have a family?"

"My work has never allowed for it, or maybe, I have never found the right person. Why do you ask? Are you applying for the job as my wife and make babies with me?"

Barbara laughed. "No, Richard and I are quite happy together. Sure, we've had our rough patches, but most do. Don't they?"

"I would not know, since I do not have a wife, but I had my moments of disagreements with mio padre. I would assume it is close to the same. Tell me, why do you not have any children since you seem so interested in my lack of offspring?"

"I'll answer your question, but first I want you to eat this wonderful fish I cooked for you. I made it special, for you. I didn't want to take the chance you'd leave town again before I could make this special meal for you."

"I am not a fish eater, but since this is likely our last meal together, for you, I will eat it."

"What do you mean our last meal? Why would you suggest such a thing Mario?"

"When we met Barbara, I told you that I do not make a habit of enjoying meals or much of anything else with other men's wives. I allowed my guard to be down with you, and it has cost me. I was not sure of my decision until now. But knowing you are making me this lovely fish as my meal has made my decision easier."

Barbara frowned and reached for Mario's hand, but he refused to accept. "I don't understand. We've never touched lips, or made any gestures to each, other than a simple flirtation once or twice. This all seems a bit sudden. But if you insist, then I too realize this is the perfect meal for you."

"Ok, I will enjoy this last lunch with you but before I do, I need to make one call. I will be right back. Put the meal on the table and I will only be a minute."

Barbara carefully made sure the deadliest part of the fish, the liver, was front and center on the plate, ready to eat. She sat in her chair, Mario returned.

"Mangiare, is that not what your mother told you at the table Mario? Eat up my dear friend, and I will explain to you my story and why I ask so many questions."

I began to eat the salad, then a few nibbles of the fish when Barbara started to tell her story.

"I see happy couples with their children every day. Ever since I was a young girl, I wanted to have a large family. I cry myself to sleep most nights now knowing I am likely never to have children of my own. Richard and I have looked into adopting, but they wouldn't have come from my womb. I want one from me, mine, my flesh and blood. I feel in some way I'm being punished and the price I pay is my barren womb. I'm being punished because of my acts in the past and the one I am about to commit. I'm evil, Mario."

I sat quietly. Barbara took notice.

"Richard and I have tried for many years to have a family of our own. I've spoken to my doctor about it and he believes it's because of mine and Richard's stress levels. He also changed my diet, since his tests proved I'm borderline diabetic. The doctors have all their theories, for me, I know evil has entered my soul."

Barbara looked deeply into my eyes, a frightened, broken woman. I wanted to fix her, to tell her that all would be right in the world. That she would have children of her own one day, but I knew that day had passed. She spoke the truth. I could see the evil in her, despite the tears pouring from her eyes. I sat motionless not knowing what to do at that moment.

"I have a paper I want you to sign. It leaves your winery to your beloved employees. You know the ones, who are your family, but not your real children. Much of your money will be left to one of my charities. I set up a few children's charities around town, and when I find money from despicable men like you, I give it to the children."

I sat wondering how I could have been so foolish in misjudging Barbara. She deserved to lose her soul. However, I permitted her to continue.

"Do you think I care about your money, Mario? Hardly. I'm a smart woman, and can make my own money. In case you haven't noticed, my husband does very well. I don't need or want your money. No, I want to steal it and award it to the children who have lost their families in tragic accidents. I despise men like you, who could give a child a beautiful home. You have all the power and resources to offer them, but you're too busy working with your investments, or landscaping or wineries. I've seen so many like you who come to my husband's office. They complain about how busy they are with work and can't afford time to find a wife and make a family. Now sign the paper and I'll make your pain goes away, you horrible man."

She took Mario's hand and helped him sign the paper. She continued with her rant about how men, who have the resources, and won't father a child, are the lowest forms of creature on earth. It was now clear why Elder Orcus could not see her for who she was fully, nor could I. I wanted to see the good in her, but when this side of her was exposed, I could not walk away and allow her to continue murdering innocent men. I allowed her to release all her venom in my direction before speaking.

"I am not who you think I am, Barbara. I do one day intend on having children, but it will be on my time schedule, not yours. I have much longer to father a child than you think and one day it will happen. However, thank you for telling me your story. I will no longer feel badly about what must be done."

Barbara's jaw dropped, her eyes widened, as I as Mario took another gulp of the fish. "Could you pass the tartar sauce please, I do enjoy it when I eat fish. I will admit though, I have never eaten the Fugu fish.

Barbara sat wide-eyed as Mario continued.

"Detective Nesstor was informed by a man, who owns a Japanese restaurant downtown, that he has been selling the same fish to someone fitting your description. Only this woman wears a blonde wig. No one from the Chicago police force knew the fish was poison and leaves people to suffocate, yet once rigor mortis sets in, it can be very difficult for the local doctors to detect. I have to applaud you in your efforts."

"How can you still be talking?" Barbara asked.

"We will get to that. You did a wonderful job hiding your crimes. The detective told me he researched the charities the men left their money, and nowhere do any papers have your name on them. He told me the attorney you have been using to set up your charities, gave you up. It seems lawyer do not jail time."

"Rat, bastard," Barbara said as Mario went on.

"Me, I think using your old law firm's letter head was where your plan started to unwind. To have two of the men as clients of your husband's, and all the Wills signed by the same notary, foolish my dear. The worst part of it all, besides those senseless killings of course, is that I really wanted to believe you were a good person. I cannot tell you how much it is going to pain me in what I must now do."

"How, how is it you are not suffocating like the others? I watched them all die in front of me. You, you looked motionless for a time and now you sit here and act as if you never took one mouthful. I watched you eat it. Why aren't you suffering?"

"I pity you for what you are about to lose, besides your freedom. Oh, it must have never come up in conversation, but that Detective I told you about earlier, Nesstor, he is sitting outside the front door waiting to enter as soon as I call for him. Anyway, back to your question. One of the Wills you left behind, I believe his name was Carl something, anyway, there was a partial fingerprint on that paper they could not identify. The Detective has been watching me, watching you, imagine that. He approached me the other day while I was leaving a downtown office. He thought I was some bigwig record company executive, because I was coming from their office, too funny. Well, he then asked me if I had anything that might have your fingerprints on them. When I asked why, he started in with all kinds of questions about how I knew you, or if you have ever invited me over for a Japanese fish dinner. I told him no, but I would call him if you ever did."

"But you ate the damn fish."

"Yes I did. So, I called Nesstor earlier. He told me he would be outside the door waiting for you to serve me the meal and see if you had me sign a document. I cannot express how sorry I am that he is correct in his assumptions about you. He told me under no circumstances to eat the fish, only act as if I did, but I am not a good actor, and I was hungry. Before I call for the Detective, one last thing I will tell you. It seems I have a rare blood form, it is nearly impossible for me to get ill from poisons or even get the common cold. Can you imagine, never getting the flu in your entire life? I called my father and had him look up the toxin found in the Fugu fish. You can never be too careful you know. It seems I am immune from that one too. The good detective told me if you were serving the Fugu fish you meant to kill me. Again, it pains me to think what happened to you and what I must do to you."

Barbara let out a loud screech and Nesstor and two other officers came charging through the door. I had to dodge a swipe of the knife that she attempted to stick in my belly before the officers could reach her. My reflexes were excellent for a man over fifty.

"Detective, I think we had an agreement if I helped you with Barbara."

"We did. Take your photograph."

CHAPT3R T3И

"Tell me, Mr. Espendari. Why did it take you almost three hours to find your way to our police station, when it's a five minute walk down the street?" Nesstor asked. "You told me you'd be right behind us. I trust you're an honest man. Am I mistaken?"

"I apologize, Detective Nesstor. I had a small portion of the fish, in error of course, maybe it made me ill. I could not breathe for a moment. However, I feel much better now."

"You're a curious man to me. I noticed quite a bit of the fish was eaten, or am I mistaken?"

"Possibly I had a few mouthfuls, but it does affect everyone differently, Detective. Does it not?"

"Yes. Dead and more dead if you eat as much as seemed to be missing from you plate."

"Tell me, Detective. How exactly would you know my portions before you came in and why the questions? I helped you apprehend Mrs. Gifford, did I not? I did all you asked of me, and now you act as though I am the criminal?"

"Funny thing about the other day, when we met, another Detective who works with me, claims the building you were walking out of is the exact one where he claims you work. Yet, when I asked you about it, you told me no."

"Please enlighten me, Detective. What does any of this have to do with Barbara?"

"I don't know if it does or not. However, I find it very odd that I followed you on more than one occasion, while you were following Mrs. Gifford. If you knew her so well, why follow her? That can wait. Tell me about the Checkers record company. Do you know Johnny Joe Jackson? The building you were coming out of the other day is the same building where they have their office. Tell me, Mr. Espendari, why were you in that building?"

"I really don't feel I need to answer all these questions of yours, Detective. Have I broken a law, because I entered a downtown office building?"

"No, but see that man standing against the wall with the white shirt and black tie?"

"I see several men with white shirts and black ties, can you be more specific?"

Nesstor sighed. "Look, pal. I don't know who you really are, or what you have to do with two ongoing murder investigations, but I don't like the idea that you seem to be associated with the two people I'm now investigating for murder."

"Two investigations? Surely, Detective, you cannot link me with more than Mrs. Gifford, and I only knew her casually through my business dealings."

"And what are those businesses again? Refresh my memory will you please, Mr. Espendari, or is it Amison today?"

"Do I need to speak with an attorney, Detective? Is this how you harass all, who attempt to help you do your job in stopping criminals? You asked for my help and I gave it, and now you are playing a game of twenty questions. This messiness seems so unfortunate."

"Mr. Espendari, we checked our records, we can't find a record of you anywhere. Barbara Gifford told us that you came to her for marketing advice for a wine company. Espendari Wines. No one has ever heard of it, not even in Italy. Believe me that long distance call was not easy for me to get the Chief to approve around here. Finding someone who speaks Italian was even more difficult. Is there something you want to tell me here, Mr. Whoever you are?"

"I am who I say I am. Now if you would like to question me about Mrs. Gifford I will try to assist you. If not, I believe my next appointment is calling me."

"Why does that man standing over there swear to me that you tried to sign his brother to a recording contract? The same record company that has its offices in the building you were walking out of the other day. If you answer me that, you can leave. I don't need any more information from you about Barbara Gifford. She agreed to plead to all she knows as long as we leave her charity money alone."

"I cannot account for your associates eye issues or perhaps mistaken identity, Detective. I can only assure you I am not the man he thinks I am, and I am certainly not the man you think I am."

"We took the glass you were using at the table, Mr. Espendari. I'll have our lab dust it for prints. I'll find out your true identity and connect the dots to the murder of Mrs. Simpson and Mr. Clive Johnson. I thought all along it was Johnny Jackson, who killed those people, but maybe I was wrong. May I see some identification please Mr.?"

"Detective, I am not a citizen of your country, so I do not have any local identification that would be of any use to you. I have a passport, but sadly it is not with me."

"Perhaps we can have Officer Piker escort you back to where it is. Then we can allow you to continue with your day. That is once you prove to me who you say you are."

"Detective Nesstor, assuming of course you are who you say you are. You asked me to let you know if Barbara Gifford ever attempted to poison me and I did. You asked me with help with her fingerprints and I provided you a set. I am positive you have never seen me commit a crime in your town or you would not be allowing me to leave even to find my identification. Now, if you want to charge me with something please do, otherwise I am walking out of here."

"Yes, whether you are either in handcuffs or not will be your choice, but either way, Officer Piker is going with you."

"Fine Detective, have your Officer walk me back to my room. I will show him my passport. But after I show him my passport, please don't bother me again."

"I'm not making any promises, Mr. Espendari, Oh I'm sorry; I meant to say Amison."

Once back to my apartment, I really didn't have any issues showing Officer Piker my passport. I did have one as Amison and one as Espendari. I only had to hope I opened the right one if he was looking over my shoulder.

"Here you are, Officer. My identification, now if there is nothing more, I will bid you a good day and safe journey back to your station."

The burly officer frowned and flipped through the pages of the passport several times. "I don't know about this passport. You claim to be from Italy, yet the first marking has you leaving the United States, not entering. Possibly we should have Detective Nesstor take a closer look. You need to come with me."

Officer Piker led me back to the street. On your way to the police station, old man with white hair suddenly fell to the ground at Officer Piker's feet.

"Help me, kind sirs. I think I've broken a hip with my fall. Please, call for help."

With all the excitement and a small crowd now watching what the officer might do to aid the broken man, he forgot all about me and started to speak to the bystanders.

"Don't move, old man," Pike said. "I'll get some assistance. No one touch him. I'll be right back with help."

Officer Piker ran down the street leaving me behind. The old man with long white hair immediately stood up and gave me a long stare. He then smiled and said, "You didn't think I'd allow you to be locked up did you? Now you need to leave and so do I. No time for questions. Get lost."

I ran back to the place I was staying, grabbed up my personal belongings and like a ghost, I disappeared from the streets of Chicago and back to our compound.

"Caeles, the Council understands this assignment took a heavy toll on you. Your subject masked her true soul well. However, in doing your duty to our people, you offered a needed jolt to our resources. We thank you for your work. In your report, you spoke of a man who was following you, a Detective. Are you suggesting he will be a problem for us in the future?"

"I do not think so Elder Orcus. As long as I stay away from the Chicago area for a while. Despites his words, he really did not have anything to connect me to the other murders. He might have my fingerprints, but they cannot connect me to any murders."

"As you know," Orcus said, "our finger prints aren't on file anywhere in the world. Nor are our birth records. He will never be able to find you through them. However, for security measures, I will have your prints stolen from the crime lab. After all, if we can steal souls, what is one set of fingerprints? Now, you have worked hard for several months. This is not a punishment, but a reward for good service. Take some time far from Chicago and restore your mind. We have a home on the island of Oahu in Hawaii. It suits our needs and we chose it because the nickname of Oahu is The Gathering Place. We will be in contact with your next assignment."

Hawaii was as beautiful as I had imagined. I would peddle the bicycle I found in the house, down to the beach early in the morning, and allow my body to soak up the tropical sun until it was time for lunch. Later I would sit on the porch and either read or take an afternoon nap. There were times my mind would wander back to Johnny, Barbara or even Alexis wondering what was going on in their lives. My connection to the world was a Philco clock radio that sat on a small wooden table just inside the front door of the house. It received a signal from two stations. News of Chicago murder investigations were not the lead stories.

One afternoon, I decided to visit the newly built International Market Place along Kalakaua Avenue in Honolulu. While chatting with one of the merchants, a beautiful woman approached me about a camera issue she as experiencing.

"Sorry to disturb your conversation, but my camera shutter appears to be stuck and that man over there told me you would able to fix it for me. Is that true?"

I scanned the area, but could not recognize a familiar face. "What man was that?"

"I'm not sure who he was," the petite beauty said. "I was taking a photo, and my shutter froze up. A man walked up behind me and insisted that even though he could not help me, he was sure you could. He pointed right to you as if you two were friends."

I looked around again. "Where is the man now? What did he look like?"

The bronzed beauty stomped her sandal. "Who cares who the man was, or what he looked like? Can you help me or not? I'm in a real hurry to get the picture I need for a project I'm working on today."

"Yes, I think I can, but I am curious who the man was or why he thought I could help you? No one on this island knows that I have tools to fix cameras. No one."

"He was standing over there on the street corner, but he's not there now. Please can you help me? I don't have time to debate if you knew the man or not. I'm in a real hurry."

I took one look, barely touched the camera and the shutter released itself almost as if it fixed itself, or was magic. I guess in her haste, she did not give a second thought to the fact that I barely touched her camera and it worked.

"Thank you so much, you have no idea how much of a hassle you saved me. Please let me pay you for your troubles."

"No. It is fine really. I hope you can finish taking your photo now."

The twenty-something looking woman hustled away. She returned three minutes later.

"Damn. I missed my chance," she said wiping her brow. "I need a moment to cool my temper. Let me buy you something to drink or maybe some lunch. I could use a break from work now that I missed my assignment today. Please, have some lunch with me. Maybe this day can turn around, because so far, it's been a lousy frigging day."

I studied the beautiful creature standing in my shadow. The first thing I noticed was her jade colored eyes, which had a Polynesian shape to them. Then I spied her long black hair that flowed from her head down to the tip of her waistline. I would have been an utter fool not to want to dine with such a woman.

"Thank you. Sure, I would enjoy getting out of the sun myself and spending some time with you. I'm Cale. It is a pleasure meeting you."

"Hello Cale, nice to meet you too. My name is Kalani."

"What a beautiful name, so fitting for such a beautiful lady."

"Thank you. In Hawaiian, the name means, The Heavens. My father gave me the name because he was sure I was a gift from above."

I didn't know why, but there was an instant feeling that I had not met anyone like Kalani in my past. We walked slowly along the crowded avenue, until we found a quiet street café that seemed perfect.

"Tell me about yourself, Kalani. Do you live here, or are you on vacation?"

She giggled at my question. I felt the breeze in my hair, the smell of the salt air from the ocean across the street. I could hear the idle chatter from the table next to us, the touch of the cold glass on my fingertips. My imagination could taste her lip-gloss against my lips. All my senses were alive sitting across from her.

"Vacation? Me? No. I was born in the hospital down the street. I've lived on most of the Islands of Hawaii. I understand these islands like few others. I'm a freelance photographer, who takes photos, mostly scenic images, to promote tourism for our Island nation. I work with a local agency, who sells my work to magazines and occasionally to the government for promotional uses. I've traveled to the Philippines, Malaysia and Australia for my work. I would love to visit China, but I've yet to get any assignments there yet. One day, I'll get there, or even Japan. I would love to explore all of the Orient before I leave this earth."

She smiled and asked, "What about you Cale? You don't look like the typical man from Hawaii. I think that silly shirt you're wearing screams tourist. Are you from the mainland and here on vacation?"

I laughed and became even more alive sitting across from her. "I tend to move around quite a bit. I was born in Europe, but I have been living in the States recently. My work keeps me moving from one place to the next."

"Oh, what type of work do you do?"

"Hard to explain really, but I would consider myself an entrepreneur. I have owned a few businesses and tend to move where I think my talents best used. Photography is a hobby of mine. I am still curious why that man told you I knew about cameras, but I am so happy he did. What did the guy look like?"

"Gee, Cale. I'm really not sure, it happened so fast. But, I don't think he was from here either. He had pale skin. I think he had either gray. Maybe white hair, but I really didn't get a good look. I was so upset that my camera froze the instant I needed it. As soon as he said you could help, I walked right over to you."

"You could have gone back and taken the photo. I would have gladly waited for you to make sure it really was working."

"If you know about photography, Cale, then you realize it's all about a moment in time. My time to take the photo had passed. I was taking one of an important man, but he moved away as my shutter froze. He disappeared into the crowd. My moment in time had passed."

I smirked. "I hate when that happens. Maybe you will notice another who looks like your past subject and you can get the image another time."

Kalani sighed. "I doubt it. I was working on a special project and I needed that one particular person alone in the photo. I missed my chance."

We spent the better part of the next three hours sitting and watching the crowd stroll by as we learned about each other. We laughed and told photography stories. We learned we both get upset when others think you set up the camera, take the shot and that is all you have to know about photography. We found we had a lot in common. Our personalities seem to mesh. For the first time in my life, I felt comfortable with a woman, who in many ways was very similar to me.

After spending an afternoon with a beautiful woman, I realized how, despite my years of life experiences and education, that Barbara had manipulated me. She had no real connection with me on an emotional level, it was all about her desire to get close and destroy me for not having children. With Kalani, it came so natural, so enjoyable. I knew I could not allow her to leave me. Before I could act to cement our relationship, she did.

She offered to take me to parts of the island of Oahu that I had not seen to take scenic photos. My mouth could not move quickly enough to accept her proposal. I think she noticed my excitement when she teased me, "Down boy, or I might leave you lost up there."

I didn't care to hide my emotion. The woman made me smile inside and out.

We had spent the better part of four days together, when she informed me of an event she had to attend in the evening. She was hired by the local newspaper to get photos of a social gathering being held to encourage people to vote in the upcoming election. It would decide if Hawaii would become a state, or remain a territory of the United States.

Several politicians from the mainland were expected to attend, as well as officials from the islands. It was a formal affair. I wanted to tag along, but I realized Kalani had work to do.

That same evening, I felt a rush of power come over my body. Since it was while I was thinking about our date for the next morning, I wasn't sure if it was a rush of happiness or someone had taken a soul. It didn't matter. I was usually a detailed and cautious person, yet I couldn't stop feeling the joy that rushed through my body like I had never experienced.

The following morning, we met for our date that she described as a bike ride. Kalani showed me a route she took many mornings that winds along the coastline where you get to see some of the most beautiful sunrises. We pulled over for a moment to take a seat and listen to the waves roll on to the beach. While watching a few surfers attempt to catch the morning waves, soul stealing, Elder Orcus, Chicago, my parents, none of that was on my mind in that glorious moment. I sat with the most beautiful woman in the world, enjoying something that most will never get to experience. I felt so grateful. So satisfied.

We jumped back on our bikes and entered the winding road, when a car came out of nowhere. It shoved Kalani and her bike off the road. The corner of the car grazed me enough to eject me into midair and back on the beach fifteen feet from Kalani.

After a few moments, I regained my composure and noticed the man getting out of his car and moving towards Kalani. I thought he was checking to see if she was ok. As I was trying to stand and regain my balance, I saw a baseball bat in the man's hands.

He lifted the bat and whacked Kalani across both legs. I had never witnessed or been in an attack before, but instinctively I grabbed my camera and took his photo. He fell to the ground.

Before he could take another swing at Kalani, I felt myself almost fly through the air, lunging myself at him. I grabbed the bat, and took my personal swipes at his very wide body. Sports were never my strong suit. My first swipe missed. I continued to swing furiously, until he backed away. I cursed at him to stay away. He cursed at Kalani.

"You stay away from Mr. Kapena, or death to you, and your family, bitch," he yelled.

The attacker stumbled back to the car with his hand on his chest and drove off. I felt power rush through me, as if I had taken the man's soul. Between the feeling knowing I had taken a soul forbidden to remove, and the adrenaline running through me from the attack, I sat in the sand for several minutes attempting to control my senses. Kalani sat crying a few feet away. I knew I had to take control of the situation, despite being barely able to move.

"Are you injured badly, Kalani? We need to get you to the hospital."

"No, Cale. Give me a few minutes to regain my composure. I'll be fine after my body calms down."

"We need to report this to the police. What did that man want with you? Why was he trying to harm you?"

"No police. I can handle this on my own."

I inched towards her. "Kalani, the man tried to kill you. He wants to bring death to your family. Why would you not want the police to know what happened?"

"Cale, please give me a few moments and I will tell you what you want to know, but my body is shaking, I need time."

I dragged my body through the sand and wrapped my arms around her. I wasn't sure if it was only my body, or hers as well, but that feeling of stealing a soul was still running through me. I was hoping she could not feel me still sweating and pulsating. I'm not sure how long we sat, but it was over an hour. Neither of us said a word until I could stand.

"Let's see if you can stand, Kalani. If not I am going to get you to a doctor."

She stood up slowly, but wasn't in control of her body. Her bike to twisted to ride, we walked to the closest phone and called a taxi to get her home. She insisted she would be fine and I was not to call a doctor.

"My father is a doctor. I will have him come over later and check me out. I don't think anything is broken, but no question that I'll have bruises for a while. Can I tell my father my new boyfriend thought it was his birthday and I was his personal piñata?"

"That depends on if you consider me your boyfriend or not? So if I am, who was that man? Maybe I can help you. You would be surprised at what I can do."

"Yeah, I noticed. I'm being beaten and you take his picture. What the heck was that all about? You're girlfriend is being struck with a large piece of wood by a brute, and you stop and take pictures?"

"It got him to stop didn't it?"

"How did you do that? Did the flash go off in his face or something, Mr. Wizard?"

"One day I will tell you the trick, but for now, you tell me about that man. What did he want with you?"

"Cale, there are rare times I get put in some bad situations in doing my work. I'm working a story about a really bad guy who has moved onto our island home. He's smuggling women from the Orient promising wealth and fame. When they arrive, they're sold into slavery and prostitution. He's a violent and dangerous man who needs to be stopped."

"Another reason to call the police about today, before you or your family is injured seriously or killed. Let me call the police, please."

"The police know all about him. The problem is that they can't identify him with certainty, or catch him near any of the girls and tie him to the crimes. He's careful never to be in the same place with them. Some don't believe he is a real person, but maybe a small group of people running the smuggling organization. I know he's one person and I can identify him. I've been tracking him for over two years now. I sit on the side of the hill and watch everything that moves coming and going from where I believe he lives on Oahu. The police caught his men one time on the docks smuggling in girls in the hull of a freighter. I think it was a set up to let the police think they had discovered clues to track them. I believe there were many more than four girls being smuggled that same day. I was sitting high up on the hill watching. I saw enough girls to fill the back of a small pineapple truck, led off a smaller fishing boat on the other side of the docks, while all the police were searching the larger ship."

We waited for the cab as she went on with her story.

"My neighbor works for Honolulu police as a detective. He knows I'm working an editorial project for the paper. He was attempting to help and told me about the raid. He also insisted I not be anywhere near the docks, so not to expose him as my informant. When that truck left with the women, I followed it from above to a location near the docks, where the women were led into a building.

The day we met, I know it was Kapena at the market. I was trying to get his photo for my assignment. I don't want to go to the police, other than my neighbor and alert them that I'm following Kapena. He's an evil man and I have my assignment to fulfill. This project is very important to me, Cale. You can't under any circumstances get in my way or go to the police and let them know I'm following Kapena. I'm trained to handle myself. Earlier, I was caught off guard because I was with you, and not paying attention. I won't let that happen again. I'm a strong woman, capable of handling this on my own."

"If you say so, but I am a pretty capable person too, Kalani."

"Don't' underestimate me, Cale. There are things you can't understand that are in play. If I told you about them, you think I was a crazy woman and run from me. For now, sit here until the taxi can come. While we are waiting, you can explain to me why it was important that you needed to stop and take a picture of someone attacking me? You couldn't run to my rescue before taking a photo?"

"You have your secrets. I have mine."

CHAPT3R 3L3V3N

"Caeles Novo, you have broken our most sacred of laws. You took a soul not authorized by this Council. Each stolen soul has a purpose. Do you have any words to defend your actions?"

Peering up and the men on the Council made me uneasy. "It was done on impulse, Elder Orcus. Nothing more. Someone I cared was about being hurt and I reacted poorly. I was protecting my own body as well as the woman I was attempting to save. I will be more careful in the future."

"Everyone on this Council understands who we are as a people. We fully understand our beginnings as purely human form and realize those emotions still run deep inside every one of us. I do have empathy for your situation, but that is not an excuse. You have signed on for a life of taking only in extreme situations. There are enough of these cases still on earth so we do not need to take from common criminals, only people who lost their way. We can't stop you from living your life, but we can punish you when you break our laws because of your emotions. Do you have any more words before I sentence you?"

"Yes, Elder Orcus. I would like you to search for Kalu Kapena. If he needs his soul to be taken, I would beg the Council that I am the one to steal it."

"Kapena has already been marked and someone has been assigned. You are to stay away from this man. Your next assignment will come after your punishment. It will not be Kapena. He has an experienced agent of ours, who already has the Council's orders to remove his soul. Under no circumstances are you to take his soul, is that understood?"

With a disappointed tone I replied, "Yes, Elder."

"Good, now as for your punishment, you're to stay here with us for one week. You're forbidden contact with the outside world and are forbidden to utter a sound to anyone for any reason during that time. You will spend that week reading our laws, until they burn into your brain. This mistake will never happen again. After you say yes to my command, it will be the last syllable you utter for one week. For every word you speak, your time will be extended another week. Do I make myself clear?"

"Yes."

"You will now be taken to your quarters. Food and water will be supplied, but if you so much as even pretend to say thank you or look at whom is delivering your meals, your time will be extended. You will read, and then you will read more. Now, leave our presence. I hope for your sake, you will be permitted to return to the outside world in only one week's time."

Being in solitude didn't bother me. Not being able to contact Kalani, that bothered me. What could she be thinking? We were developing a relationship and I disappear. I was helpless to help her with Kapena or to tell her I needed to travel on short notice.

My space consisted of one room with a bed, a chair and one light. I was able to walk outside for sunlight and feel nature during the day, but my short path ended with a large wall. I could walk for about five minutes in any direction from my room, until I reached a wall or others who I knew I had to avoid. It was easier to sit in my room.

I fulfilled my punishment. I read our laws. Then I read them again. A crusty old book filled with hundreds of pages, it was written in Latin. The first two times while reading the pages, I glided over them with my mind closed to the words since I had read the book many times in my training. I could almost recite what each word on each page, before I flipped to the next.

However, the third time, I actually read the words carefully. A small verse jumped out at me that I could swear was never in my edition of the book. One small line sat in the middle of all the other rulings deep inside the books pages.

It stated. "No creature or human large or small shall remain without a soul for more than the time deemed necessary to replenish and restore." It made no sense to me. There was no mention of restoring souls anywhere else in the book or in any of my training. No one had ever told me that this was even possible. One line now had all my attention. Was our mission to take and restore long ago? Was this only in print because originally, that was the goal, but the powers were never granted?

The remaining three days under probation were horrible for me. I could not speak to anyone or ask questions about what I had read. Did I want to discuss this with anyone on the Council? Were they hiding something from our past? Was it nothing but words on a page that meant nothing? These questions churned in my brain until solitary confinement was not something I aspired to do again. I wanted out of this place badly, yet I wanted to know the answer to my questions.

Anyone who passes certain aptitude skills early in our training to steal souls were brought to the compound for six months of extensive training and education. My father once told me, "only about fifty percent will finish the six months of training and be taken to the compound."

Training at the compound involved mental, survival and physical skills to evaluate if I was ready to advance. I hadn't forgotten that time in my life. However, to me, it was another six months before reaching what I considered our highest honor. I recalled visiting a library, during my training at the compound.

Occasionally, I had no choice but to visit the small room at the end of the hallway. It is close to the living quarters of Elder Orcus. I decided my punishment didn't preclude me from visiting the library as long as I didn't look or speak to anyone. I needed to scour the library, to check and see, if there were any more books that mentioned restoration.

There was not need to avoid security guards. The few in the compound were allowed to take your soul our homeland came under attack.

Long after nightfall, I found my way into the library. I wasn't sure how many were in the compound, but I knew I had to move rapidly. The problem was that I was not sure if what I was looking for even existed. I spent as much time as I could flipping through old parchments and tired books, but could not find anything written about restoration. The only thing I did notice on one of the parchments was it seemed the numbers ran sequentially, with one page missing. But in reading from one page to the next there did not seem anything missing from the text. I left not knowing any more than I did when I entered.

"Your punishment has ended, Caeles. Your next assignment is on the table inside the library. It seems you know how to find your way there. David Blake is your subject. He's a rogue CIA agent, who left Viet Nam and has been suspected of executing business executives and top officials around the globe. We suspect that he has killed at least three men, possibly more. No one knows where he is right now. From what the report will tell you, he constantly changes his appearance. My sources tell me that the United States government will not admit he exists, but I know from reliable sources he is on the government kill list if sighted. He is very dangerous and under no circumstances are you to put yourself in jeopardy. His soul is as dark and ruined as I have seen in many years, Caeles. His high school yearbook photo is in the library as well as a copy of a report we had our internal source steal from inside the CIA. You don't need the Council's permission any more than you have now to steal on sight. Only be positive of your target, he is hard to identify. Good luck, now go."

The report had listed one man suspected of being killed by Blake in California. Since the California execution was the closest to Hawaii, yet not exactly along my way, it would be foolish to tempt the Council so soon, but then again, Elder Orcus did tell me they really didn't know where to find him. I assumed Honolulu was as good of a place to start as any.

"I am so sorry to leave so quickly, Kalani. My work detained much longer than I was expecting. Can I make it up to you and take you out for a nice dinner?"

Kalani stood with crossed arms, but with a wrinkle of a smile. "Do you really think you can leave for almost two weeks with no word, and show up on my door step with that sad face and expect me to believe you couldn't contact me? At least one simple, hey sorry, I had to leave town, but I'll see you soon."

"I don't know what to say, I really don't. Sometimes my work takes me places I was not expecting for longer than I want, without a way of communicating. I swear, had I been able to contact you, I would have."

"What kind of job is this again, Cale? You told me that you are some kind of free spirit and that you go where you think you're needed. I don't need liars and free spirits in my life. I need a man who doesn't disappear the moment I'm injured. What happened, were you afraid the big man who you had to take a picture of would come looking for you and your silly camera?"

"Trust me, Kalani. That man is no threat to me, and that was not my reason for leaving. I know, I know, I so wish I could have let you know I would be away. I am so sorry. Please, let me take you out for nice evening and I will try to make it up to you."

"My job takes me strange places too, Cale, but it really hurt that you ran when I was in trouble."

"Stop right there. I was never running from you. I was called away by someone very important. I was not expecting to be away this long. Honest and truly, if there was a way of contacting you, I would have."

"I will go out with you, Cale, on one condition. You tell me exactly where you had to go and why they kept you. Tell me and I will go. If not, please don't bang on my door ever again."

"Kalina, I want to tell you. I want to tell you all I know. I do. However, if I tell you, it will ruin our relationship. In time, I will tell you everything, but for now you have to trust that I could not contact you. Please be understanding and offer me the benefit of the doubt, this one time."

"I have enough mystery in my own life, Cale. I'm sorry but I don't need yours, and I am not into handing out benefits. Good bye."

I sat on her doorstep for hours. I wanted to bang on that door, but what would I tell her? Hello, Kalani. I travel the world stealing souls by taking photographs. I'm expected to live another two hundred years, and I answer to a High Council in a place I am unable to disclose to you. The Council held me captive in our compound and I couldn't speak to anyone for a week as a punishment because I took a photo of your attacker so that he would stop hitting you with that bat. In doing so, the reason he looked like he had a heart attack was because I took his soul and for that, I was being punished. I decided to sit feeling like a broken-hearted fool than tell that story.

While sitting there, I could feel her eyes piercing through my back as she peered from her window, but she never came back outside. I never turned to look. Eventually, I left assuming it was the last time I would see her. Maybe my life is too complicated for a lover. And now, I was chasing a man, who I didn't know what he looked like, where he was on earth, or where he may be next. I didn't want to end up losing my right to steal souls and let everyone down, who relies on me, including my own family. I needed to walk away and never return.

My first stop was Los Angeles, California to gather information on the most recent murder by Blake. The CIA report noted the deceased was the CEO of a weapons company used by the United States military. My identity changed to FBI agent John Latens. It wasn't easy to get credentials, but who knew the FBI and the CIA didn't always share information. Our contact inside the CIA, not only got us a copy of Blake's report, but smuggled information to an FBI friend, in exchange for a set of fake credentials for me. They were in the package with my report. I knew whoever got us the fake credentials, knew his Latin since the word "latens" means "hidden or unknown." I found it quite amusing he chose that name for me.

The other thing that I came to discover was that the LAPD did not like the boys from the FBI looking into their cases. The lead detective on the case was Patrick Wilson. His courtesy towards me was uglier than his terrible suit and overweight physique.

"Listen close, Special Agent Latens. This is my case. I'll be the one slapping the bracelets on whoever did this, not some shiny suit from Washington. Do you understood? If so, nod once. Otherwise, get your ass out of my office. The only reason I'm tolerating the stench of your fancy cologne in my space, is because the Chief once worked for you boys back in the day, and he told me to play nice."

"Thank you kindly for all your hospitalities, Detective. I give you my word, should I find this fellow before you, the first call will be to you, so that as you say, you can slap the bracelets on him."

"Now why would a big shot Bureau man like you want to give up a high profile collar to me?"

"My mission is to have the perpetrator atone from his sins, not make a name for myself. In fact, I would prefer my name not be mentioned in your report, once we do bring him to justice.

However, I would like to be there to take a photo for my records, when he is booked. If you give me a head's up after you and your men are in place for the arrest, I will update you if I should find him first. Can we agree on that?"

"I've been around too long and trust few men, so I'm not agreeing to anything just yet. One last question, Latens? How come you aren't carrying a gun?"

"Who says I am not carrying what I need to carry out my mission? Like I said, Detective, if you cooperate with me, you will be the arresting officer, should he be arrested in your town, not me."

"What makes you think he's left this town, Latens?"

"Tell me what you do know, Detective, and I will tell you why I do not think he is anywhere near California right now."

Wilson frowned. "The hit was on a gun manufacturer VP. He was in town visiting friends. He was shot in the head while getting in his car leaving a nightclub, just before two a.m. There were no witnesses and no one heard gunfire. The bullet is from an AK 47, one of the new long range types."

"Does that not tell you it was done by a trained killer, Detective? Possibly military? The killer knew his trade. My guess is that this was a paid hit. If so, the killer is a pro. I pro would never stay around. I'm not telling you something you do not know, so stop playing games with me."

After leaving the long time detective Wilson, I went to the murder scene looking for evidence. Wilson had showed me the photos taken the morning after the crime. The angle the bullet came from behind the victim. There were a line of trees and bushes behind where Wilson believes the deceased was standing when shot.

It had been a month since the crime. I wasn't expecting to find much, but I did. Lodged in some mud, next to a large rock rested a shell casing. I wondered how the detectives could have missed it. I didn't know if it would match the deadly bullet, but I took it to Wilson as a sign of goodwill. It broke the ice with Wilson. He parted with more information.

"We think this guy is ex-military too," he said. "You aren't the first Federal agent to come wandering into my office. You boys must want this guy bad. In fact, one of you Feds offered up the name David Blake and showed me a photo taken from his military file. You all are sending a lot of top guys in here trying to find this nut job. I'm figuring he's anted for more than this one killing."

"I can't tell you that with any certainty, Detective, but it is assumed this was at least his third shooting. Washington is putting a lot heat on us to find Blake, assuming he's our man."

"Why Blake? What makes you Feds think this is the guy who's doing all the killing?"

I needed Wilson on my side, so I returned his information with my own. "All I can tell you is that at least three murders were done with the same rifle, the same one Blake was trained on before heading off to Viet Nam and all three happened after he went missing. No one is certain that Blake is responsible, but the first person murdered was a US diplomat, who was in Saigon when he was shot. Blake worked in Saigon at the same time, but went missing five days after the murder. The next was a US General who was on leave in Japan and then the dead gun maker. All three were involved in escalating the Viet Nam conflict. Blake is a highly skilled marksman, who was trained for missions just like these murders."

Wilson rubbed his chin and nodded. "Thanks for the intel, Latens. None of the other Feds gave up much more than a name and a photo. I assumed Blake was wanted for more than this murder, but no one would tell me."

I turned to look for the exit when Wilson kept talking.

"Since you seem to be keeping your word on updating me, I'll tell ya something I didn't tell your other Fed pals. We had a tip yesterday from an anonymous caller, stating Blake was in a hotel room not far from where that murder happened. I have no idea why they called here. We haven't made any statement to the press or released any names. It's odd Blake was mentioned by name staying in that dump. I've had my men sitting on the place since the call, but they haven't seen anyone come or go since. The office manager says by the picture we showed him, that it could be Blake, but he wasn't certain. Now, if try to enter that room, my cheery personality ends. Are we clear?"

"We are clear, Detective. Like I have told you more than once, I only want to see the man for identification purposes before he is shipped off to jail, nothing more. I have zero interest in bringing him in, nor will I stand in your way of arresting him."

"You ain't really a regular FBI, Latens?"

"I am as interested in justice as you, Detective Wilson. Mine is let's say, more spiritual than physical. I'll tell you what, I won't even ask for the name of the hotel as long as you promise to call me if you see him coming or going from the room. If you call this number and leave a message, someone will get it to me. Thank you for your time Detective."

Originally, I had planned on heading to Japan to get information on the second murder, but with the possibility of Blake actually still being in the area, I thought I would stay put.

While waiting around in town, I contacted a few old classmates of Blake and his family to see if anyone could offer some insight as to where he might be, or why he might have gone AWOL. It was a mixed bag of reactions, but the two things that did stand out were that his father told me he was a history buff. The younger Blake read all he could about history and wars. The second thing that friends stated was that he always wanted to live near the beach, any beach. So maybe he was still in California, or maybe he knew if he tried to leave the country, he would be stopped.

CHAPT3R TW3LV3

"She cries for you. Go to her. Wake now, Caeles. She cries out in need. "

Four nights in a row, I awoke from the same dream. He had returned, the mysterious man, who had appeared in my past, and now nightly in my dreams. He was hovering over my bed, watching me as I opened my eyes.

He begged me to help someone. I saw myself, in my dream, lying in my bed with the unidentified man hovering over me. He had long white hair, with a hint of the color of pearl, and a long flowing white robe floating in mid-air, attempting to wake me with his words.

The curtains in the window rustled, yet the window was closed. His words replayed several times in my dream.

"Wake now, Caeles. Time is running out. Go today, or she will die."

I sat up in bed, now fully awake. The curtains calmed. No one else was in the room. I tried to focus my eyes. In the mirror, across the room was a faint image of the same man as in my dreams. He was holding Kalani in his arms, only she looked haggard. The light in her eye faded. I heard his voice shout at me, "Go to her. She is dying a slow death." I rubbed my eyes hoping to get a better view. The image disappeared.

It was past nine in the morning. I rarely sleep that long. I called Detective Wilson. His men had entered Blake's suspected the motel room, but no one was there. However, he told that there were signs of recently eaten food. They never bothered to watch the back door of the motel. Whoever was staying there, was coming and going through a back door for days.

I called Kalani's home number, but no answer. It was now past six in the morning in Hawaii, but she usually started her bike ride promptly at six. It wasn't surprising that she didn't answer.

I paced my room for hours trying to make sense of my dream and the vision. I then switched thoughts wondering how they never knew there was a back door at the hotel and if Blake was ever there. I wanted to believe Blake was close, but it could have been anyone staying in the room.

Wilson said his crew dusted for prints. Had Blake been in the room, he would have seen the police out front. I called Kalani again. No answer. I remembered her agent's name and called that office number.

A friendly female voice answered. "We're sorry, but we can't give out personal information about our clients over the telephone."

I was torn between my duty, and someone, who last time we spoke, wouldn't even allow me to pass the shadow of her front door. However, I couldn't take another night of dreams. I informed Detective Wilson that I was leaving town for a few days and begged him to call me if they found evidence of David Blake still in the area. I wasn't convinced he would since his men entered the room without any advanced warning as he promised. His excuse was that his men thought they heard a shot fired. Whatever. Good thing Orcus and the Council didn't remove souls for lying.

I grew weary of the waiting game with Blake. I sent my report to the Council, so they knew I was on the case, but told them I had to travel to Honolulu. My mind would not allow me to rest until I knew Kalani was out of harm's way. I had to see her beautiful face unharmed, before I could rest easy.

Her small home looked vacant. I walked around it until a male came out from the house next door and began quizzing me.

"I am looking for Kalani Inoke. I am a friend of hers, and I am worried something has happened. Have you seen her recently?"

"Kalani hasn't been home in over two weeks. She travels a lot, so it's not unusual for her to not be around. If you are her friend, then you'd know she comes and goes without much warning."

"Are you her neighbor she spoke about, who works for the Honolulu police? The one who is a detective?"

He stared me down before responding. "Yeah, who is asking?"

"I am her friend Cale. I know she was looking into a dangerous man, Kalu Kapena. I am afraid something may have happened to her. She was attacked by one his men a few weeks ago."

"Kalani's a smart girl. She can handle herself and what do you know about Kapena?"

It was my turn to size up the man in my presence. He looked two shades under six foot, with dark features. He wore a gun and holster hanging for all to see.

Do I remember Kalani telling me that your name is Paulo Kopona?" I asked.

"It's not a national secret who I am," he said with a smirk. "What did she tell you about Kapena and why he any of your business?"

"I know he is a suspected smuggler of women. Kalani was working on a story about prostitution and smuggling on this island and maybe other places. I know Kapena has a dark soul and needs a spiritual makeover before he hurts her and others."

"Mr. Cale, let me offer you a word or two of advice. Stay away from Kapena and Kalani. We know all about him and his operations, the police are getting close to locking him up for a long time. If you know her, as you say, then you know she's been watching him. However, right now, she'ss likely on one of the other islands taking her photographs for clients. She dashes off on assignments all the time."

"Yes, she told me, but did she leave any notes, or say good bye, or ask you to watch her house? I don't notice her bicycle anywhere, do you? It seems odd that it is not against the wall in her house. If she was gone for work, why is her bike missing?"

"After her accident on the road, it was sent to be repaired, maybe it's not back yet. I don't know. All I do know is that I'm late for work and you shouldn't ask so many questions. If you were really her close friend, you would know these answers. I don't want to see you here when I return, or I'll have you locked up for trespassing."

My body was exhausted. I had barely slept in five nights. I checked into a local hotel. I had another dream. This time the man had his arms around Kalani, but she was barely clothed. There were hands reaching for her. Her hair had lost its luster.

"She is close, Caeles. Wake up."

I rose from my bed, sweat was pouring down my unshaven face. I was trembling. A voice shouted at me.

"She is close Caeles. Seek her now."

"Where, where is she? Tell me now," I yelled back. My mind raced with thoughts about where she might be. I remembered the nightclub that Kalani showed me from high on the hill, where some of the girls would be taken to dance at night. It was near Pearl Harbor, not far from where I was staying. I looked at the clock and it was just past one in the morning. I rushed to put on some clothes and made my dash to the nightclub.

The room was dark, full of smoke. Sailors filled the barstools. There were two lights shining down in the center of the bar on a small square platform, with a long pole, and single dancer twisting and curving her body around it.

As I moved closer to the stage, my eyes wandered around the room, searching for any clues of Kalani. An old man with a foul stench yelled at the stage, "Take it all off, whore."

I looked to see, whom he was yelling at. It was Kalani. All I could see was sadness dancing on the platform. Her dancing pace quickened. She tossed her top, as the men hooted for more. Kalani resembled a shell of her former beauty. She didn't show any marks on her body from being beaten, but as I stared into her eyes, I could tell she was mentally shattered. She wasn't the same defiant and confident woman, who refused to allow me in her home.

I lingered in the area for her routine to be over. I then followed her over to where she left the stage. "Kalani, what have they done to you," I cried to her. As she turned to look at me, a huge man with a barrel chest and forearms the size of my thighs pushed me aside.

"No talking with the performers," the brute said. I tried to get closer, but was pushed to the floor. "Touch her, and I slit your throat, asshole."

I didn't know what to do. She was escorted to another room, with only one door and no windows. I went outside to see if maybe they would take her out through a back door at closing time.

I waited about an hour when finally a truck pulled up with two men inside. Two minutes after they arrived, the back door opened and five women in bathrobes and another man walked out of the door. I rushed to get close, but was beaten back. Kalani offered me a nothing but a blank stare. They piled the girls into the truck and were gone.

After daybreak, I went to Kalani's neighbor Kopono to tell him I had witnessed in the nightclub. "She needs our help. Please send in the police to get her away from these criminals. I am sure they have done something to her. I saw her up close. They have taken her against her will. I am sure of it."

"Mr. Cale, I warned you to stay away. She is likely working an angle to get closer to Kapena. We are under direct orders from our boss not to go inside. All I will say is that we have one man working the case from the inside. I'm sure if she was in danger he would know. We've been working this case for two years. Don't do anything to disrupt our investigation."

Since he would not help me, I turned to Kalani's father. I had met his once at Kalani's house when she was healing with her leg. He was a handsome man, who appeared to be in late forties. His clean-shaven look fit his profession.

"My daughter does work you would not understand, Cale. She's a rare person, trained in many skills. I'm sure they haven't harmed her."

"What is it with everyone?" I asked. "Doctor Inoke, I can assure you that your daughter is in need of our help. I am trained in ways you would not understand either, and I am telling you that your daughter is in serious trouble. Who knows how long she will even remain on this island. She is in the hands of a dangerous smuggler. She could be being shipped off this island at any time. Please, go see for yourself."

"I have someone, who handles incidents like this for me. I'll go with him tonight and see if she is in any danger. If so, we'll get her back. If I think she is working undercover for her work, and wants us to leave her, then we'll not involve ourselves in her affairs. Like I've told you, she sometimes puts herself in harm's way. Yes, I know all about Kapena and the threats he makes on my family. He is of little concern to me."

"Doctor, I know you don't know me well, but I know when a person has lost their desire to live or cannot function properly. That is your daughter right now. I will get her from those people with or without your help."

"I'll be there tonight to see if I believe she's in any danger, Cale. Do not touch her until I can see my daughter."

I went back to my hotel wondering what was wrong with these people. Kalani was in obvious need of help and no one, not even her own father wanted to believe me. I tried to sleep, but every time I would get close to sleeping that voice would be in head.

"She cries inside, save her." I knew something had to be done, but running around snapping photos wasn't the answer. It would only land me in the compound for a very long time or worse. Was I missing something? Was it all an act by her to get closer to Kapena's network?

I went back inside the club the next evening to be sure Kalani was dancing again. She was. Again, there was little life or spirit in her eyes. Again, I tried to get close after she came off stage, only to be warded off by the same huge man from the previous night. I did all I could to gain eye contact with her.

"Look, fool, I told you last night to back off, next time you won't walk out of this building alive."

The more I thought about what they had done to that woman, the more furious I became. I felt as alone as Kalani must have felt inside.

I waited outside for the pickup truck to arrive. I sat out of sight waiting for the back door to open. I wanted a clear view of Kalani. The truck arrived. Minutes seemed like hours, finally the door opened. There was about twenty feet between the door and the truck on a dirt lot. As the back door closed, I lit the fuse and sent rags full of gasoline onto the back of the truck.

I lit the fuse on the ground and watched the flames engulf the truck. The two people inside the vehicle were in ring of fire. There was one man on the outside of the fire and before he knew what was going on, I slugged him as hard as I could with a baseball bat across his back. The two in the truck ran from the fire and truck. One was on fire. I grabbed Kalani and started to run. Her high heels were preventing her from running. I stopped and ripped off her shoes. She went limp and fell into my arms.

"Come on, Kalani," I said. "I need you to focus for only a few minutes. Please hold my hand and run with me. As we struggled to reach the front of the building, I was about to toss her in my car when another car almost ran us over.

"Get in now." Gunshots rang out. I shoved Kalani into her father's car. Inside the car was a man shooting back at the men shooting at us. One of the bullets hit me in the leg as I shoved Kalani into the back seat.

"I told you not to go near her, Cale, her father said as we sped away. "However, I'm thankful you did. After we saw her on stage, we knew we had to act. She's safe now, that's all that matters. I didn't see you inside, or I would have warned you. I have some place safe to take you both. They'll be looking for you and my daughter. Kapena won't take kindly to the mess you created outside his club."

Kalina's father took us to a small home on the other side of the island. After only a few minutes, he knew.

"She's been turned into a heroin addict. They have poisoned her with this garbage. I know I can heal her, but she still needs to go through some withdrawals like any other addict. I cannot tell you why, Cale, but heroin's one of the few toxins that can destroy my daughter. She's immune to most earthly drugs. However, in a few days I can make her whole again. I can fix your leg too. It's not serious."

Not serious? Maybe he would have liked to change places with me, as he removed the slug and stitched up my leg. I didn't want to tell him that I healed faster than an average human. It would be healed in less than a week, but I didn't want him to know. Then again, I had never been shot before, so I was only going on what I had been taught. Then I considered what he meant by Kalani not reacting to most drugs.

For the first time in a week, I had no dreams to wake me. I awoke several hours later on the floor, watching Kalani sweat and become very anxious. She begged her father to make it all stop, but he pressed her to be strong. Her anxiety was obvious as she attempted to rid her body of the poison. Watching her only made me angrier with the people who did this to her. It took three days before Kalani started to regain her former self and recognized I was there with her.

"My father tells me you're the one who saved me, Cale. Is this true? I know it might sound strange, but I knew you would return. I know you were upset with my father, but he's under strict orders not to interfere with my work. He's seen me in some extreme situations before, but I'm happy you came back."

"There are so many things I want to tell you Kalani, but all I will say is that the man, who told you that I could fix your camera, came to me in a dream. He revealed to me you were in trouble. I know that sounds ridiculous, but it is not nearly as crazy as why I had to leave you the first time and where I have been since. Now, just rest. I won't leave you this time until you are fully healed. I promise."

Kalani put her hand in mine. "I'm worried about you, Cale. Kapena's not going to rest until he finds you. You need to get off this island to a safe spot until he's arrested. You need to disappear. I'll understand this time. Kapena's got connections all over this island. You're not safe here."

"It's fine. He doesn't know who I am, Kalani. Those men that night, they didn't see my face. It was too dark, and with the fire and the confusion, I don't think they could identify me."

"I wouldn't be so sure, Cale. He's a very powerful and resourceful man. He has eyes and ears all over this island. If he wants to find you, he will."

"What about you? You promised me you would be safe and keep your distance, how did they capture you?"

Kalani placed a cool cloth in her forehead. "I was on the hill with my binoculars and someone came up behind me. They stuffed a rag in my mouth and knocked me out. The next thing I knew, I was sitting in front of Kapena and some of his goons. They started to shoot me with this filth in my veins. My system must have been fighting it, because his man was complaining that it took too much of this junk to make me high. My body fights off most toxins and poisons, Cale. Well, better than most humans. Next thing I knew, I was taken to a private room where Kapena ripped off my clothes and then I am not sure what happened. I must have passed out from the drugs. When I woke up, I was in a cage in some room with the other women. I heard them begging for a fix. Eventually, I did the same. This went on for a few days I think, before they told me, if I danced they will take care of my needs. I would have done anything at that point to feel better. I feel so ashamed. I'm a strong person, but I gave into the drugs and those criminals."

"Sssh, rest now. I'm going to make him pay for what he did to you."

"Cale, you can't go near that man. I've not finished my assignment, until I do, please do not go near him. You can't understand how important this is to me and to others that I finish my task."

"Nothing can be more important than your safety, Kalani, especially after what he did to you. I'm going to make that man suffer by making him pay with his soul. Trust me."

"What did you say?" Kalani asked.

"I said I'm going to make him suffer for what he did."

"No. I think you said you were going to make him pay with his soul."

I smiled. "Did I? Well, it's only an expression. Get some rest."

"Cale, promise me, you will stay away from Kapena. I'll be better soon and I'll finish my assignment. When I do, that man will not hurt me or anyone else again."

After two more days, Kalani was close to her former self. Her smile and beauty had returned and my leg had healed. It didn't go unnoticed. I gave the doc all the credit for how well he treated the wound and stitched me up.

Having gone close to a week without outside communications, I had to get to my room and check any messages. One of the doc's associates went by the club and picked up my car. I drove over to my hotel room after the sun went down. When I arrived, I wasn't alone.

"I was starting to think you were never going to return. You owe Mr. Kapena an apology for blowing up his truck and attacking his men. Don't you think, Mr. Cale?"

"Kopono. How did you get in here? Wait, silly question. But, why? Wait, that was even a dumber question. At least I know now how Kapena's thug knew where to find Kalani the day on our bike ride and where she sat on the hill."

"I warned you we had people in that strip joint. I warned you to stay away from your little girlfriend. Mr. Kapena has taken a liking to that sweet body of hers, and he's sent me on a mission for her safe return."

I showed a lot patience in not dropping the traitor by taking his soul. He had shown enough evil to me, but I didn't want anymore confinement. I tried the tough guy approach. "Her return will never happen."

Kalani's neighbor chuckled. "I suggest that you tell me where she's hiding out. If you're lucky, Mr. Kapena will only beat you, turn you into a junkie and then I'll arrest you. If you don't talk, well then, he will use you as shark bait on the side of his boat and let them rip you limb from limb, while you slowly die. Either way, I suggest you tell me quickly, or the pain will only be worse. Mr. Kapena really does not like it when people steal from him."

"Since you have badly overstated my emotions for the girl, sure I'll take you right to her. Since I know Kapena would never release me to you or anyone else, after I show you where she is, you will release me, or no deal. You had me all wrong, Kopono. She had stolen from me. I only wanted back what he stole from me. If you promise to let me collect a few things on the table over there, and let me go once you see her, I will take you to Kalani, and you will never see me again."

Kopono twisted his neck. "Maybe you're not listening to me, asshole. You're going to suffer one way or the other. No picking up your items. No telling me how this is going to play out. I'm in control here."

He handcuffed me. He then led me to the front door. He shoved me through the doorway, following closely behind. I heard a thud. I turned to see Kopono on the ground.

"Let me get those cuffs off of you. Help me tie up this dirty cop. Then get your things and get off this island. We'll dump him on the other side of the island where it will take him hours to walk to the closest phone. You're too hot to stay here now. I'll tell Kalani I took you and you can call her once you are safely away."

The Doctor's bodyguard had been ordered to check on me. Before he could knock on the door, he heard voices. Seconds later, Kopono led me out, and struck Kopono. I grabbed up my belongings and called for my messages. I had one from Detective Wilson in Los Angeles.

We left Kopono on a deserted beach and headed for the airport. The guard was under orders from the Doc to wait with me until I boarded a plane. We sat through the night, hoping the dirty cop couldn't reach us before I could get off the island.

"There he is," the guard said, while we sat at the departure gate.

I was half-asleep when I looked around and noticed a wall of people walking towards us. "Who, who is that?"

"That's Kapena. No doubt about it. That's Kapena."

"Where's my bag. I need my bag, hurry," I said.

"What are you doing? What's in your bag, Cale?"

"I need my camera bag. It's next to you on the floor. Hurry I need a photo of him."

We followed Kapena and his men to the end of the waiting area. Kapena waited by a doorway, while a small plane pulled up on the tarmac. I knew the door would be opening soon and he would be gone. I needed him alone in the photo. I knew I would be punished severely for this photo, and it was possible I would not see Kalani again once I released the shutter. However, in that moment, my rage for the man over shadowed any future punishments. This man had to pay with his soul not only for what he had done to Kalani, but all the women he had enslaved.

I pulled my cap down and sat in a chair within a close enough range to steal his soul. Kapena moved away from the others. I raised my camera and click. I heard a shutter release, but it wasn't mine.

"I asked you to leave this to me, Cale. I told you I would handle it. Is this how our relationship is going to go? You don't listen to a damn thing I tell you. Do you?"

It didn't matter what Kalani was saying. My body began to shake and power came rushing through me. I could see in the foreground, Kapena drop to the ground with people calling for assistance. He was having difficulty breathing, but I was having a hard time doing anything.

Kalani's body was shaking, along with the bodyguard. People were taking notice of the three of us. We knew we had to move. It was still another thirty minutes before I could board the plane.

The three of us made it to a coffee shop in the airport terminal. We sat there staring at each other, now knowing we shared a common bond. "If you knew why didn't you tell me, Kalani?"

"How could I be sure? It's not like I meet another like me every day," she said with a giggle. "In fact, you're the first one. I suspected it when you took a photo of my attacker, but hey maybe you wanted it for identification purposes and were thinking ahead. However, the other day when you said you wanted to steal his soul, and your wound healed within days, it became obvious."

"I have to admit Kalani, it barely crossed my mind that maybe you had the power too. I mean you did shake off the addiction fast, but that's not impossible. I was more surprised they addicted you at all now that I think about it. Someone tried to poison me a few months ago and it barely hit me. But then again, I took it in a small dose."

"They shot me up with five times the normal amount to make someone addicted, so I would guess that's why. We're not immune from all drugs and toxins as you likely know, assuming you weren't sleeping that day in class."

She loved having a laugh at my expense, but that was ok. I turned to Kono, the man who had been watching over me. "So what about you? Do you have the power too?"

"I did for a while, but I lost it. No one really knows why, but after about ten thefts, I lost the ability. I know no one told you, but I am the Doc's brother and Kalani's uncle. It is one reason why I stay close with them."

"Does your father steal too, Kalani?"

"He never wanted to steal. He was always more interested in healing. He never finsihed his training. Ever since he was young, he wanted to be a doctor. I wish I was there when he was in medical school, and he had the appearance of a ten year old. Elder Orcus had him work at the compound until he aged enough to where people were comfortable with him as their doctor. He did tell me that he thought your name sounded familiar and that maybe he did some work on your family."

"I'll have to ask if my dad knows your dad," I said. "I guess now I can tell you that I was locked up in the compound during that time you thought I abandoned you. I was being punished for taking that guy's soul who hit your leg. What was I supposed to tell you? I stole a guy's soul protecting you and some all-powerful Oz sent me to my room for a week? I mean really, think about it."

Kalani smiled and gave me hug. "Ok, you're forgiven, but you still need to get off this island, Cale."

"By the way, your neighbor is on Kapena's payroll. Stay away from him."

"I was afraid of that," Kalani said. "I think he's the one, who put the rag to my face. He wears a very distinctive aftershave. Whoever it was that kidnapped me that day was using that same aftershave. I didn't want to believe it was him, but I guess I have no choice now. I hear them calling your flight. You need get off this island. Kono and I will handle Paulo Kapono."

You be safe, Kalani. I'll call you when I reach California and tell you all about who I'm chasing. At least now, we can be honest with each other."

CHAPT3R TH!RT33N

"I don't want to hear a damn thing from you, Latens," Wilson said upon my return to his office. "I left you a message. We had Blake but he got away. The fingerprints in his room matched what you Feds had on file. And one more thing, how come no one in your office has ever heard of you?"

"It is a big office, Detective. Does everyone in the LAPD know your name? Besides, I asked you to keep my name out of your reports."

"I want to see your credentials again, Special Agent Latens. Let's make sure you really are who you claim to be, before I share any more details of my case with you."

"Detective Wilson, don't you have more important work to do than to chase down my credentials?"

"Let me see 'em before you see how comfortable the inside of our jail cells can be."

"Fine, Detective, but please after you do this, can you realize that I have shared everything with you, and you are the one not playing nice here."

"Just hand them over, my mother was always disappointed with me because I never did learn how to play well with others."

He asked me to sit in the hallway, where I sat for nearly two hours waiting for a response from the FBI. While sitting, I started to reflect and be concerned about what was happening with

Kalani and her family. I hadn't been able to reach them since I arrived in California.

I noticed a newspaper lying on the table next to me. There was a small story about suspected mobster Kalu Kapena, who he was resting comfortably in a Honolulu hospital after a suspected stroke. The story continued how the police raided a nightclub, where six women were in custody charged with prostitution. Several kilos of heroin were discovered in a safe. It went on to say the investigation was still ongoing.

"Ok, Latens. Your friends wouldn't tell me much, other than you were on their payroll and worked in a special department. It appears you work cases alone. Here's your credentials back. You're free to go."

"I was not aware I was in custody, Detective. I was only here to read your newspapers and drink some of the terrible coffee you have for your honored guests. Now, would you please tell me what you know about Blake?"

"Blake's gone. It's what I get for putting a couple of rookies in front of the motel. They didn't have the sense to check for a backdoor. I should have knocked that door in much sooner, but I wasn't certain Blake was even in there. A judge might have released him without probable cause. I don't think we'll be lucky enough to get another call letting us know where he might be. If you get a lead, you be sure to let me know, Latens. You promised me that you would let us bring him in."

"Yeah sure, Wilson. I'll keep you informed, just after I call your boss to check your credentials. Have a good day, Detective."

When I started to train for stealing souls, I never imagined I would be chasing criminals across the globe. Nor did I ever suspect I would start a record company or share poison fish with a woman merely because I had not fathered a child. Here I was in the middle of Los Angeles, not having any idea where my subject was or what my next move should be. It was one of those days where I wanted to run off and never return, but too many were counting on me to do my job. I needed to focus.

I read Blake's file, trying to find a common thread, other than the obvious association with Viet Nam. He surely knew he alone could not stop any wars by killing diplomats, gun makers and generals. Was he acting alone or with another? His mental health came out clean in his most recent tests before he went AWOL. To suddenly disappear and go on a killing spree didn't make sense. I kept reading the file until I fell asleep.

The next morning, I received a call from Kalani. "I'm back from the compound and I have a few weeks before my next assignment. How would you like to spend time with me?"

"I would love that, but I am not sure where I have to travel to next. I have no idea where my subject is right now, but if we can meet up once I know my destination."

"You really suck at this don't you, Caeles. I mean you don't even know where your subject is in the world. Yes, Orcus was not happy with me, once he discovered that you and I were spending time together. But I did finish my task, there wasn't much he could say to me. Don't be surprised if he gets in your ear too. He told me all about what a pain in the ass you are Caeles Novo. Should I still call you Cale or what? Or come up with a nick name for someone who tries to steal more souls from non-assigned targets than actual assignments."

"Is this your way of attempting to convince me we should spend more time together?" I asked. "What's going on with Kapena? What about your neighbor, did they arrest that bum yet?"

"I got back in town last night, but Kono tells me that Kapena has lost his frigging mind. They're running all kinds of tests on the jerk. I guess they don't have one yet to look for his lost soul. See, that's the difference between you and me Cale. When I steal from someone, I do a number on them. You please, your lady is singing like a bird in prison and your singer is still making records. My people, I turn them into mush. If you promise me a nice dinner, I might show you how to take a soul for real, because obviously you need some work."

"Whatever," I said.

"As far as Detective Kopono, no one has any evidence linking him with Kapena. I think you're right. I do think he was the person, who captured me, but I never saw his face and he was not in the room when they drugged me. I asked Orcus about Kopono, but he's not on the list, at least not yet."

I laughed over the phone. "Well, like you said. Not being on a list has never stopped me before.

"It's best that you don't come back to Hawaii until Kopono is arrested. Kono has heard on the streets now that Kapena has crushed pineapple for brains, there's a power struggle to take over his business. It would not surprise me if Kopono is in that fight. There were two murders on the island last week. Now, do you want to finally take me on that dinner you promised weeks ago, or do you have some poor unsuspecting grandma you need to sneak up on and steal her soul?"

"You know, I am starting to think I liked you better as a naked, mindless bimbo wrapped around a pole, but I'll be in California a few more days if you think your ego will fit inside a jumbo jet."

Kalani giggled. "Let's hope you can pick a restaurant better than you can complete your tasks without having the Council confine you to the outhouse for a week, eh Champ?"

I was beginning to learn she always had to have the last word.

We spent the next week together swapping stories about Elder Orcus, the Council, the training and life in general. As much as Kalani loved her life, she felt something was still missing. Her parents had been married for more than one hundred years.

Kalani had a brother, but he was killed taking a soul. She only gave the basics of the death. He died before we could take souls from a distance with a camera. In the past, we had to make actual contact with the subject. The subject was the leader of a developing nation, and when her brother got too close, a bodyguard killed her brother. It was a reminder that what we do can be dangerous. He lived in an era, where many were lost due to close contact and the evolution of firearms.

Before she left, she took a look at Blake's file. She wanted to know if there was any connection to any of Blake's jobs in the States during his training, before being shipped to Viet Nam. The only one where he had much contact was a three-week assignment of protecting the President during social events outside of the White House, like when he played golf, or attended State dinners. I wasn't sure I could make a connection but it was worth checking out.

It was hard to let her go, but she had a new task. Her next stop was New Zealand, to look into a politician, who was shaking down people for money in return for favors within the government. I thought if that was now meeting the criteria, we'd stay busy forever.

I headed off to Langley, Virginia, to meet with our contact within the agency. He searched through Blake's assignments to try to discover connections between the murders. There it was on a golf log. All three murders were people who played golf on the same day with the President. Blake was assigned as a trainee to follow along with the Secret Service in the security force. We now had our connection. I wondered why Blake would want to murder those three, and could the President be next on his list? Evan Crowe, my contact inside the CIA, who was one of us, alerted the Secret Service to be on the lookout for David Blake. He gave me the President's itinerary for the next few days. However, the President wasn't scheduled to appear in public or leave the White House.

Four days later, a United States Congressman from Illinois was executed walking from his home to his car. There were no witnesses. Washington was abuzz with the killing. All local police and federal agencies were on high alert. Crowe and I looked through all the logs, but there didn't seem to be any connection. Jim Dorsey the Congressman, who was gunned down, never played golf with the President, nor had he ever met him in private. Security around the President was tripled after the murder. If he was a target, it would be even more difficult to get near him. The only connection we could find was Dorsey was on the Armed Services Committee. Time to dig deeper.

Dorsey had an unproductive career in the House of Representatives. He hadn't presented any bills of any substance in his five years, nor had he cast any votes that went against the party lines, or were considered controversial. This was a head scratcher of a murder. Maybe there was no connection between Blake, and the other three murders. It would be a few days before I could get my eyes on the ballistics report to match a weapon.

Thankfully, a break came with a call from Kalani. "Did you find your guy yet? I'm heading back from New Zealand. My subject was so foul and corrupt, and the idiot was always in public. I got a photo of that jerk in two days. He fell over like a sack of beans. Damn, I'm so good at my job. Speak up, did you even locate your target or not?"

I could hear her giggling, but it was ok. "It seems Orcus gives you all the easy tasks," I said, "and leaves the real work for us pros. Maybe next time he will give you one where you can just trip over your subject."

"Yeah right. Like I would ever need your help to track someone. You know what, Cale. I'm going to create a picture book and call it, "Where's Walton, or Willie, or something and make a small fortune. It will be photos of all the exotic locations around the world with people filling up the picture and one is your target.

We can give it a subtitle of where in the world is Cale Novo's subject."

"Keep it up, girl. One day if you ever get an assignment, where the target is not right in your lap, I will be right beside you, helping you find them, not! Besides, didn't it take you over two years to steal from Kapena? If memory serves me, I had to rescue you and your big mouth from him. So keep it up. You might be beautiful on the outside, but underneath you have an evil quality about you, don't you?"

"Remind me again what you do for a living my naïve, Cale. All who steal have some evil in them. Don't you think?"

Kalani wanted to meet me in Sydney, Australia for a week, but I had to finish my task. With people being murdered every few weeks, Blake had to be found and the sooner the better.

I worked with Evan Crowe to figure out Blake's next move. Why would someone murder a do nothing legislator from Illinois? I asked.

"Maybe we're going in the wrong direction," Evan said. "Maybe he's not trying to stop the escalation of a war, maybe he's promoting it? In reading a recent speech given by Dorsey on the House Floor, he was threatening to vote to pull funding to the military budget without more proof we had a reason to be in Viet Nam. Sources tell me the General, who was killed was recommending to the President not to install more troops without a better strategy in place. The diplomat was on his way to peace talks. I think whoever it is behind this, Blake or not, they want the fighting in Viet Nam to continue, not stop. The next target is probably someone looking to stop the fighting, not promote it. I don't think the President is a target. He's recommending we send more troops."

"You make a good case, Evan. If that is true, then who could be the next target?"

We attempted to narrow down a list from hundreds of potential names when Kalani gave me another call. "Hey, did you find your shooter yet? I wanted to let you know that I'm in Maui overlooking the beach in my swim suit. Maybe your subject is hiding in the bushes near my hut. Don't you think you should come and find out?"

"I would love to, trust me, but I think we are getting close to finding this guy. After this assignment is over, we can spend more time together. And why are on Maui?"

"They put Kapena in a mental ward. The man is now certifiably whacko. Like I told you, when I remove souls from these people, I don't mess around. I know you have that little pea shooter of a camera that barely feeds us for a moment or two, but I do it right."

"Yeah yeah, but really, what are you are doing in Maui and why are you not at home?"

"Oahu has exploded into a major drug war. With Kapena all locked up, rumor is that Kopono is running things now. I had my uncle ride past my house a few times and Kopono has not been seen near his home for weeks. I don't want him coming after me. I did my job with Kapena, but I'm not the police, and what has resulted from Kapena going down is not my fight. My father and mother have moved from the island as well. They moved to Tahiti. Orcus got him a job in a hospital over there as a surgeon. I'm going to hide out on Maui until my next task."

"Ok, but if Kapena had his people everywhere in Hawaii, and Kopono really did take over, then he must have his connections too. You keep your pretty head low and out of sight. And don't go flashing that bathing suit to any of the locals."

"I won't. I really only called to see if I could get you jealous. Mission accomplished, sucker."

The girl really did learn how to push my buttons, and she loved to get the last word.

I tried staying focused on my task, but the thought of sitting on a tropical beach with Kalani was hard to resist. However, I knew contacting the Council and asking for a break would be one of the worst ideas I had in a while, and I've had more than my share of bad ones. Crowe and I narrowed the list to who we thought might be the top twenty-five possible targets for Blake. We also got notice that the bullet taken from the dead Congressman did not match the others. Did Blake switch weapons to put doubt in investigators minds or was it another shooter?

The next day, a message arrived for me. "I know where David Blake is, I need your help, Special Agent Latens. When you reach Los Angeles, call the number I have given you."

I caught the first flight back to California. I thought about calling Wilson, but decided maybe it was better I waited until I knew more about the message and who left it I landed in California and made the call.

"Agent Latens, we spoke a couple of months ago. You called my home asking questions about my son. I know where he is, but you have to give me your word that you'll make sure he is brought to the proper authorities without being detained in any jail cell. I know there is a kill order for my son should he surface in the public eye. I don't believe he would even make it out of a jail cell alive. If you can get back to me with your plan, I will tell you where to meet the two of us."

"Mr. Blake, I am not sure I can give you those assurances, but maybe there is a way we can hold him in solitary confinement, until we get him to whoever it is you think he needs to speak with, but it seems to me he is going to jail for a very long time."

"Agent Latens, I was in the military years ago. As you know, we all have a chain of command. My son was following orders. He is not the cold-blooded killer people think he is. Please, call someone and see if you can arrange for him to speak with the President."

"The President? Are you kidding me? I don't have access to the President. Even if I did, why would he consider seeing your son?"

"Make the call. Give me a number where I can contact you tomorrow at three in the afternoon. And before you think you can trace this call or give the number to anyone, it's a pay phone, not even in the same town as my son."

"Mr. Blake, you have to give me more to go on, other than I need to contact the President. Even if I can find a contact, who can get to speak directly with him, I can't tell him an ex-agent who went AWOL, and murdered at least four people, wants to meet with him. He would never do it."

"He will do it. You tell him to think back on the day he played golf with those men and my son was there. Tell him to remember what they did directly after the round, not while playing. He will meet with my son."

I had no idea how to get to the President, or what I would say. I knew I could trust Evan Crowe, but past him, I wasn't sure. I didn't think I could even trust Detective Wilson, since I knew he really didn't care about Blake other than slapping bracelets on him.

I called my partner inside the CIA. "What do you think, Evan? Is there anyone you can trust all the way to the President to get his attention and not have this all blow up along the way?"

"Cale, this guy is on the kill on sight list from all of our agents and the FBI. I don't know what is going on, but there is no way they want this guy to ever see the light of day or talk with anyone, especially the President. I don't see that happening unless you can get more information from the dad."

I took the call from Blake's father promptly at three as promised. "What have you got for me, Agent Latens?"

"Mr. Blake, I made the only call I could make to someone I trusted, and he said he can get word to the President, but not with the little information you gave me about some golf outing. He won't do it. If anything were to happen to the President before or during meeting your son, everyone would lose their jobs or more. It is too high a risk. You have got to give me more."

"Meet me in front of the Chinese place across from your hotel in two hours. I'll be wearing a fedora with a red feather. Be there or my son will be gone forever."

I called Kalani to let her know where I was going and with whom, in case I disappeared. I knew I could trust her. She was not thrilled with my plan, but I didn't have a choice. She was on notice to call Wilson and Crowe in four hours if I didn't call her back by then.

I met Mr. Blake in front of the restaurant. We asked me to get into his car. We drove for twenty minutes, until he pulled over and made sure I wasn't carrying any weapons as promised. He insisted on tying my hands, or there would be no meeting. I agreed. He wanted to know why I had a camera.

"That enters the room," he said. "I can' take any chances with my son."

We drove another ten minutes, until we arrived at a small apartment complex. I was led into Apartment 102. When we entered, I noticed a sofa and coffee table, a television, several empty pizza boxes and slender man wearing a white tee shirt and blue jeans, who stood up and greeted me.

"Hello, Agent Latens. I'm Agent David Blake. I understand you've been looking for me. My dad for some strange reason thinks you can help me. First of all, I didn't kill that Congressman. I have no idea who it was that shot that man, but from what I saw on the news, it was an execution from a real pro. He was originally on my list, but things were changed with my orders."

"David, look, you have to tell me what is going on here, because as you know, every Federal Agent alive has orders to shoot you on sight."

Blake's father asked me to sit on the sofa, along with his son. We each sat.

Blake sighed. "I shot those three men, not the fourth. I shot them under orders from my boss. My mission was to kill those men. I didn't ask why. I followed my orders. I was sent to Viet Nam to make it look like I was assigned there. I was ordered to make it seem like I deserted, but I was only doing my duty as given. One day, I was on detail with the President, after his golf game. There were six men, who met with the President in a private room. The arrangements called for at his three golf partners and three others right to meet. The three others were the Vice President, my boss and a four star general, who I didn't recognize. After everyone left, my boss gave me the assignment to execute the three men. When I fulfilled my mission and called my boss, I knew something wasn't right. He wanted to know my exact location. The entire phone call was all very odd. I made a call to my buddy, who I trained with, and he told me I was on the kill list. I have been hiding out ever since. I am telling you, Agent Latens. I was doing my duty. I know my mission might seem morbid to you, but I was trained to kill. I didn't like killing those people, but it was my duty. I need the President to hear my story, because he's the only one who can save me. I can leave the country, but I'd be looking over my shoulder for the rest of my life. I need the President to hear me out and make this all go away."

"Blake I can sympathize with you, but what makes you think the President can help you? How do you know he's not the one who gave the order to kill in the first place?"

"I would rather die, than believe the President of the United States of America ordered the execution of private citizens. I have to believe it came from someone else, who knows, maybe even the Vice President. Maybe my boss was acting alone, I don't know, but kill me right now if my President ordered those hits."

"I'll see what I can do for you Blake."

I left wondering what I could do for David Blake or if I believed any of this story. He refused to tell me the name of his boss. First, I went back to the compound.

"Council Members, I think you have it all wrong with my subject, David Blake. I ask you to search the man's soul again. I spoke with him, and looked him right in the eye. He was doing his duty in executing those people. I do not believe we should take his soul. You have to understand a military mind. To him he was doing what he was ordered to do."

"How dare you come before us and question our judgment, Novo. We put much thought into our decisions, and only take a soul once it's long past saving. You know this. This Council rejects your request."

"I would like to protest," I said.

Orcus moved forward in his seat and said, "Blake has fooled you into thinking he had no choice with his command. Everyone has a choice. The man could have resigned his position. The same as you can right now. You have a choice in life. Now, if you are to remain strong with us, you will finish your duty and take his soul. We're not asking you to kill him, or turn him over to his superiors. Your mission is to remove his soul. Do what is now your duty and finish your assignment."

I headed back to California and sat in my room for a day searching for an answer. I know he killed three innocent people. My mission should have been an easy task. However, the man truly believed he was following orders. People are killed every day in wars by others following orders. I know this wasn't really war, but I was still perplexed. In the end, I knew I had to take his soul. My only other questions would be, should I turn Blake in to the authorities or try to contact the President? I placed a call seeking advice.

"Evan, the man said he was following orders. He told me his boss ordered the executions. He wants to tell the President and hope he was not the one who ordered the deaths. If the President did, you know Blake is as good as dead. Hell, he's likely dead no matter what happens to him now. The Council ordered me to take his soul even knowing the background of the story. Do you have any ideas? Is there any way we can get this to the President?"

"Don't try to be the savior here, Cale. That's my advice. If the Council told you to take his soul, do it and don't look back. I'm starting to think you're not really one of us. Any other soul stealer would do it and not think twice. I can't risk my cover and attempt to contact the President. My mission here is vital to our kind. You know that. I gather valuable information all the time for our stealers. I'm sorry but I can't help you on this one. People are already beginning to ask questions about you around here."

I called Kalani, but with pretty much the same result. "You have a big heart, too big. Me, I wouldn't think twice. I'd zap that man so fast and move on to my next mission. Finish him off. Come sit on the beach with me. I promise; you won't be disappointed if you do."

I called Blake's father and asked for another meeting. I told him I had news, but I couldn't offer it over the phone. He picked me up, only this time I was blindfolded. It was a longer trip, so I assumed he was moving his son around town.

"David, I spoke with the people I know, and they want your photo to prove I have actually seen you. I'm going to deliver it and see if I can arrange a meeting for you but, in case it does not work out, I obtained a new passport and a new identification for you. I have people, who can do these things. I also have some money for you. It will get you to Tahiti. There is a hospital there. You are to see a Doctor Inoke. He knows you are coming and will give you a job in the hospital. I know it is not what you want to hear, but my inside source thinks if you meet with the President you are as good as dead."

"I don't like this plan," Blake's father said. I brushed aside the old man's comments and continued.

"Give me two days to try to set up the meeting. If I can't, then you need to get out of town. Don't fly out of Los Angeles, the local police are looking for you. Have your dad take you to Colorado, or somewhere far from here. I know it's not safe for you to travel, but it's your best option.

"Hold on, Latens, I think you're lying to me," the younger Blake said. "This isn't making sense. You need my picture to possibly get a meeting with the President? If not, I need to go to Tahiti and work in a hospital? Why would I want to do that?"

"David, I know you were following your orders and that has significance to me. If not, I would have called the local police and they would already be outside. I need your photo. After that, you're on your own. If you don't wait for my call, then fine. If I were you, I would leave tonight for Tahiti. I am giving you a heads up that your life is about to change, and in a weird way, I am trying to make sure you have a place to land. It's not going to be easy for you. I don't think the President's going to meet with you. I don't. However, let me take your photo and see what I can do."

I turned on extra lights to allow enough light in the room and snap. I followed my orders. I sat in the chair, my body twitching. Blake ran into the bathroom convulsing along the way. His father began yelling at me. "What did you do to my son? What was in that camera? Give me that camera, Latens."

I got up and tried to get out the door. My body was surging with power. I was able to fight him off enough to get out the door. I made it to the parking lot where he again attempted to knock me over and snatch my camera. We were both rolling on the ground when I heard sirens in the distance. "Those sirens are for your son. I called them and they followed us."

"Damn you, Latens, I trusted you. I'll hunt you down and kill you for this."

"I did what was best for your son."

He left me and ran to get his son. He was still convulsing and could barely walk, but they got in the car and drove off. Lucky for me, there were sirens in the background. I can never be sure who they were for, but not for David Blake, not on that day.

CHAPT3R FOURT33N

My reward for stealing Blake's soul was time off to meet Kalani. We met in San Francisco for a long weekend. Her next assignment was days away, so this would be the last time we would likely see each other for an extended period.

"Cale, you can't get so involved in your subject's lives the way you do," she said as we took in Giant's baseball game. "Our mission is to take a soul and get out. We don't question if it is the right decision or not. You're not on the Council. You have sworn an oath, like me. I beg you to do what is required of you or give up being a soul stealer. I fear it's only going to put you in the mental ward next to Kapena. Please, Cale, think about what everyone is telling you.

I tried to watch the game, but she kept up until I responded. "I know, Kalani. I do. However, something is not right with our all our teachings. It seems with each theft, I see goodness still inside their souls. I believe I can restore these people if given the chance. For example, your politician, yeah he was shaking people down for money, but did it rise to the level of taking his soul?"

"I don't know, Cale. It's not my job to question it. I do my job, as should you."

We later walked along the wharf after taking in the afternoon game a nice dinner, watching gentle ripples in the water across the bay, when a man, who I instantly recognized walked up to us and began to speak.

"It's time we formally met. Don't be alarmed. I bring you no harm. My name is Mikael Sano. My responsibility is to watch over the two of you. I'm breaking the rules by making this contact, but I feel it's important that we meet. Yes, Cale, I was the one in your dreams and yes, Kalani, I'm the one who pushed you to Cale at the market place. I've watched over both of you since your births."

Kalani looked at each other and back at the old man in our paths.

"I bring you news, Cale. What you see in your heart is true. It's also true that you can see into others souls, not a power developed by Kalani or anyone other than Council members. You've not developed it fully yet, but over time you will. You were chosen generations ago to lead the rebirth of what was to be the original mission of the Elders and the Council.

"Huh," I mumbled.

"Him?" Kalani said.

Do not fight him, Kalani. It is his mission to reclaim the Council. They are not what they seem. The Doctor has the answers you seek, Cale. You and Kalani have always been destined to be together."

Kalani and I stood stone-faced listening to him deliver his message. He came from nowhere and when he was finished, he vanished into the brisk San Francisco breeze.

"Well, thank you once again for an interesting evening, Caeles Novo. How much did you pay the man to deliver that timely speech?"

"Come on, honey. You don't honestly believe I put that guy up to it, do you?"

"I'm not sure what to believe," Kalani said. However, I don't think my father has anything to do with any of this. Some creepy old man comes walking up to us talking about you being some kind of savior and vanishes. You don't find that a little too convenient after how we just talked about you doing your mission and nothing more?"

"Honey, I assure you. I had nothing to do with that man showing up again. However, he has popped in and out of my life for years. He helped me after I took my first soul and he helped me save you. I don't know anything about taking over the Council, that's all nonsense to me, but I have seen him before. Admit it, so have you."

"I don't know. I'm going to leave for my next assignment in the morning. I suggest you forget about the old fart, and do your duty to our kind and the Council. And keep my father out of all of your running off and saving the military sharp shooters for a better life. And one more thing, if I see that creepy old man go near my dad, I'll take his soul, assuming he has one."

"Now look who is talking about taking unauthorized souls. Chill out, I didn't put anyone up to anything here. I have no intentions of you disturbing your father. Now let's enjoy our last evening together and forget about missions and souls and be happy."

"Fine, but if I ever find out you paid that creep to do that, you will never see me again."

Always the last word. My emotional lady was lucky I cared for her the way I did.

Over the next several years, I did my duty and stole soul after soul. I tried not to think too much about it since most were bad people. There were rapists, murderers, and child pornographers amongst the group. I saw some horrific things over the next several years. There were times I got an assignment, read the file, and was so upset over what vile and disgusting people I had to steal from, that it would only take me hours to complete my task. I never gave it a second thought. There were times it took longer for various reasons, but for the most part, I took everyone's advice and stole without remorse.

Kalani and I spent as much time together as possible, but the Council kept us on opposite sides of the globe most of the time. We were convinced it was intentional. We were both doing our jobs with much success, so the Council really couldn't complain when we did see each other. Besides in the past, others who had stolen for our kind had married. We wouldn't be the first to do so in our history. Kalani and I both talked about getting married and having children, but we also knew one would likely have to give up stealing. We were apart too much to have a healthy marriage.

After months of being apart from Kalani, I became depressed. I left my latest assignment and met up with her in Tokyo, Japan. We talked it over and decided that it was time to make a change. We were willing to compromise with ourselves, and the Council. We would go to them as a couple, and tell them that if they wanted the both of us to continue stealing, the Council would have to change our territories to make it easier for the two of us to live together. If that worked, we would get married, but something had to change with us being apart so often.

"The two of you stand before the Highest Council and threaten us with your demands?"

"No Council Members. We only ask that you understand that our work has started to suffer from being apart. Yes, I keep up with assignments as does Kalani, but we both fear in time this will change. We are only asking that rather than keep us so far apart, you rearrange our assignments to be closer. We are seeking a compromise, since we both see the value in continuing our duty to the Council and our kind. We think it is a fair request."

"It is true the Council has kept the two of you apart as much as possible, but with good reason. We don't believe the two of you are making a wise decision in wanting to be together. It will cloud your decisions in your work. We don't see good coming from your choice. However, since the two of you have decided that you believe it is what is best. Your request is granted. But be warned, should the time come when your work suffers, you will pay for the request the two of you are asking of the Council today."

We left hearing the warning and knew the consequences, but we felt it was the proper thing for the two of us. Kalani wanted to be a mother and I wanted to be a father. We knew if this worked, marriage would be soon. Since she still wanted to work the Pacific Rim and I had been working mostly in the United States and Western Europe, we decided to live in California. The Council was true to their word and it was easier to see each other more often. We had more time to see each other during our breaks. On rare occasions, we even worked the same cities. After a year of working this way, we decided to marry.

We had a small ceremony in Greece. My parents, as well as Kalani's were in attendance. Kono, her uncle joined us, as did some on the Council and Magister Verax, who instructed both of us as children. There were a few others, who were friends of our parents, who were like us, but the crowd was less than fifteen people. A Council member married us. We had a small dinner party for our guests later in the evening.

As the evening ended, I realized I hadn't seen my mother at her table next to my father for an extended time. I went and asked my father if everything was ok. He assured me that my mother was fine. He said she went out for some fresh air.

I walked outside to see if I could find her. She was talking with a man, who covered his face. When I approached them, the man quickly scurried off.

"Who was that man mother and what did he want with you?"

"It's perfectly fine, dear. He's an old family friend, who reminded me that it was your destiny to marry Kalani."

"What the heck does that mean? Where did he come from?"

"Caeles, my dear boy, we all have our paths in life. I don't think you know where yours is going to take you yet. I knew mine at an early age. It was to be with your father. Part of yours is to spend the remainder of your years on earth with your new wife. However, as my friend reminded me, yours is so much more."

"Oh, so now you, and some white haired guy, who pops in and out of life and now some stranger knows my destiny. Why are you all hiding it from me? Will someone please tell me what is going on here, Mother?"

"There are things that just happen in life. When they happen to you, then you will seek and find your destiny. For now, be happy, enjoy your new bride, raise a family, be who you are. One day your destiny will appear."

"Have you hit the wine too much, Mom? I mean seriously, I know we are in Greece and if you look into the distance, you can see The Parthenon, but you are not Socrates and I am in no mood to play this game. Come inside and sit down, I think the wine has gone to your head."

"I have never felt better and you should not talk to your mother this way. I don't care if you think you are a big shot now because you have taken so many souls. That was never the story you were to write."

"I really think you and the old white haired dude need to quit with all of this destiny nonsense. Now please, let me enjoy one day without thinking about taking someone's soul or my destiny. I want to have a dance or two with my wife and retire to our honeymoon suite. You can go talk with dad about all your philosophies and my destiny."

"Your father knows too. I don't need to tell him. It's why he was my destiny and Kalani is yours in marriage."

"Ok, Mom, whatever. Can we please, go inside and enjoy what remains of the party?"

As I turned, my new bride was standing a few feet away with a smirk on her face.

"I turn my back for five minutes and my husband runs away? What happened, you saw some hot looking Greek Goddess outside and figured you would have one last fling?"

"I wish it were that easy, and I never did flings. No, my mother was talking with some strange man outside, then immediately started mumbling on about my destiny. My destiny is to put a smile on my beautiful wife's face."

"You sometimes say some pretty dumb things, my dear husband, but that time you sounded pretty smart."

It was bad enough when I was single, now I know I have no chance at the last word.

After the evening, we all went our separate ways. Kalani and I went back to California and continued our careers in taking souls. To me, it was becoming more of a chore than something I had trained for all my life. I had become so much better at taking them quickly as had Kalani, but I also felt an emptiness creep inside me.

I would talk about it with my wife, but to her she saw it as an opportunity to secure the future of our race and was honored to do so. I felt the same way most days, but also knew at times, some we took from might not be suitable candidates.

"Cale the Council has a very difficult job," Kalani said. "I don't think you have given them enough credit for what they do. Since the balance of our kind has shifted from more people not having the power to steal, than the ones like us who can, we have to work harder each day to maintain our race. I know the Council is only looking out for our best interest when they assign our missions. I will be a mother soon and you a father. It will be one more added responsibility for you once I have our child. I know I will need some time off to be a mother. Look on the bright side of me being away, you can actually steal more souls than me. Well, maybe for one year."

There were days I questioned why I married her. Good thing I rarely felt compelled to need the last word.

CHAPT3R F!FT33N

"Hello, Mr. James. I'm Doctor Summers. I'll be overseeing your mental health here in our facility. Please tell me a little bit about your background and why you are here."

"Why, you can't read it all on that chart of yours?" the rock and roll star said.

"Mr. James, I am here to help you. Actually, I don't need a chart to notice you think something has been lost in your life, but I can assure you it is not."

"Yeah, and what is it that you think I am missing there, Doc?"

"In time, I will be happy to render my opinion, but we have a lot of work to do. In speaking with your wife and friend Gordy, some around you have suggested maybe you have lost your way, even your soul. I am here to assure you it is not possible, despite what others might suggest. Injuries like yours manifest themselves in many different ways, like your current anger issues. My job is to assist you in understanding where your anger is coming from and in time release it."

"Oh really. So in thirty seconds after walking in here, you think you know what my trauma is and now you can mark that pretty chart of yours and go off spewing your medical garbage to the next person eh, Doc?"

"Mr. James, may I call you Dylan perhaps?"

"You can call me whatever you like, people have called me far worse lately, broken down guitar player, bad father, bad husband, terrible friend. You name it."

"Well, Dylan, I am not here to call you names or accuse you of being a bad anything. I am here to help you recognize why you are having a difficult time returning to your former life. My job is to make that as painless as possible. However you must open your mind to our sessions."

"I'll sit here and listen, because if I don't my wife will take my kids and leave me. But I don't have to open up my mind to jack shit."

Pretending to be a therapist was new to me. I had to be careful not to blow my cover. There was a glass window where I could see through and speakers to hear every word. Dylan James was my latest target, but he was not a bad person. He was an angry one. My ability to see into others souls was now growing and in looking into his, I saw his anger raging, but not evil. This surely was not a candidate to lose his soul. I watched and listened for the remainder of his thirty-minute session. Unless I was missing something, I could not steal from this man.

I followed him to his home. His wife had driven him to the therapy center and as they were leaving, I noticed his limp. There were still visual and mental signs from his accident. Not being a trained mental health person, I would think trauma like he suffered would lead to anger in some cases, but I thought the Council was really overreaching in Dylan's case.

"Council Members, I am here to ask you to take a second look into my subject's soul. I have done so as well. I see anger, but nothing more. There must be better targets on your list. This man has a wife and children. He has not hurt anyone, other than himself. I would think with proper therapy he can turn his life back around."

Elder Orcus exploded from the dais. "How many times do you think you can question our decisions before you end up staying in this compound forever? Everyone on our list is there for a reason. Your responsibility is to steal, not to question our authority."

I then realized I let something slip. Orcus didn't miss it.

"Why do you think you can see into someone's soul? Is this even more lunacy from your mouth that needs to be punished? There are six, and six alone who can see into a soul on this earth. You might think you have the ability, but make no mistake, you do not."

"With all due respect, if one of you were to die, would you not need someone else to have that ability to join the Council? Where would they come from? How can you say it is impossible, yet all of you have the power? It must come from somewhere does it not?"

I watched as the six men huddled together and then retook their seats.

"If it were prudent for you to understand and know those answers, we would tell you," Orcus said, "but it's not. Now we strongly suggest you watch your tongue. I can assure you it's your imagination gone wild and your desire to believe this man isn't a candidate that makes you believe you have the power. Now, you can either take the man's soul or call your wife and inform her that you will be spending time with us on an extended book reading in the library. I'm sure you've not forgotten how much you enjoyed your last extended visit."

"I have another option as well, one that you, Elder Orcus told me about years ago. I have free will to resign."

"Caeles, you're a father now, and a husband. You have responsibilities to your family and to all of us. We are depleted within the ranks of soul stealers and you know it. If not for that fact, you disobedience would have been punished. Your years of constant insubordination will end. You have become one of our best remaining agents in the field. I can't allow you to just walk away. Yes, you have free will, but you also must suffer the consequences of your decisions."

"What would I suffer from? Spending even more time with my wife and son and live a peaceful life without trotting across the globe? Then feeling that every time I take from someone like Dylan James, I lose a part of my own soul. Tell me, Elder Orcus, what is it you think you can do to make me continue?"

"You really are a foolish one. For all your abilities, you think you have always been the one in control of your own destiny, when it was this Council all along pushing and prodding you. Do not dare stand before us and declare your independence from your kind with your free will. You will go back to your subject, you will steal his soul, and you will do it soon. That is your destiny. I don't care if you believe it was done using your free will or not."

"I find it very odd that everyone seems to know or deems to have created my destiny for me. However, the longer you sit behind that dais and tell me what my destiny is, the more I reject your words. I quit!"

I began walking for the large marble doors when I heard Orcus speak behind me.

"Caeles Novo, you have left us with few options. It is the ruling of this Council that should you decide to leave the ranks of soul stealer, this will be the last day your son retains his soul. If you insist on rambling on about how this Council doesn't know your destiny, we will add your mother, your father, whoever else we deem necessary for you to understand that yes, you have your free will, but it comes at a price. Now leave this area immediately before you anger us further. Go take Dylan James' soul before we take one to compensate for what you think is your free will and the stupid notion that you could ever quit."

I dragged myself home. As expected, my wife had little sympathy for the position.

"We have gone over this so many times, Cale. Take the soul and go. Would you rather a total stranger keep his soul than your own child?"

"Of course not, and you know that's not my issue. However, I do see a pattern, for every three souls we take, one of them does not seem right to me. I mean this man is pissed at the world because he can't play his music right now and he does not understand why. He is pissed at God and his world. So what? If every time someone was pissed at the world and we swooped in and took their soul, humans with souls would be a small population on earth now wouldn't they? Dylan does not deserve to have his soul taken. It will only spiral him into a deeper depression and ruin not only his life but his wife and children's as well. Do you not care that we take without any real cause?"

"Cale, I can't worry for every lost soul in this world. I'm a mother, a wife, and soon I'll be back working my missions again. All I know is that if my son loses his soul to the Council because you won't do what is expected of us, I will never forgive you."

"Kalani, something is not adding up here. Why is it that so many of our kind either can't steal or refuse to steal, which only makes it harder for the likes of you and I to live our lives? For every one of us, there are fifty, who cannot steal. I know some try and fail. I know all of it. However, is the Council insisting we remove marginal souls, in order to keep others properly nourished?"

Kalani crossed her arms and gave me her evil stare. "Cale, you have a mission. I love seeing you. I love when you are home, but we have our own race to protect. I don't care about, who is marginal and who is not. I get my orders and I execute them. Go do your mission and protect this family. Keep in mind that all those others, who don't steal for whatever reason, including our own parents, they support us with a very hefty wage. How could we fly around the world, take nice vacations, and live in this home, if they didn't appreciate our powers and work to support us. Each side benefits from what we do and you know it. I have to believe that we're creatures, guided by truth, doing what was ordained centuries ago. If I can't hold on that belief, then I have nothing."

"Nothing? You have nothing without the Council and our laws? What about me and our son?"

"Stop it. You know what I mean, now go take the man's soul and let's go on one last trip before I have to go back to work."

I headed back to North Carolina where Dylan James resided and followed him for several few days. I could still see the anger, but I also think it was the fear of the unknown for him. He was struggling with who he was as a person. He believed he knew his destiny. When he realized maybe he was wrong, he became confused and angry. He wasn't unlike many others, who think they know what their life is all about. His destiny changed from his expectations, so it was easy for him to become disillusioned. Maybe that's why I never became angry at the world, only people. I knew as a young child, my mission was to follow in the footsteps of our ancestors, but if it turned out I could not steal, I would find another calling. Maybe it is because I never worried about my destiny from day to day. I lived my life and allowed destiny find me.

One day, as Dylan was leaving his therapy session, I asked if I could take his photo as a fan of the band. His wife was with him.

"I'm not really in the mood to stop for a photo, besides the nurse inside probably told you who I am. She has a big mouth you know. She has asked me to sign so many photos and record albums for her, it gets ridiculous."

His pretty wife jumped into the conversation, "Dylan, the man asked politely for a photo, we have the time."

"Yeah sure, you can take my photo, but under one condition. This pretty lady next to me, tell me, who she is and what instrument she plays? If you can do that, you can take both of our photos, not just mine. After all, she played with some of the finest orchestras in the world. Me, I'm a sad excuse for a bandleader and guitar player. It's her photo you should want, not mine. So go ahead, tell me hot shot, who is this beautiful woman next to me and what instrument does she play? We'll see if you are really a fan or just wanting a picture for a magazine to show how pathetic I am now."

"Mr. James, I don't want a photo of you and her, only you. However, the lovely lady is your wife Elise, and she is a wonderful violinist. I don't want a photo of you with her, only yours. I know this is going to sound wrong, but she does not deserve to be in a photo with you today."

"Get out of here then," Dylan snapped. "If you can't take a photo of the two of us, you can't have mine. Let's go Elise."

I could have snapped the photo as he was getting into the car. It would have been simple, clean, but the love she had for him in her eyes, there was no way I could steal from him at that moment. I would wait for another day.

The Council wasn't happy with the delay, and neither was Kalani. "Take the photo, Cale, please, come home. I miss you, as does your son, Nick. Who knows how long Orcus will be patient. This is not a difficult assignment for you. The man has the same routine almost daily and can barely walk to the car. He has no security and is at the therapy center almost daily. Finish this and stop second guessing all of the Council's decisions."

I called my father for some guidance and he told me about some of the people he had met as soul stealers. The one thing they all had in common was they all did their jobs without questioning authority. Their mental makeup was more of a paid killer. They didn't know the word remorse. It seems at times, I could be that way, but with Dylan, I knew it was wrong. However, even my father told me to finish the job and go home.

The next day when Dylan arrived for his therapy session, I went inside again posing as a therapist in training. I watched as his wife carefully assisted him out of the car and into the building. I knew this was more than taking a soul. I was taking a father and husband, but it was my mission. I muttered to myself to take the damn photo, as I watched him from behind the glass window in his therapy session.

As I readied my camera, I could feel someone standing behind me. I turned and could see Dylan's wife looking at me with her sad eyes.

"I'm sorry for my husband's outburst the other day. He was in a terrible accident. He's now struggling to find himself. He's a good person with a big heart. I know it was in the news about his work supporting the troops, but not many know how much he did behind the scenes. How many times he went places like this one, with his guitar and play for hours, his only pay being smiles on an otherwise broken face. If you wait around today, I'm sure I can get him to give you your photo. I will even take it for you and you can be in the photo with him if you like. I have great faith he will be the person he was again, but for now, all I can do is love him, and wait until the real Stu returns to me. Please don't judge my husband by what you see now, he really is a good man."

"I know you are right. Mrs. James. I can't say I'm a big fan, but before I got into this line of work, I too dabbled in the music industry. I have an appreciation for how much musicians sacrifice to entertain others. If I could take a photo and bring him back to you again, I would. I am a new father with a beautiful wife. I don't know what I would do without them in my life, so I don't envy you and the pain you are suffering. As silly as it sounds, I know your husband has a good soul, I have seen it. His soul can be restored to all its glory. It is only broken right now. I give you my word, if it is ever possible for me to help restore Dylan's soul I will. I won't bother him outside for a photo. I suspect he is going to need some extra rest tonight. Watch over him."

"Thank you, I'm going to get something to drink, would you like me to get you something?"

"No, thank you," I said. "I am about to leave, but I promise if the day ever arrives that I can restore him to you, I will."

With a heavy heart and much remorse, I quietly raised my camera and snapped the photo through the glass. At first, I wasn't sure it worked. I didn't see any difference in his outward appearance or speech patterns. After a few moments, I felt the surge. I knew it had worked. I sat in a chair trying not to arouse unwanted attention.

"Are you ok? Can I get you anything?"

"No, Mrs. James. Thank you, I'll be fine. I have been working double shifts this week and I think it caught up with me for a few moments."

"Dylan will be finished in a few minutes if you still would like that photo?"

"No, I should have been more understanding of what the two of you are going through right now and not asked for a photo."

"Oh don't worry. He is asked all the time. He was just being a cranky jerk the other day. He has his moods, but today he was much better. Please, let me introduce you, while his mood is on the uptick."

"I am late for another appointment, Mrs. James. I do wish you all the best."

I left the facility, filed my report with the Council and headed home. I boarded the plane and within a few moments, I fell asleep and started to dream. In my dream, there was a man, the same white haired man telling me about how I could obtain the power to restore Dylan's soul. It felt so real, more as if the older man was sitting next to me on the plane and we were having a real conversation.

"Caeles, I know I have told you before, but it is now time for you to believe that you can obtain the power not only to steal but to restore. I know you looked in the books in the library. The truth is in there. The doctor knows the truth. He is afraid to tell others, but he knows his destiny was always to protect the truth. Go to him and ask. There you will discover your destiny."

"Look dude, my destiny is to steal. It has always been my destiny."

"Caeles, we've met before on the wharf and other places, and I've told you my name is Mikael Sano, so please don't call me dude. I watch over you, as I have others for centuries. I admit I don't predict or see into the future, but I do know what has been written. If you don't believe me ask Magister Verax, or your mother. Now wake up, the plane has landed."

I woke to the hustle and bustle of people collecting their bags from the overhead bins. As my eyes opened wide, I could see someone who looked exactly like Mikael Sano leaving the plane. I jumped up from my seat and tried to leave to find him, but by the time I could weave my way through the crowd, he was gone.

CHAPT3R S!XT33N

After arriving back home, Kalani didn't want to hear anything about Mikael Sano or restoring souls. "I've told you before, do your job. Orcus and the Council have been good to us."

My warm homecoming put me in the mood to do what all new parents do; we took our son to Disneyland. Does it matter to the parents that their child couldn't walk or understand anything about the trip? No, I guess it was more trying to be like a normal family for a few days before going back to work. Besides, my wife looked cute wearing mouse ears.

After two days of banging my head against the wall trying to remove, "It's a Small World" out my brain, it was time for both Kalani and I to go back to work. We both had assignments locally, so we split parenting duties as much as possible with our newborn son, Nicon. We called him Nick for short. It would be hard to explain to a babysitter over time why he was not aging like a normal child. Even at a tender age, our kind still ages three times slower than your average person.

My next assignment was to track and find a subject, who would scheme with an accomplice to steal millions of dollars from unsuspecting investors. Robert Rapio was raised on a farm in rural Nebraska with his parents and seven siblings. As a youngster, Robert excelled in sports and was well known throughout his small community.

By the time he reached his senior year in high school, the local newspaper ran a story about Robert's potential.

"Robert Rapio has the world at his command, despite having never been outside of the state of Nebraska. His understated charm and handsome looks are only outmatched by his intellect. It was hard to imagine that Robert was confined to working a farm much of his young life, and could still achieve all that he had before his college years. A state champion in wrestling, as well as a four-year starter for the boy's-varsity baseball team. Robert had also been recognized for his outstanding work on the debate team. Do not be surprised if one day in the future, we read about Robert all across front pages of the newspapers throughout the land. Go make us all proud Robert."

Robert refused several athletic scholarships to accept an academic one at Northwestern University located just north of Chicago, Illinois. He majored in economics and finance. He went on to graduate at the top of his class. After graduation, he worked for a law firm in New York. He managed contracts and finances, for many sports and entertainment clients.

Robert's boss sent many accolades in Robert's direction. "Despite only forming this department within our firm recently, you've made it one of the premier sports and entertainment management firms in the nation, not just New York. If you need anything, bang on my door."

"Thank you Mr. Peterson, I will."

Not only did Robert's first months go well, so did his first two years. He not only became well acquainted with how to acquire clients, but also the inner working of Wall Street. In his third year working with the Pruitt law firm, Robert became responsible for managing all the retirement options for the firm's clients. He would also make suggestions on stock investments. Robert had proven at a young age that he had a talented financial mind. However, at times, he did have his detractors, like one of the law firm's biggest clients.

"Carl, I don't understand what you see in Robert. Stop looking at his pressed suit and look closer at him. I can't explain it. There is something about that man that I don't trust. It's like he is all out for him and not for me. What happened to that kid you had picking investments a few months ago? You know the college kid, George McAdams? I know I busted his ass in the beginning but when I looked that kid in the eye, I could tell he was really looking out for me. This Rapio guy, not so much. I want George to look over my investments not Robert Rapio.

"Dan, I love you as a quarterback," Carl Peterson, Robert's boss said, "but you need to worry about reading defenses and not who I hire in this office. You worry about Super Bowl's and I'll worry about my employees. I love to watch you play on Sundays, but sometimes you are a royal pain in my ass. I had George McAdams work for you and you wanted someone else. I give you Robert and you want someone else. George has to finish college. Robert has already proven to be very creative in retirement plans and tax shelters. I'm trying to get George back after he graduates and you know that, but the kid has to finish school. Now listen to Robert, the man is sharp, Dan. You need to give him a chance."

"The guy is a con artist, Carl. He's going to bite you in the ass one day, mark my words. And tell George to hurry up and graduate and start picking my investments again. I don't plan on retiring any time soon, and Linda wants a nice house in Biscayne Bay, so I need cash now, not thirty years from now."

"You need both. Now stop bitching and get out of my office. Robert knows what he's doing."

Robert Rapio lived and breathed retirement plans and economics for years. He would study everything from elections across the globe, to oil prices, and everything in between. He tracked how everything affected the jittery stock markets. He was never one to analyze individual stocks like some brokers would, but was a master for recognizing trends. His specialty was timing commodity prices like wheat, gold, oil. Robert would make recommendations on when to buy and sell investments related to those fields.

Something soon started to eat away at Robert while his ego grew as large as his client's wealth. It wasn't that Robert was poor by any standards, but compared to his millionaire clients, he paled in comparison. He realized he was watching their portfolio's grow, while he didn't have the same resources to make his assets grow as quickly as his famous clients. He felt they weren't paying him proper homage for all the success he was delivering to their bank accounts. He thought his clients the professional athletes in particular, would understand it was impossible to be correct on every assumption or trend. Robert felt he was being treated poorly when one of his suggestions failed and received little acclaim when one was a success.

"Robert, you have to get over the idea that all your clients will forever love you," his boss said. "They're in it for themselves, not you. You fail to recognize that most of them have been coddled and cared for most of their careers. Most don't give a damn about you, me or this firm, but I recognize that fact. You should too. They aren't here to be your friend. They're here to do business and there is a huge distinction. If you don't get that, you are doomed to be disappointed with your career here. Now, get over it."

"I know that, Carl. I do, but some recognition from them would be nice."

"How many times have you been to Yankee Stadium sitting in the box seats over the dug out? That's their way of showing you appreciation. It is not that they're bad people Robert. However, your job is to make sure when they blow out a knee, or their music hits the discount racks, they have a few bucks saved. Their job is to throw touchdowns, hit home runs or sell out Madison Square Garden. How many times did you send Reggie Jackson a thank you card for a game winning home run? Do your work here, Robert and be satisfied that every year you seem to get a bump in salary and we as a firm recognize the job you do here."

"It should be more, Carl. It should be about respect. I'm as good as Reggie Jackson in what I do and no one notices me like they do him."

"Robert, take satisfaction in knowing that long after Reggie is done hitting home runs, you will still be at the top of your game, maybe even better than you are now. Your talents will allow you to continue long after many of them are mere faded baseball cards collecting dust in someone's attic."

Months passed, but Robert wanted more. He wanted the glitz and glamour that his high profile clients experienced. He did his best to be featured in the, "Wall Street Journal," or any other paper or magazine that would print one of his stories. He started to claim that he had a system that would guarantee a minimum of twelve percent return on their investment even in a downward market.

"Robert, you realize you can't tell your clients you can guarantee a certain return on their investments, "Carl Peterson said. "It will only lead to a lot of trouble for you and our firm. We're not going to allow you to offer such returns. If you would like to quote what you have done in the past for your clients, then fine, but you're forbidden to work here and quote a fixed return."

"With all due respect, I can do it. I have a system that has worked for over six months now. There is no reason why it won't continue."

"Robert, I'm your biggest fan, you know that. But I can't jeopardize the reputation of this firm with your bogus claims. It ends today."

"Carl, I appreciate all that this firm and you have done for me, but the only thing that will end today is my employment here."

What Robert didn't tell Carl Peterson was that he had been considering a move to California for months. One of his clients, who was a successful film actor based in Hollywood, explained to

Robert that he would gain plenty of clients, if he was based in California. Since Robert had his new system, he knew deep down it was time to make the move. Besides, Robert knew if you wanted to be noticed, why not move to one of the most famous places on earth to be seen?

Once in California, Robert tried to keep his overhead low, and didn't immediately open up a private office. He did much of his work over the phone or in local restaurants. His friend was true to his word and introduced him to several clients quickly to start his west coast business. With every meeting, the sales pitch was the same. "I will guarantee your money is one hundred percent secure, and will grow at no less than twelve percent each and every year."

Over the course of the next year, Robert's promises held true. All of client's money grew at a minimum of twelve percent. The word started to spread quickly and because actors tend to be on sets around the world, Robert became less visible, not more. He hired a down on her luck actress Jackie Monet, to help him with daily secretarial items.

"Bobby, you're like the most famous man in Hollywood that is rarely seen in public," Jackie said. "How cool is that? All these other people pretend they want to hide from a camera, yet they stand there smiling for a horde of paparazzi, but you, all the money people come to you, but don't get to see you. I think you're the bomb."

This was never Robert Rapio's plan in moving to California, but it did make sense in an odd way. He could become famous for not being seen. Why fight for all the attention in the public view in a town where you had to be seen? Why not be famous for not being seen? It was a hard pill to swallow for him at first, but the more distant from the public eye he became, the more people wanted his services.

He turned the tables on fame and gave the impression he was far too important and intelligent to have time to attend parties and be one of the crowd. The joke was that a few times, he would attend larger gatherings and put on a fake mustache, have his good looking secretary on his arm and no one even noticed him.

At first, he despised it, but eventually he warmed to the idea of being famous for not being seen. When clients would call asking for a face to face meeting before turning over millions of dollars to be invested in his can't miss plan, his response would now be, "I have my rules, if you don't like them, go somewhere else."

As silly as that seemed, it worked. When Robert acted like he didn't want or need their business. Hollywood couldn't wait to give Robert their cash to invest.

CHAPT3R $3V3NT33N

Robert Rapio and Carl Peterson became adversaries. Robert took a few of Carl's clients with him when he left the law firm. He also didn't live up to his employment contract on several points. Threats of litigation were pushed in each direction, but Peterson's law firm came to an agreement. The law firm wanted to distance themselves from Robert's twelve percent plan.

Robert's business thrived with high profile clients from movie stars, to owners of professional sports franchises. Robert became, "Hollywood's Financial Shadow." When he did travel beyond his office or residential walls, it was in disguise. His clients didn't care. Some were making as much as a whopping twenty five percent return, while newer clients were still getting their twelve percent.

"Tell me the secret, Robert," a high ranking official asked. "How's it possible that you can keep up this track record of such high returns over several years now?"

"There's no secret or trick. I studied economic trends for several years, and it seems I have a knack for predicting the market. It's all I can tell you."

"I really can't complain with the results, but I just don't see how this is all sustainable. I'm a former Wall Street man myself. I just don't see how this is possible."

"I don't know what to tell you, Mr. Treasury Secretary. I'm the Hank Aaron of financial home runs."

"I'd like to meet with you in person, so you can at least give me some idea of how you spot a trend or a better idea of how all this works. I can't explain it, other than I'm good at picking trends won't cut it here in Washington."

"Are you accusing me of fraud or deceit, Mr. Secretary?"

"Should I be, Robert?"

The battle of egos escalated. "You're welcome to send auditors from the Security and Exchange Commission if you like, however as you are aware, I do not take meetings with anyone."

"You will if Congress subpoena's your ass to appear in Washington. That I can promise you."

"My record speaks for itself. I've never been accused of a crime, and I've been audited in the past. I don't like the tone of this conversation. So it is now over."

Many were curious about Robert and his trends. Others saw their accounts grow fatter and never questioned the results. However, pressure mounted on Robert from Washington to prove there was no fraud. Auditors arrived from California to review Robert's records. When they visited two years previous, they found nothing but legitimate trades, and solid investments, and all within the boundaries of the law.

Robert was on a hot streak of analyzing trends. It wasn't that he really had a system as much as he was good at what he did. However, over time, the rate of returns started to slip. Robert's promises of twelve percent would sometimes evaporate. The auditors wanted to check to make sure Robert wasn't running a Ponzi scheme, where he was taking funds from new investors and allocating them to older client's accounts.

Robert didn't hit on every trend. Eventually, the growth rate of clients slowed. It became harder to keep up with the twelve percent growth rates. The fear was that Robert was robbing Peter to pay Paul when he could not keep up with the growth rates promised. He knew if he could not get back on his winning ways, he might lose clients and his tag of being a genius with numbers.

This time when the Security and Exchange auditors arrived at Robert's office, all they found were a few dead bugs and a sign on the door that read, "Gone Fishin." In speaking with Robert's landlord, no one had seen activity in the office for many months, however the rent came in a timely manner. The address on the lease led the investigators to an abandoned warehouse. The office phone number was shut down the day before their arrival. Robert and his secretary were now ghosts. The FBI and local officials were being brought in to locate Robert Rapio and Jackie Monet.

"Caeles, the soul of your subject is now very dark," Elder Orcus said. "It's time for you to remove his soul. You've read the file and know his previous addresses. Our informants don't have any more information than you just read. You don't have to call for permission once your subject is in sight. Do your duty."

I headed over to Robert's office looking for any clues. Nothing. The place was stripped cleaner than a used dog bone. I decided to head over to an old friend's precinct, Detective Wilson to see if he had any information about the disappearance of Robert and Jackie.

"Agent Latens, I never thought I would see you again after letting that fugitive get away. What was his name, oh yea Blake. I know you met with him and his father. I had one of my men follow you around for a couple of days. You let that many escape, Latens. Don't deny it. You promised me a collar, but you allowed him to get away."

"That's not true. Well, not all of it. I did meet with him and his father, that part is true. But I wanted to hear his side of the story before I called you. He wanted assurances his head was not going to be blown to pieces the moment he stepped out the door. Before I could call to set it all up, they overpowered me and disappeared."

"That's a load of crap and you know it. You let that murdering son of a bitch get away. I would have locked your ass up that day, but I had my man try to stay on Blake and his father. By the time back up arrived, you were gone. I should still lock you up now, but let's hear what you have to say first."

"Detective, I can't blame you for being pissed at me, but I didn't let the guy escape without consequences. He is paying for his sins. You will have to trust me, but that is not why I am here. I am looking for Robert Rapio and his secretary. I know your department has an APB out on them. What can you tell me?"

"I can tell you that I don't trust you farther than I can spit. Even if I had anything on either of them, I wouldn't be spilling it to you. If you had any sense at all, you would turn around and never come through my precinct again. Besides, I thought you Fed's already assigned someone to find him. Another uptight Bureau man with the same dark suit as you, came asking me about Rapio two days ago."

Wilson scrambled around some papers on his wooden desk.

"Let me look at his card. Nesstor, that's the guy. He tried to cozy up to me claiming he was just like me in Chicago, before he got asked to join with you Fed boys after he cracked some big murder case. He thought he could get more information from me by acting like he's still a local cop. I told him I was burned by you Fed boys once and it wouldn't happen again. If I was thinking straight at the time, I would of told him your name. Now, like I said, remove your face from my presence, before I find something to charge you with and hold you at least overnight. You and me, we got nothing more to say to each other."

I called our informant inside the CIA and had him do a check on Rapio's and Monet's passports. It turns out neither ever applied for one, at least not under their birth names. It was possible both were still in the States. Since the trail was cold, I had to follow the old adage, to follow the money. I started to make calls to the few, who I knew were clients of Robert.

"Detective, even if I knew where Rob was hiding, I wouldn't tell you. He made me quite a bit of money over the past few years. Yes, I know they claim he's hiding somewhere, but he never stole one dime from me. I had complete access to my money at all times. In fact, just to be on the safe side, after I heard the cops were looking for him, I had my accountant move the funds I had with his company into a new account. It was all there, every penny. Robert is not a thief. I felt bad about moving it, but he didn't return my calls. I've known him since his days back in New York. I was working on a soap opera, when he was assigned to my account. He had just graduated college and I wasn't real happy Peterson dumped Rob on me, but he came through big time. Soon after I landed my big role in, "Three Long Days." Rob was always an odd fella, but he's not a crook."

"I am of the understanding you are the reason he relocated to Hollywood, Mr. Westwood. Is that true?"

"Rob always made his own decisions. I did set him up with a few friends from my soap days and some people I had met out here, that is true, but he's his own man."

"Is there anything you can tell me about his secretary, Jackie Monet?"

"I only met her a few times. She came here with Rob. Even after everyone claimed Rob went into seclusion, he would stop by for dinner about once a month. She came a few times with him. That was the big joke Detective. Rob was never in seclusion. He would go to sporting events, parties wherever he wanted. He was all over this town. He was living the dream. He would put on some silly costume and go out in public all the time. He would come dressed as an old man, a woman, I never knew what to expect from the guy. But as far as his girlfriend, I really can't offer much."

"Hold one here, Mr. Westwood. You said his girlfriend. We are talking about Jackie Monet, his secretary right?"

"You can call her what you like, but she was more than his secretary."

"I appreciate your time, Mr. Westwood. If Mr. Rapio or Miss Monet contacts you, would you please let me know? I would like to ask them a few questions."

"Rob is a good friend. He didn't steal my money, and I don't want to see him hurt. You have a good day, Mr. Latens."

I contacted several of Rapio's clients and they all said the same thing. "The guy is a genius with money. When you find him, please bring him back, he's been the best broker I have ever known."

A few days later, while sitting at home with Kalani and Nicon, the phone rang with a sorrowful voice on the other end, "A friend tells me you are calling around looking for me."

"Yes, I am. I would like to meet with you and help you out of the mess you are in right now."

"Agent Latens, I'm not stupid enough to think you're out to help me, but I'll meet with you and try to set the record straight. I'm in Los Angeles. There's a Dodger game tonight. I'll meet you in the parking lot at section seven, row seven at seven p.m., if I see anything that looks like trouble, you'll never hear from me again."

Kalani didn't like the arrangement because with all the people walking into the ball park, it would be hard to get a photo without someone else jumping into the frame. It's possible for our kind to take photos of people without stealing a soul, but anytime we're taking a photo with intent to steal, anyone else in the frame loses their soul as well. She was right. It was a risky site. I was standing at the marked site long before the appointed time.

The parking lot filled with fans heading into Dodger Stadium. The game was against the rival Giants from San Francisco. Fifty thousand men, women and children were streaming through the turnstiles from all directions. Kids were tossing balls with their dads before game time. A few fans had set up grills and were munching on burgers and Dodger Dogs. Radios were blasting all types of music as well as the pregame talk show. I was somewhat anxious not knowing what to expect with so many people around and not sure what my subject would even look like. All I could do was to stand against the pole and wait.

"Don't turn around, Agent Latens. If you do, I'll mix in with the crowd and be gone for good. I wanted someone to hear my side of the story. You know, to set the record straight. These people, they trusted us with their money, and I stole it. I didn't take much compared to what I could have taken. The business took its fee off the top. There was plenty to go around."

I took all my patience not to turn around and see who was behind the voice, but I held firm as the story continued.

"These entertainers and movie moguls, they have so much, and not just money. Everyone knows them and loves them, why would they miss a few dollars here and there? I wanted to be them and since I couldn't, I grabbed their money. The minute Robert noticed that I was stealing from his clients, he was furious with me. He'd given me all I could have wanted, except for one thing. He even tried to give me that. He begged some of his clients to give me one more chance at stardom. When they wouldn't even let me read for a part, I had my revenge. I stole from those movie makers, who refused to give me my real dream. Fame. I only stole from three accounts, Agent Latens. You must believe me. I don't know how much it was really, maybe five million dollars, I didn't keep track."

I could hear the lineups being introduced from the ballpark as she continued.'

Robert was so embarrassed with it all. He was trying to replace the money and put it back in the accounts before the auditors arrived, but he ran out of time. I gave him back what I still had left. I think he called one of them to apologize, but I don't know where Robert is now. I know he loves me very much, but I messed it all up. I'm not sure what is worse for him, my betrayal or letting people know that his secretary could steal millions of dollars right under his nose. But please believe me, he's completely innocent."

"I'm not here in search of Robert or the money. I'm only searching for you Jackie. Others can judge you and Robert in court. That is not my mission."

"You don't understand. I wanted to be on the big screen with all my being. Robert believed in me, and did all he could to help my dream come true. I admit it. I loved the idea of being a star more than thinking about what all of this would do to Robert. Once he realized what I was doing, I thought he would have me arrested. To my surprise, he told me to stay in town for a couple of weeks and he would handle it. He didn't want me to go to jail, but he didn't want others to think his client's money wasn't safe with him either. He wanted to find a way to put it all back. You have to believe me, Agent Latens. He has no idea I contacted you. I called one of his friends to see if they knew where he was. They told me that you and another agent have been calling around looking for Robert and me. Don't let him go to jail over all of this."

I could hear her sobbing. I thought this would be a good time to turn and snap her photo. I wasn't sure I could identify her if others were near, but I didn't hear any ambient noise since the game had begun. Most fans were now inside the stadium. I had to try. I turned and only saw one person behind me. A beautiful woman, donning a baseball cap and wiping the tears from her eyes. I raised the camera and took the shot. She fell to the ground. I motioned for Detective Wilson and his men to come over as I tried to get away. I could feel my body start to get the rush of energy. It is a sensation almost too hard to explain. Even though you feel the rush, your body can't handle it for a minute or two. It was in those brief moments that Wilson came charging over and arrested Jackie Monet.

"I'm surprised, but you did what you said you would this time, Latens. You're almost back in my good graces."

"Give me a moment, Detective. I need to catch my breath. I promised you if Monet admitted her guilt, I would call you over and I did. She confessed to it all."

I could see them start to load Monet into the police car with another vehicle pulling into view. I still didn't have all my senses back, but I did feel much stronger and more alive. I did my best to stall Wilson with idle chat while attempting to get myself back to feeling normal.

"Agent Latens, meet Special Agent Elliot Nesstor. I promised him he could take Miss Monet away after I got the credit for the arrest. It's kinda funny. I feel like I am the middle man between the two of you."

"Monet admitted to me that she is responsible for taking the money. Rapio is innocent. I figured I owed you a favor Wilson, and I delivered. I am sorry that everyone was putting so many resources into finding Rapio, but Jackie is your criminal. Now, like we agreed, get your story straight. She called you directly Wilson, not me, to explain her case, you arrested her. Now keep my name from your report as promised."

Nesstor jumped into the conversation. "Wait. Why wouldn't you want credit in the arrest?"

"Let it go," I said. "Detective Wilson is under the impression that I owed him an arrest, so I was helping him out. I work this area and I wanted to keep a good relationship with the local detectives."

"No, no, no, that's not how all this works. I was looking for her and Rapio just like you and Wilson. The FBI should get the credit for the arrest. You were the arresting officer and Wilson told me you work with us."

Nesstor's face morph into something from an alien invasion movie. "Holy crap. It's you. I thought you looked familiar to me. Now I know why. Wilson, how long have you known this guy?"

"I don't know, a year or more. Why?"

"I knew this person back in Chicago. He showed up at two murder scenes and now he's out here posing as FBI. This man is not FBI. I don't know who he is, but I can assure you, he's not with the Bureau."

"I thought that too, Nesstor," Wilson said. "I ran his credentials. He's one of you Fed boys. I'm not sticking him in a car and taking him with me. I got what I wanted and I gave him my word he would walk free after I got Monet. You two argue over, who each of you really might be, but keep me out of it. Nesstor, if you want to speak with Monet later, you know where to find her. Latens, thanks for the tip, I'm outa here."

CHAPT3R 3!GHT33И

"Ok, so it's Agent Latens, this time? You're not getting out of my sight until you come clean about who you really are and why you seem to turn up around so many criminals."

I smiled and put on the charm. "Congrats on getting a position with the Bureau, Agent Nesstor. How long have you been working with us now?"

"Cut the bull right now, before I take you in for impersonating a federal officer. Tell me who you are and what's going on here, and maybe I'll ask the judge to go easy on you."

"Nesstor, if I really told you who I was, or what this was all about, you would assume that I was totally deranged. So, let us part as friends and who knows, maybe we will bump into each other again. You never know, who I might decide to be on that day."

"You're joking right? You escaped from me once. There is no way in hell it's going to happen again. You can either get in the back seat of my car without the bracelets, or I can slap them on you and make them really tight."

After getting into his car, Nesstor drove me to a nondescript office building in downtown Los Angeles. Three other agents were already seated when I entered the second floor room with Nesstor.

"This is the guy I called in about, Sir. I'm sure I've seen him in Chicago near two other crime scenes, and now he was talking with an admitted embezzler. He claims to be working with us on secret missions. Did you pull his records?"

"I did, but there's not much in it. I've been making calls to everyone and no one has ever met this man. Even on the dates in his file, where it shows he went to the academy, no one can remember this clown. My guess is he's working in a highly classified department as his file indicates, or all his records are a total forgery. We need to keep him locked up until I can run across someone who actually met him."

Nesstor escorted me to a small room with no windows and one door. There was a small camera perched in the corner of the ceiling just to my right side. After being chained to a metal table, I was tossed into a grey metal chair and told to sit. Agent Nesstor sat across the table from me in another grey chair. We sat silently, while I watched the second hand on the clock above his head tick away. Four minutes and thirty-eight seconds later, another man walked in and sat in the other chair across the table. He motioned for Nesstor to leave the room.

The looked to be in his early to late sixties, dark hair with traces of grey, black rimmed glasses and a coffee stain over the left side of his upper chest on his white shirt. He wore dark blue pants and a very plain black tie with a small gold clip to keep it in place.

"Mr. Latens, I'm Agent Jerry Hopkins. I'm the regional director for the Federal Bureau of Investigations, Western District. I apologize for our less than cordial treatment of you, but Agent Nesstor has reason to believe you're not one of our agents."

I shrugged as Hopkins went on.

"He claims to have met you in the Chicago area posing as two different people. Now you show up in my district claiming to be working here. I've done a background check and despite finding documents suggesting that you are gainfully employed by the Bureau, no one has ever met you. If you can shed some light on this, I'll be more than pleased to release you and allow you to be on your way. Until that time, I'm afraid you'll remain as our guest. Is there anything you would like to tell me?"

"Agent Hopkins, is it your policy to detain every agent of the Bureau, who dares to enter your district and not report to you?"

Hopkins smirked. "Don't get cute. We have every reason to believe your records are forged. Why don't you tell me why Agent Nesstor believes you're not who you say you are."

"I can't speak for Agent Nesstor's faulty memory; maybe I have a common face, I don't know."

"It's responses like that, which will keep you as our special guest for a very long time, Mr. Latens."

I could see this tact was getting me nowhere so it was time to change course. "Are you a man of your word Agent Hopkins?"

"I would like to believe I am. Why do you ask?"

"I'll make you an offer and we'll see if you really are a man of your word. I will answer each and every question of yours with complete honesty, if you see no laws have been broken, will you release me?"

"I guess that depends on if I believe your answers, but you're welcome to try."

"Ask away, Agent Hopkins. I can only hope you listen with an open mind because all my responses will be accurate." I looked into Hopkins's eyes as he offered his best poker stare.

"Is your real name Latens and are you currently an employee of the FBI?"

"My name is Caeles Novo. You will not find records of my birth or any existence of me in your database. Do not bother trying. I am not paid by the FBI, but I do have proper credentials under the name Latens, in order to gain access to information when I am working on a mission."

"What type of missions do you work on, Mr. Novo?"

"Agent Hopkins, I have no doubt you are as good a man as I know Agent Nesstor is. I have seen his work up close, when we were back in Chicago. I admit he has seen me pose as other people. However, if I were to tell you my true mission, you would never believe me. I realize you have no reason to trust me, but we are on the same side. Your mission is to arrest criminals and put them in your jail cells. My mission is to shackle them with their personal chains for as long as they walk this earth."

Hopkins frowned. "I don't need some intellectual bull shit from you, Novo. Just tell me what the hell it is you are doing hanging around with known criminals?"

"My mission is to steal souls from people who cannot see the beauty in life, or appreciate all that has been given to them. I do not break any of your laws, and I have been given the right to do so by the heavens above. I will continue my mission for well over one hundred years or more after you are dead and buried. Odds are that you now think you have a crazy lunatic sitting across from you, but I assure you every word I have spoken is true. I will also tell you that I have others, who will assist me in leaving this building unharmed and unchained. I do not know when or where, but it will happen. Agent Nesstor can continue to chase me across the globe for as long as he likes, but I have broken no laws. So with all due respect, I suggest you release me."

I sat daring myself not to show fear or break a sweat as Agent Hopkins continued to stare directly into my eyes, almost begging me to change my story.

"Mr. Novo, I believe you've been impersonating a federal officer. That is a crime and you will be charged on those grounds. Besides, what should I tell my superiors back in Washington? We had Mr. Wizard in our possession, but I was afraid he would turn me into toad, so I had to release him. Come on, you have to do better than you fly around the world stealing souls and there is no record of you on earth. Do you take me for a fool?"

I again shrugged. "Agent Hopkins, my credentials with the FBI are real. Besides, I never said that I can fly. I take the same modes of transportation as you. Despite my current position and desire to be released, I still cannot turn you into a toad. In fact, if I took your soul with the sole intention of being released, I would be punished. I promised to offer the truth if you would release me. I did my part, even if I did not expect you to live up to yours. I know how silly it sounds, however I can assure you, I am a highly educated being, who is fluent in several languages. I am knowledgeable in world politics, and have been to over one hundred countries on earth. I am of sound mind. I have tracked down and found criminals that even your people could not locate like James Blake and Miss Monet. I am not a crazy person, but I am one, who is losing his patience. I am going to ask you one last time in a calm and rationale way to kindly release me."

Another pause ensued with Hopkins, still staring my way, before sitting back in his chair and wiping his brow.

"Mr. Novo, we get all kinds in here. Some are delusional from drugs and alcohol; others have serious mental challenges, while a percentage of them are just downright stupid. We do run into a few sophisticated criminals from time to time, yet still I have no idea what category you seem to fit. You don't seem like you want to harm anyone and even Nesstor admitted that he does not think you committed any crimes back in Chicago. I don't know what to think about you. I know I can't release you after hearing your story, but if your credentials are real, I'm not sure how to detain you. But until someone can identify you, or you can come up with a better story than the one you're selling now, you're going to remain our guest."

I could hear the second hand on the clock behind Hopkins' head ticking away, making me more impatient with every tock.

Since honesty didn't work, it was time I realized I would be staying longer than first anticipated.

"If I am going to be detained, then I assume I can make a phone call? I would like to call my wife and let her know where I am. She will be expecting me home soon. I don't want her to worry about me."

"We will call her for you, Mr. Novo. Please give me the number. Besides, don't you have some way of communicating through brain waves with all of your special soul powers?"

"Agent Hopkins, I have been very respectful of you and your job, I would appreciate some of the same courtesies. Now, may I have my phone call or not? Let's not forget, the only reason why Nesstor located me again was because I was assisting in the apprehension of a criminal. One day, you might need my assistance in locating another one. You would be foolish to doubt my skills. Those facts alone, I do believe, should garner me a phone call."

"I don't know who you really are pal, but you did take a slow night and turn it into something entertaining. Ok, you can call Mrs. Wizard and let her know you won't be home for the séance tonight."

"I do believe one day you are going to rue your words, Agent Hopkins. Please hand me the phone, my super powers don't allow me to dial from across the room."

I called Kalani to let her know what happened. I assured her I would find a way home within a few hours. I could hear the phone click off before I hung up. I knew someone was listening from within the office. After my call, I was unchained from the desk, but was locked in the small white room with the camera's red light watching me twist and turn in the chair. I was in a very uncomfortable mood throughout the early morning hours.

"Let's go, Novo. We're moving you to a secure location."

I lifted my head from the cold metal desk. There was a hint of drool dripping from the right side of my mouth as my eyes focused on the clock long enough to realize it was just past five in the morning. I was in no mood to be shuffled off to another location, but what choice did I have?

"Is this all necessary, Agent Nesstor? Have I shown even one sign of violence or an attempt to escape? Besides, I have not even called my attorney yet. Have you guys even charged me with a crime? I know I have not been read my rights. What kind of cops are you anyway?"

"Novo, I am sure once we get a handle on who or what you are, we will release you back to the magical kingdom of fairies and goblins, but for now the chief says you are to be held in a cell until we know more about you.

"I have already told you all there is to know about me and you won't find any more. We take great care in protecting our identity and there is a chance if the Council ever finds out how much I told you people, I will be punished. However, I wanted to go home, so I took a wild shot that someone would believe me. I have done nothing wrong. In fact, I'll make you an offer, Nesstor. I'll bet it's eating at you that you don't know who killed that poor lady in the rocking chair back in Chicago. If you release me, I will tell you who suffocated that poor woman. Now mind you, I was not there and I could never be an eyewitness, but I am certain I could help you. I did give you the lady killer, Barbara."

"I'm no longer associated with the Chicago Police, but I'll pass along the information if you have something to offer me."

"Oh, no, it does not work that way. You go to your boss, have him release me, and I will tell you who did it."

"You have no idea who committed that murder, Novo. No deal."

"Have it your way, but once my lawyer gets here, I will be walking free anyway. You might as well save us both some aggravation of the paper work and all the nastiness of my name put in the public records. It will only disappear soon after I am released, and you are left with your prick in your hands. But then again, maybe you like that?"

"Alright, Merlin, that's enough from you. Don't try to do anything stupid between here and the padded cell we will find for you. There is a nice doctor who wants to meet you."

"Nesstor, I know my rights and having me carted off like this is not on the list. Now I insist on calling my lawyer before you take me anywhere."

"You've not been charged, so no reason for a call. Talk with the nice doctor then maybe if you're a good boy, he will give you a new magic wand to play with."

"You know Nesstor, I asked about you. I was told you have a clean soul and you were not on the list. I think I am going to double check again once I get released. And by the way, if you see an old guy with white hair, you might want to duck. I have no idea if he will be outside or not, but he seems to show up when I get in trouble. He comes to me in my dreams and every once in a while, he meets in person, while I am awake. His name is Mikael Sano, but whatever you do, don't call him dude. He really gets upset when you do. If you don't let me call my lawyer, I am guessing he will find a way to get me out of this mess. Then again, I have not seen him in a couple of years, so who knows. Oh well, you were warned."

"You really do need some time away from society, pal. Now get in the elevator."

It was an hour before dawn. The streets were dim. A nearby street lamp lit the path from the front door to the parked car a few feet away. I was being pushed towards the car door, when Nesstor dropped face first to the ground.

"Hurry, Cale, before we start to feel the effects. Grab his gun and keys and unlock yourself. We only have a moment. Hurry."

"Kalani, what have you done?"

"Hush, and get yourself free. You can be mad with me later, but for now, do as I say."

I found the keys and released myself as I started my body started to quiver. Kalani was in full shake. We jumped into a car driven by a friend of hers and pulled away. Nesstor was still flat on the ground, with his head hanging over the curb. We were out of view before we both stopped shaking.

"Kalani, I don't want to sound ungrateful, but why did you do that? I was fine. They were only trying to mess with me for a while, before releasing me later today. They had no reason to keep me and didn't even charge me. There was no reason to go to such extreme measures."

"You're dead wrong. I had a call from Even Crowe, our man back east. He had a call from his source inside the FBI and you were being transferred to a mental hospital with locks and bars on the doors. I called Orcus, but he said he couldn't do anything and would figure out a way to get you out once in the mental ward. I couldn't take the chance they would do something to you before we could get you out. I panicked, Baby. I didn't know what else to do, so I took his soul. I knew you would be upset with me, but it was my only option on short notice. I'll answer to the Council. If we're lucky, it won't affect him too much, and he can live a near normal life."

CHAPTER NINETEEN

Kalani upset me for what she had done, however being brought in front of the Council for yet another scolding, upset me more. We were both hoping Kalani would be given probation, or be held in the compound for a short time. We wished to get on with our lives.

"Kalani Inoke Novo, you have mocked this Council with your actions. Not only did you break a sacred law, you did it for personal reasons. You've both been warned many times the perils you would face if you ever altered the fate of a human without permission. You leave us with no other choice. The two of you will be a reminder for all eternity for all, who believe you can mix your duty and love for each other. Before you were joined in your union, you were lectured that your marriage would fail. Now it has. You must pay for your failings. Kalani Inoke Novo, kneel before this Council and accept your punishment."

Seconds later, I fell to the floor. Any other time a soul is taken, I would feel power rush through my veins, and then allow a time for my body to readjust. This time nothing but hatred, despair, sorrow, and pain filled my being like never before. Not only was it cruel for the Council to rule with such a vindictive force, but to do it so suddenly.

The only person other than our son and parents, who I truly loved, had been taken from me. It took every ounce of energy left in my body to peer up at the Council and beg them to undo what they had just done. All I could see was the disgusting sneer on the face of Elder Orcus. He seemed to take pleasure in removing my beautiful Kalani's soul and even more pleasure in making me watch. I wanted to kill every one of the six men looking down on us. The anger and pain was overwhelming.

Exhausted, I slowly pushed my body to stand, pointing my finger at the six men, who would now be my enemies until my last breath.

"Why?" I asked. "Why would you commit such a heinous act on someone, who lived within your rules every waking moment? She was protecting me. I beg you to give back her soul and remove mine. I am the one who deserves to suffer."

"But you are paying for your sins, Caeles. The Council knows it is far worse for you to watch her suffer every day. It would be too easy for you if we removed your soul too. This is your punishment. As for her, she knew the risks. She contacted me and told me your situation and I gave her a strict command not to leave your home. She disobeyed my command."

I wanted to jump up on the dais and slit the throat of all six men. The rage pulsating through me was an emotion I had never previously experienced. As I took a step towards them, a warning bellowed in my direction.

"Should you take one more step, you can join your wife with your soul in the abyss. I know you feel anger and despair but it will soon pass. When it does, you will continue with your duty. The emotions you are experiencing will only aid you to become more efficient with your work."

I knew he was right in that I could never reach him before they removed my soul, but remaining a soul stealer was never going to happen.

"With all due respect to you, Elder Orcus and High Council, my time as a soul stealer ended the second you removed Kalani's soul. I will not accept any more assignments."

"Caeles, you might be an educated creature, but you're not very smart. You will continue your missions or more pain and suffering will enter your world. Should you decide to stop stealing, the next to suffer will be your son. If you do not accept the next mission, we will strip his soul in your presence. The next will be your mother, your father. Anyone who represents joy will be taken from you. Do not stand there thinking you can dictate to this Council what you will and will not do. You will continue your duty and will do it with honor. If not, we will destroy everything you love. Now, pick up what remains of your failed past and wait for your next mission."

I eyed Kalani, knowing my wife would never recover. I felt dead inside. It was as if I had lost my own soul and more. I sat next to her on the cold stone floor and pulled her into my lap. There was little sign of life in her eyes. Her body lay limp against mine. I pulled her into my chest, tears gushing down my face. I begged her to utter a word, anything. Nothing, she was motionless.

Her heart beat against my chest, but it was the only sign of life. Hate now consumed my body. I again looked at the wretched men who did this to her. They were all sitting high in their chairs looking down at the floor watching me clutch her in my arms. My resolve to kill them all was now as hard as the stone floor underneath me.

Hours passed. I couldn't move a muscle. The Council had departed the chamber, leaving me alone with Kalani draped around me. During those hours when I could focus my mind, it wavered between revenge and the good times I shared with my wife and family. She started to gain some of her former self, but not much.

She could speak slowly, but with little meaning. The few words that I could decipher made little sense to me. Her once strong and vibrant personality had transformed into someone I could now sense was fearful of her surroundings. When I looked deeply into her eyes, as I had so many times in the past, I saw emptiness. I knew I had to be strong for her. I also knew it would be impossible to explain to my young son why his mother might never again be able to communicate with him.

I hired a private plane to get her back home. Kalani was in no condition to travel on a commercial airline without drawing suspicion. It wasn't an easy trek home.

No one has ever been able to explain to me why everyone seems to act differently should their soul be taken. Maybe it's the more you believe, the more you feel the loss. All I knew was that Kalani was not the same person.

I was forced back to work or risk losing more of my loved ones. Maybe the Council would not really take my son's soul, but I couldn't take that risk. Kalani's mother and father had been taking care of our son in our home. They were there when we arrived back in California.

Her father was raised and educated to heal, but within seconds he fell to the floor in despair. Her mother's sorrow manifested itself as she pounded her fists in my chest in anger until she no longer had the energy. It was the second hardest day of my life. Kalani would desperately attempt to communicate, but it was maddening trying to understand her. After the initial shock of it all, we decided to move Kalani and my son to Tahiti, where her dad had his hospital, and Kalani could get care from her mother. I was in no position to raise my son at this time.

The night before we were to transport them to Tahiti, Mikael Sano again came to me in a dream.

"Caeles, develop your powers. Speak with the Doctor. He knows the secret. It's a difficult journey but one you must take."

This replayed in my brain, until I could no longer stay asleep. I woke to a cold sweat with Kalani's warm body neatly pressed against me. I didn't understand my dream, but it was worth questioning her father to see if he knew more.

"Doc, I had a strange dream about developing some type of power and you could help me. Does that mean anything to you?"

"What type of power, Cale?"

"I really don't know, but as odd as this might sound, it was delivered by someone or something that has come to me before. I almost think I am being told to develop the power to restore Kalani's soul. Does any of that make sense to you?"

"It makes perfect sense to me. It's your guilty conscience trying to lead you down an empty path. My daughter will never be the same and there's nothing you can do to repair her. I suggest you accept it and move on. You'll have to live with what you did to my only daughter and not let your guilt crush you. In time, maybe I will forgive you, but not today."

"Hold on, my guilt? I didn't do this to her. I didn't want her anywhere near that place."

"Then why did you call her, Cale? You knew she wouldn't harm find you. The same way you fought to save her back in Hawaii. Did you believe she would do less for you?" Face it. You put her in a position to choose between you or our laws."

"I did no such thing. I called her to update her. I would have never allowed her to take someone's soul to rescue me."

"Oh, you did that for her, and you also set a truck on fire with people inside."

"Can you help me or not, Doc?"

"I can help you by taking my daughter and my grandson back home with me, other than that you are on your own."

The next few months, I ripped out a soul every few days. To me they were all faceless people, who meant nothing to me. I no longer cared if I thought they were deserving of it or not.

I was doing exactly what the Council wanted in becoming a heartless monster, but that is not the way it was seen. I was doing my duty in keeping our kind alive. The one thing that I did notice was that because I was stealing more than a soul a week, my mind was becoming sharper, my body stronger. However, even though my body and mind were never stronger, my life had no meaning. I felt nothing. I raced from mission to mission making sure my son would be safe. I considered suicide once, but the thought of leaving my son and even Kalani behind was too painful.

While on a mission in Florida, I stopped in to visit with my parents. I told my mother about the dreams I was having and about Mikael .

"Yes, I know Mikael ", my mother said. "He's our family guardian. It's time you heard the truth. It was preordained that you would be joined with Kalani. Mikael assisted in seeing that it happened."

I sat up and moved to the front of my chair.

"What are you telling me? It was an arranged marriage made without our knowledge? How did that happen and why would anyone care if we were married?"

"Caeles my darling son, it's time you learned the truth about our family and the history of our kind. I'm not sure Kalani's family knows the truth. I assume they do, but I have never spoke with them in fear if they didn't know, it could cause major concerns with the Council."

"Spit it out, Mom. What are you trying to tell me?"

"How did you meet Kalani?"

I was getting very anxious as to where this was leading. "You know how we met. I was on holiday in Hawaii, wandering around the market place and she asked me for help with her camera."

"Exactly, and who nudged her in your direction telling Kalani that you were the one who could help her. Who was it?"

"Are you telling me that Mikael made sure that I met Kalani and kept nudging us together?"

"Yes that's what I'm telling you."

"Why? What's all this about?"

My mother took a deep sigh and looked at me with that soft caring look that only a mother could offer.

"The short answer is that your blood is a perfect match with Kalani in order to create more children who can restore souls, like you my son."

"I don't restore souls, mom. I take them, or have you forgotten? Stop holding back and tell me what is going on here."

My patience was running short and my anxiety level was rising.

"Caeles, if you were ever to repeat what I'm about to tell you, it could lead to your immediate death at the hands of the Council. I haven't told you because I was afraid you would not be able to keep it to yourself. This is not to be taken lightly. If the Council knew your true identity, you would be executed."

Her words were met with great speculation on my part.

"The Council loves my work. There is no way they would harm me as long as I keep stealing souls for our kind."

"You're not listening to me. Our family bloodlines have been manipulated for the past three generations. It was done to significantly increase the odds that you would develop the power to restore souls."

"Mom, there were times I felt uneasy taking a soul and yes a few times I would have liked to have given it back.Now with Kalani, I would do anything I could to return her soul, but I do not have the power. I do not think the Council does either. Do they?"

My mother let out a long sigh, as if to encourage me to listen closer to her words.

"The mission of the original one hundred, who were given the power to steal, also had the power to restore. The mission was never about theft, Caeles. The original mission was one of redemption. The original one hundred of our kind would take a soul only long enough to offer redemption and later return it. Most humans, even if they deny it at first, will seek a second chance to see the beauty in our world. Rarely will anyone turn down redemption."

"If your story is true, then what happened to our powers?"

"As time passed, some did not seek redemption. The Elders recognized that when we kept the souls for ourselves, our own powers grew stronger. Over time, we fed on the poor choices of others and became ever dependent on that power. Eventually, there was no turning back. The power to restore souls was destroyed by the Council. However, they were smart about it. They slowly eroded our powers so that few noticed and greed for more power consumed our kind. As long as we were fed with the souls of others, our kind didn't care who we stole from. The Council made sure the bloodlines were thinned out and anyone who still had the power to restore was sent on dangerous missions and were killed. The others were so dependent on the souls of others that no one saw the horror around them."

I sat back in my chair, running my hands through my hair and staring off into space, trying to imagine if all of this was true, and what it all had to do with me and possibly Kalani. I then remembered when I was in the compound and had read one small line in a book about restoration. Was it possible we really did have the power to restore?

"Caeles, why do you think the Council was so opposed to you and Kalani being married and removed her soul so quickly? She handed them the excuse they had been looking for so the rest of our kind wouldn't look harshly on their decision. The Council never encourages two, who have the power to steal to marry. They will however allow two like your father and I to join, since neither had the power to steal."

I thought she had delivered enough shocking news for one day, but there was more.

"I have the power, my son, always have. I chose not to tell the Council or your father. Your father comes from the original one hundred bloodlines with his ancestors only one time having mixed with pure human form. He should have developed the power to steal, but he has too kind of a heart. That side of him runs through you. My side of the family tree has never taken a pure human for a mate. Kalani's bloodlines are direct descendants from the original one hundred without a break in bloodlines as well. However, the records in our official documents kept by the Council don't reflect that fact. They've been altered. The Council believes they have eradicated all the pure bloodlines from the original one hundred. They are wrong. If they knew the truth, we would all be eliminated too, as would your son."

I suspected this was possible for years, but never wanted to investigate the truth.

"I'm in a bit of shock mom. Why'd you wait so long to tell me?"

"Because, you weren't ready to restore, nor did you have a burning desire to try. The master plan was that my offspring would be more likely to be able to regain the power to restore. As much as it pains me to know Kalani sleeps without her soul, I believe it has a purpose."

"How were the documents altered?"

"As you know, all of our history of births and bloodlines are kept secure near the site where our original power was granted. As the years passed, our God grew angry with the Council's decision to eradicate our original mission of redemption. Mikael tells me that rather than destroying us, being a merciful God, we too have been given the chance at redemption. In 1693, there was an earthquake. For several days, no one was able to reach the official documents. Mikael was given the chore to alter the records and make it look like the few remaining families who had not mated with humans did so and remove any chance the Council would find ways to have them mate with pure humans. Mikael asked every other generation not to steal souls to have it appear as if our powers were weakened. This is the reason why I don't steal. Mikael has been joining those few families since 1693. It has taken this long to regain our original powers. I'm not certain you'll develop the power of restoration, but you must try."

"How do you know all of this is true mom? Who told you?"

"Mikael of course. He's been sent from the heavens to restore our original powers."

I sat chuckling in my seat, not so sure all that she told me was true.

"Caeles, I know you are unsure of Mikael . I know your faith is weak right now. You grow stronger in mind and body with every theft. I can see it. However, it's wrong. You must believe in Mikael . He's a strong spirit sent from the heavens. He knows how to proceed past the gatekeeper, where all lost souls remain, while their owners are alive on earth. I believe him and you must too. Embrace your dreams when Mikael comes to you with his words. Even you must admit he helped you save Kalani back in Hawaii and you in Chicago. Yes, I know about it, he told me. It's time to take the new path he has laid out for you long before you were even born."

CHAPT3R TW3NTY

For the next several weeks, the dreams continued to torment my rest. It was always the same message.

"The doctor knows the truth."

I hadn't seen Kalani or my son for several months. I begged the Council for a respite in my duties and one was granted. I caught the first flight to Tahiti to visit with my family.

The greeting at the door by my mother in law was less than warm, the one from my father in law wasn't much better. My son was still a very young child and was beginning to form words. I could now communicate with him on a different level than the last time I had seen him.

Kalani remained the same. When I would pull her closer to my chest, I could feel the beat of her heart quicken. I wanted to believe she knew it was her husband. Still, it was very painful to feel her so close, knowing she was so far away. Later that evening, I tried to reason with my father in law.

"Doc, the dreams continue. They grow more intense every night. I have to believe that you are the one who can help. I am starting to believe it is possible to restore Kalani's soul, as well as others. I need you to think hard about what you may have read or overheard while you were a doctor in the compound. Please try to recall anything you can so you can help me and your daughter."

"Cale, don't you think I want to help my daughter? I'm the one who has to see her day after day, a vegetable in her own skin, while you trek across the globe destroying others in your wake.

Then you come to me asking for help, and to what ends? Do you really believe you're some kind of savior to the world? Or, you can rescue my daughter from the hell she's in? I'm the one, who has to look at her knowing, who she was before she was destroyed because she loved you. I have what remains of my family to think about. You have no idea how powerful the Council has become. They have spies everywhere. You don't know what they see and don't see. If I were to help you, not only would my life and my wife's be in jeopardy, but so would the life of my grandson. Go do what you need to do, if you think that's your duty, but don't ask me for any assistance."

"Doc, I know your life has been as a healer and not one of pain. I am well aware you think what I do is all about destruction, but were you not proud of Kalani doing her duty? You were so proud when you thought she was keeping our kind alive, but me, I am destroying the world? I am growing more convinced every day that my mission should be about one of restoration. I can't do it without your help. You know that our kind was raised on the principles of removing souls from others who cannot see the beauty in their lives. I feel as though you are looking at me as if I was the originator of such thoughts. I know you blame me for Kalani. I am not the one who created soul stealing, including hers. However, I am starting to believe I am the one who is destined to bring back the souls for some who will want redemption and a second chance in life. Kalani loved life. She loved her family, and saw beauty all around her. She of all people deserves another chance in life. I need your help."

Kalani's father lowered his chin and peered above his wire frame glasses, offering a stare of conviction. "Cale, talk of restoring a soul is nothing but lies and innuendo. Yes, I have read passages and heard the whispers about our history. If you attempt it and the Council finds out, you will be brought up on charges and your son will lose both parents. I cannot take the chance of the Council thinking I helped you. I'm sorry. Please do not bring that talk into my home again. I wish you could bring Kalani back to us, but there is no evidence it can be done."

"Doc, now I think you are holding back. I think you know there is a chance and are afraid to tell me what it is."

"You are welcome to be a guest in my home out of respect for my daughter and your son, but if you dare bring up this topic again, I will demand you leave."

I stayed a few more days mostly to see my son and spend time with him. I tried to communicate with Kalani, but the highlight was what I perceived as a passing smile when I told her that I loved her and missed her. During that week, the dreams continued and made it near impossible for me to sleep more than two or three hours at a time.

When I returned home to California, there was a package at the door. The return address was labeled from a building in Kingston, Jamaica. I opened it up only to find a few cryptic notes about ancient laws and an address to a building. I had a few more days until my next assignment, so I headed off for Jamaica.

The address in the package directed me to a small, but well maintained building along one of the main roads in Kingston. The building was home to a man, who held the title of Custos Rotulorum.

After meeting the man, he informed me that it meant, "Keeper of the Rolls." We had a conversation about why he sent me the package. He informed me that a stranger with an island accent called him with my address and asked that he send me the enclosed information and address to his building. He didn't know why someone would care to have it sent, but he was paid a fee for sending it. The tall Jamaican man had no idea who I was or why I would come to his building, not did he know asked him to send it.

I left the building totally confused and unsure why I needed to make the long journey. There was a small park across the street. I went and sat on the bench deciding if I should take the first plane ride back home or stay a few days and relax. I started to close my eyes when someone sat on the bench next to me.

"Scuse me, Mon. I don't mean to intrude on your peace, but I was told you were looking for me."

If I thought I was perplexed a few moments ago, now I was really scratching my head.

"I didn't know I was looking for anyone, but who might you be?"

He politely smiled before saying, "I am Bastian Duvaliar, but people round here call me Doc."

I smiled back and said, "You know what, I think I am looking for you. Why do they call you Doc?"

This time a louder chuckle came from rotund man. "Because my friend, I am the one who can find your lost spirit. Have you lost your sprit?"

"Not a spirit, but what about thousands of souls?"

Bastian moved closer and placed his left hand on my right knee. "I never thought this day would happen. My father told me the story and his father before him, now the day is here."

"I don't understand, Doc. What story?"

"Enough words, do not ask any more questions. In one hour, meet me at the last house down that road. Don't' worry about the chickens out front, they don't bite. I will see you in one hour. Do not be late."

I checked into the local hotel and met Bastian at the last house on the road exactly one hour later.

"Come in, come in. Welcome to my home. I never did ask your name."

"My name is Caeles Novo. But I have a strange feeling that even if you didn't know my name, you know why I am here."

Bastian waved his arm to offer me a seat. He resided in a small wooden house with several windows that were now open and a paddle fan barely turning. The furniture was old, but well kept. Bastian appeared to be a man in his late seventies or early eighties. He was a dark skinned man, with signs of age across his face. He wore a short-sleeved white dress shirt, neatly pressed but not new, dark dress pants and polished black shoes. When he smiled, it seemed as wide as the island of Jamaica. As I sat, I noticed a small scent of burning incense waffling from somewhere across the room.

"It has been a tale told for many years that one day someone would come looking for this book. It has been stored down the street where the Custos has his office. I think you were in the building earlier. You need to read this book in my presence and then I'm to return it back where it has been stored for over one hundred years. I'm responsible for its safety. This book was smuggled into England sometime in the late half of the seventeenth century. It was brought here to the Keeper of Records in 1876. It is one of a kind. My family has been anticipating someone coming to find us for several generations.

"With all due respect, Mr. Duvaliar, all I did was to ask you if you could find lost souls. Now you invite me to your home and talk about books being smuggled and you being the keeper, how do you know what I really want?"

He smiled as wide as the Island of Jamaica. "You are the taker of souls, who wants to return them. Yes or no?"

"Yes, I am."

"Then never doubt the spirits and what they tell me about you. We have a lot of work and you have much reading. Your time is short. The story also says that when the soul taker arrives, others will follow. Now read your book, and do not anger the spirits."

The first part of the book outlined the history of our kind. It spoke about the original one hundred, who were given the power to steal. It also outlined very carefully where to place the taken souls while offering the victims a second chance. It told the story of, the "Gatekeeper of Souls," and how and where they are stored, while remaining away from their physical human body.

The second section talked about how, if the soul remains away from its human body for more than a few months, it becomes much harder to restore. When a soul is removed, it's stored in a crystal that looks like a snowflake. Each one is unique, but the Gatekeeper keeps a careful record to match each soul with its proper owner. If left alone for too long, the crystal can begin to disintegrate. The only way to return it back to its original form if already damaged is for the one returning the soul to lose a portion of their soul.

In reading the pages, it led me to believe there was a safety mechanism in place for removing a soul. The stealer would gain power from the stolen soul, however if you returned the soul in a proper timeframe, you would not lose all of the power you gained when restoring it. It was as if you shared in another's redemption.

However, the longer you waited to restore the soul after taking it from the Gatekeeper, the more difficult the mission to restore would become. The one, who took the soul, would have the best chance at restoring the soul. However, anyone with the power of restoration could attempt it. If you waited too long to restore the soul or you were not the original thief, part of your soul would be lost upon restoration.

As I read the pages, I felt there was a system in place, where if you removed the soul and restored in a proper timeframe, you would be rewarded. But if you waited too long, there would be a penalty. It seems there was not provision for the greed of never returning a lost soul, only a penalty for doing it slowly.

"You don't seem so surprised by all you read, Caeles Novo. Why is that?"

"Before enduring the evil of watching my wife's soul being stolen, I sometimes suspected the Council would remove souls, not broken or dark, only confused. Our kind was being eliminated, because so few had the power to take and even fewer had the power to see into another's soul. Once the Council ruled to remove Kalani's soul and I looked upon their eyes, I could see directly into their souls. I knew at that moment, I had the same powers as them.

"The gods have given you more than the power of sight my friend. They have given you a pure mind and the ability to reason, even against what appears to be truth. Now rest your beautiful mind. You will need it if you are to gain the powers of restoration."

I left Bastian's home for my hotel room and slept for over twelve hours straight, as if someone knew I would need it.

CHAPT3R TW3ИTY OИ3

"**W**elcome back, Caeles. I trust you enjoyed a restful evening. Are you now ready to offer redemption to your chosen soul?"

I took in a deep breath and was asked to sit in a wooden chair below a window.

"Before we begin, you must be certain you have the authentic bloodlines and have the true desire to succeed. If you are missing either of those elements, your soul will be lost forever. Are you willing to take on this risk?"

Another deep breath.

"Yes. However, I am still unclear how I can proceed beyond the gatekeeper?"

"That my friend is an answer I cannot offer you. Are you still confused? Possibly we should review the process before we begin?"

"I think that would be wise, Bastian. I know I only have one chance at restoring this soul. I refuse to accept failure because I was unprepared."

"Ok, then let us review. First, I will ask you to relax your mind. Soon after, the spirits will begin to enter your thoughts. Allow them to roam your mind with ease. Once they do, they will then lift your soul from your body and take it to its destination. I cannot explain what you will experience in your mind, since I have never done this myself. After the spirits have lifted your soul, you will meet the gatekeeper. I don't know who the gatekeeper will be. It is told there is but one gatekeeper, who takes on the image of the person the lost soul finds as a symbol of peace and harmony in his or her mind. You must be ready for anyone, Caeles. The gatekeeper has never been known to be the image of the same person twice, yet is the same being. You will be given the task of proving to the gatekeeper you are worthy of returning with the soul you seek."

Second thoughts about my mission creeped into my head, but I began believing in possibly I had found my destiny.

"What do I say, Bastian? What do I do when meeting the gatekeeper? I was very confused when reading the book yesterday. Does my soul speak to the gatekeeper?"

"The story has been handed down for centuries from others who have succeeded beyond the gatekeeper that you can communicate with them. The spirits will translate your thoughts from your mind to the gatekeeper. Allow the spirits to do their job. You must convince the gatekeeper, not only to send you to the soul you seek, but also convince the gatekeeper your intended soul seeks redemption. Not all souls want to return to their earthly bodies. If you fail at either task, there will never be a second chance. Do not fail, Caeles."

"I am aware of that part, Bastian. I intend to try with the musician I spoke about yesterday, and not my wife. I cannot risk her soul lost to me forever because of my inexperience, despite wanting her back in my arms."

Bastian nodded. "I am only here to guide you, my friend. One last time, are you certain you want to journey beyond this earth and risk losing your own soul?"

"I am."

"Let us begin. Close your eyes and open your mind."

The wind outside the windows quickened. The birds went silent. Time had come to release my soul from my earthly body and seek out the gatekeeper guarding my intended subject. Bastian would guard my body so that no one would interfere with me, while my soul was detached from my body. Should anyone attempt to waken me while my soul was away, my mission would end. There were no assurances that my soul would return to my body if awaked during the process. A second chance to succeed was not possible.

"Relax your body, Caeles. Let your mind allow the spirits to enter. Feel the universe around you. Take a deep breath, now another. I call on the spirits to remove your soul and engulf your mind."

A new chapter in my life was now set in motion. My mind was consumed with spirits, who took me to a place outside the only world I had ever known. My mind witnessed my soul being removed from my body. Shadows of dull grey resided everywhere my mind could glimpse. There was no longer the sensation of gravity pulling me in any direction, only shadows dancing from distant beams of light. Not a strong light, but dim, like just before dawn. The shadows arranged themselves into a form I was more familiar with, the form of a human body. My mind was able to make out some elements, but not all. It was working harder than it ever had before. The beams of light became stronger as I could now plainly see someone come into view.

"What is your purpose in coming to the Shadows of Souls, Caeles Novo?"

"Who are you? You seem familiar to me."

"I am the gatekeeper. No one goes beyond here without my permission."

"Please you must grant me access to the soul I seek. Show me where to find it, time is short."

The light began to fade along with an eerie silence.

"Do you deem your words to have meaning to me? I answer to no one, but the one who assigned me here. These souls are under my care, a command from you has no meaning for me."

"But I am here to offer redemption and a path back home for a vanished soul. You must not interfere with what is inevitable."

The light grew a stark white. I could now see the gatekeeper was the image of a tall thin black man with a tie dyed shirt, bellbottom blue jeans and a large afro hairstyle holding a white guitar. He peered at me with a perplexed stare.

"Inevitable you say? What makes you think your vanquished soul deserves redemption? The soul you seek is content to play music alone. His soul is waiting for death to consume his earthly body. It is then his soul will move to the next stage of existence."

"Leaving the earthly stage without seeing the beauty he left behind will not allow his soul to proceed forward," I said. "The soul must be returned to his earthly body to know beauty once more. You must let me succeed. And no disrespect to you gatekeeper, but why do you look like Jimi Hendrix?"

"I represent a symbol of life to the soul I shelter." A C chord rang from his guitar. "You have not convinced me to offer you what you seek. Why does the soul you seek deserve redemption?"

The silhouetted image of a stoic Hendrix stood against the backdrop of what had become a hue of soft purple beams. I had to try again to convince him to allow me to pass before my time would expire, or I would fail. What could I offer as a reason? What could I say to make the gatekeeper understand that the soul of Dylan James deserved to be back on earth, rather than playing solo until his earthly body ceased to exist?

"How could a man, who lost his way, not deserve a second chance at life? He did not do damage to others, only himself. He loves his family, and they are waiting for him. Please gatekeeper, show me the way to his soul."

"You tell me he only did damage to himself, yet what about the family he loves so dearly, or the band that stopped making music? What about all his followers who used his musical talents to bring joy to their lives? Your logic is flawed, Caeles Novo. Now move on."

A loud G chord rang out, but I wasn't going to be denied. I had come too far to fail. I took one last chance with the gatekeeper.

"What about the family, and the fans, Gatekeeper? Do you believe the soul you defend would rather play music alone, or with his daughters back on earth? As lost as he was on earth, I know that deep inside his soul he misses his daughters. If you allow his soul a chance at redemption, he can make amends with his family and again produce music for the entire world to hear. If his soul remains locked up, none of that is possible. That is Dylan's true path to peace and redemption. Allow that to happen, grant me contact to his soul."

Rays of light, with a hue of purple, produced a perfect rectangle made of shadows from the beams. Inside the rectangle was a pathway with no end in sight. My soul was now hovering inside the shadowy corridor, my mind again on overdrive. The pathway started to move beneath my soul, gently gliding it deeper into the rectangular hallway of purple light. Along the shadows disguised as walls were hanging crystals. At closer inspection, under each crystal read a number. Some of the crystals were white and fully formed. Others were dark and deteriorating. Some had a single faint color, while others had a mixture of all the colors in the rainbow. My mind attempted to slow down the pace of the journey to get a closer look at the shapes and names of the crystals. It was not to be.

As the hallway of purple shadows began to narrow, one soul was glowing with a radiant fire of orange, every crystal in perfect condition. It read KIN 128965. I knew that was the soul of my beautiful wife. My mind desperately attempted to stop my soul from moving beyond hers, but it failed. As my soul slid past hers, the radiant glow from hers seemed to dissipate. It was if her soul knew mine was there, but not to reclaim hers. Collecting her soul was not my mission, at least on that day.

My floating soul funneled to the end of the hallway of purple light. It was there my soul was within reach of my goal, the soul of Dylan James. My soul came to a complete standstill. It became apparent there was a casing surrounding my subject's soul. My mind became void of a single thought. It was then the casing, caring for his soul, shattered into a million tiny shards of glass. The snowflake looking crystal attached itself to my soul, as all but one of the purple shadows of light disappeared. That single beaming ray of purple light was all my mind could distinguish. My mind raced with flashbacks of the life of Dylan James. Within moments, his entire life history became branded into my brain. My soul and Dylan's pierced my body, the single ray of purple light exploded into a haze as my mind heard the sounds of a man screaming.

"Wake up, Caeles. Hurry you must leave."

As I started to become aware of my surroundings the face of Bastian Duvalier was no longer smiling. I tried to focus my mind, but it felt as though I had been given anesthesia. I attempted to stand but my legs had other ideas.

"Get out now. The tales are correct, the ones who want to stop you, I can see them getting out of the car. Hurry before they enter the house."

Still groggy, I attempted again to stand, this time being pulled from the chair by Bastian. He directed me to the back door. He shoved me down the steps and disappeared back inside his home. I could hear the sound of shouting men as I stumbled into a patch of trees behind the house.

"Take my hand. I am a friend of Bastian. Hurry, we have little time."

I was now in the back of a car with someone shoving my head down to the seat and the sound of squealing tires. I have no idea how long we drove, since I felt only semi-conscience during the car ride. All the emotions of being on stage as a rock and roll singer rushed through my thoughts, as did a pain in my hand and back. Sadness washed over me. A feeling of being lost in the world and not knowing why did too. I could now understand why Dylan felt he was a lost soul. It was my responsibility to return what was Dylan's to his physical presence on earth.

"Those men chasing you, they know why you were here. You need to restore the soul before they find you, or they will try to steal it from you. Bastian has told the story about this day for years. We did not want to believe in him. We believe him now. They are preparing a plane for you. It will deliver you to the Bahamas. From there, you are on your own."

Within a few hours of capturing another's soul, I was sitting in an airport in Nassau, Bahamas waiting for a flight to Miami. I had no idea where Dylan James could be. I only knew I had to find him before whoever was searching for me, could locate me first.

Once in Miami, I made a call to Dylan's agent Carl Peterson, who informed me he believed Dylan was wandering Europe, possibly Italy. He quizzed me why I needed to find him, and who I was, so I informed him that I was a doctor, who had seen Dylan back in North Carolina. I am not sure he believed me, but I also got the sense he wanted Dylan found, and any help would be appreciated. With my senses now fully restored, it was off to Italy.

Since Dylan's soul was carefully tucked inside my being, I attempted to channel his thoughts. I felt the presence of a woman from his past in Italy, and could see her face and town she came from, in my mind. It took two days of searching, but I could uncover her. She had seen Dylan the day before my visit, but she informed me she pushed him away. She explained how he was not himself and very depressed. She ordered him to return home to the States, but he did mention that he would stop in London on the way home. I was on the next flight to London, England.

Once in London, I contacted all the hotels. One finally admitted to having him registered as a guest. I waited patiently in the hotel lobby hoping to find him. The next morning, a man who appeared to be Dylan staggered through the hotel lobby. He seemed frail and fractured. I followed him as he paced slowly through the streets of London. We came upon The Royal Albert Hall. I watched as Dylan stood in the ticket line. I didn't want to attempt anything with so many people in the vicinity. I needed him to sit, or at least not be near others. It was obvious that he was a broken man. I needed to finish what I had started.

It was an overcast day with a light drizzle of rain. I watched as Dylan struggled, but couldn't even find the means to purchase tickets from the counter. He ambled over to the cold stone steps and sat down. With tears in his eyes, we had a brief conversation until I asked him if he wanted his soul returned to him.

"Why did you destroy my life? Why did you take so much from me? I did all I was asked to do in life. I gave to others. I gave to my family, my friends, my band and you still destroyed me."

"We don't have time for all this, Dylan. Know that it was you, who destroyed yourself, but you can have a second chance. I am here to give, not take this time. I need you to focus, please."

"Wait a minute. I do know you. You are that guy learning to be a doctor back in North Carolina. What are you doing here?"

I began to second guess myself in choosing him as my first soul to be restored. The real reason I chose him was because, he was the first soul I ever stole that I believed was wrong. I also wasn't sure any of this would work. I didn't want to practice on Kalani knowing I would have one chance and one chance only. However, if he didn't stop his incessant whining, I was going to walk away.

"Dylan James, I will ask you one time, do you want your chance at redemption, yes or no?

After a moment of silence, he looked at me with a tear in his eye, and uttered, "I want to be the man who sings a beautiful song. If I can have an encore, then my answer is yes."

The camera clicked. My body shook, as did his. I could again feel his soul pierce my body, only this time leaving me for good. I felt lifeless. Seconds later a woman, who appeared to know Dylan sat next to him. I was doing all I could not to show any outward sign of the convulsions that ran through my body.

"Dylan, it's me Feona. Do you remember me? I want to help you."

I knew Dylan would be given a second chance, but I knew if I stayed there much longer people would start to notice me. I stood up, feeling as if I had just sucked down twenty shots of whiskey. It was a feeling I didn't care to experience on a regular basis. I stumbled down the steps until a tall man, who I thought could be Mikael , told me to lean on his shoulder. The odd feeling of inebriation was instantly gone. The man spoke.

"That was the first step in restoring your kind and others, Caeles. I know it wasn't easy for you. Dylan will be fine. It is now time to get your body regulated, so it can cope with the physical swings it will take every time you do this."

My body crumbled onto a park bench desperately needing some repair. At that moment, I didn't think I could put mind and body through the process again. I became selfish, not wanting to care about others. I only wanted to keep my mind and body healthy.

"Caeles, the first time is always the hardest. Your body is not accustomed to the jolts of gaining then restoring souls. It will learn to adjust over time. You must trust me."

"Mikael , why should I believe anything you tell me? I mean seriously, you come in and out of my life every few years. Sometimes in a dream and other times, you sit next to me as if you were very much a living and breathing person. I don't know who you are, or why you come to me in my dreams, or on airplanes or park benches. You keep insisting that I have some sort of destiny in rising up against the Council. Yet all it ever accomplishes is to have me punished for breaking our laws and disobeying my leaders. You have to do better than telling me all this gets easier, because right now, there is not going to be a next time."

I stared at the people strolling past us. Something was different. All I could think about was the sensation of being a super hero and having x-ray vision. I blinked. I blinked again this time shaking my head attempting to clear the cobwebs. I assumed because my body was still adjusting.

"Embrace it, Caeles. Your powers are now complete. I realize it seems odd to you. You can now see into another's soul. That is what you are seeing. In time, you will learn to control the intensity of what you see, but for now, don't look upon it as a curse. You are the first in many generations, other than the six on the Council, with the power to see, take and restore a soul.

"Why me, Mikael ? Why not someone else? I didn't ask for this."

"Careful or you will sound like the ones you steal from, who can no longer see the beauty or appreciate all that has been given."

Perplexed would have been an understatement for my emotions. As thrilling as it seemed to have power to see into another's soul, it was still a huge responsibility. One I didn't seek.

"Mikael , I know my mother claims you are the protector of our family, but protecting from what? I don't know if you are even real or not."

"Think of me as your personal body guard no one sees. However, I am much more to you. I am the guardian of truth. My assignment is to revive the power of redemption on earth. You are the catalyst. I am as real as you make me. I am also your conscience. I do not appear on any schedule or even in human form, even if you believe I do. Kalani never physically saw me in Hawaii. I worked through her subconscious to find you. I was not on the airplane next to you. It was your mind working overtime while dreaming, like it is now. You see an image of me, but others don't. The old man in Chicago, he was real, but not me. He was an old man, who was taken ill when your mind knew you were innocent. You have strong powers, Caeles. Use them wisely. One more thing, you don't need a camera, you never did. Did they take a photo to remove Kalani's soul?"

Next thing I knew, someone with a wooden nightstick was tapping my leg.

"Sorry, sir but we do not allow sleeping on the benches. You need to move along now."

CHAPT3R TW3NTY TWO

The following day, I caught a flight back home to California, stopping in New York. By pure coincidence, Dylan was on the same flight heading back to the States. Once in the air, I asked to be moved to sit next to him. Being a frequent flyer member the airline went out of their way to make me happy.

At first, Dylan balked at me moving my seat, but I assured him all was fine. I think I wanted to speak with him more for me, to see if there was any change in his demeanor. He did seem far more at ease than the day before on the steps. He became relaxed and we he started a conversation.

"I was always a person who believed in a supreme being and that my life had a purpose on earth," Dylan said, "I don't know how much you really do know about me, but after my accident, I stopped being a believer. I still don't know if you were the person who made me stop believing, or the one who wants me to believe again, either way it's time to move on with my life again. Who are you anyway?"

"My name is Cale. I was not responsible for your accident. Maybe my job was always to make sure you could use your talents as a musician again. I am not even sure myself any more. I will tell you that I do hope you can get your life turned around. I think you have a much better chance now that we crossed paths again. Who knows, in the end, maybe you can consider me your good luck charm."

We had a nice chat almost the entire flight home. He told me about the loss of his wife. I explained to him that my wife was also ill. We talked about how neither of us had seen our children in a while. He shared many stories with me about traveling the world as a rock and roll star. I shared that at one time I had managed a few bands. I didn't want to tell him what bands since Johnny Joe Jackson and one of the others were still actively performing. In looking at my perceived age, he never would have believed that I had managed performers early in their careers who were now in their fifties and sixties. I still looked to be in my late thirties. We talked about songwriting and his band members. By the time we landed, he had invited me to his home in North Carolina. He seemed very sincere in his offer.

When we left the plane and entered the terminal, Dylan had two people waiting for him at the gate. He introduced me to his agent and a very attractive woman, who was a fellow band member. We shook hands, and I wished him all the best. He had his agent write down my name and give me his business card assuring me I could always get in touch. The flight seemed like closure for both of us.

Soon after arriving home, the men who were looking for me in Jamaica turned up on my doorstep. They were not pleased when I informed them I had already restored Dylan's soul. I knew I would have to confront my Elders and explain my actions. No need for violence, I went peacefully. I wasn't ready for another long plane ride, but I had no choice.

I stood in front of the Council, where their threats no longer had the same impression on me. They weren't going to convince me that what I had done was wrong. But there I was, in front of the men who I despised, attempting to lay judgment on me.

"One would think after we took your wife's soul that you would not disobey us so quickly, Caeles."

"With all due respect, Council Members, the reason I did was because you did take her soul. I really had not decided to explore the possibility of restoring anyone's soul until you took hers. And so there is no miscommunication, I intend to restore her soul next. Dylan's was only a test to see if it worked and I could actually do it. And because it was a success, Kalani is next."

Elder Orcus pounded on the dais, yelling at me, "You will do no such thing. Her soul will remain where it is. Besides, I am the one who took it. I am the one who needs to restore it and I refuse."

"I beg to differ with you, Elder Orcus. I can restore it. It is written that it would be easier for you, but not impossible for me. It is a risk I am willing to take, since I am well aware you will never restore my wife's soul."

"Caeles, you need to heed my words. Kalani was broken. We allowed her to keep her soul much longer than we should have, only because she was so good at her job. You will not attempt to restore her soul."

"Don't lie to me. She was not broken or a bad soul. Your lies will only encourage me to act quicker."

In my mind, I bet on the idea my newly developed skills would have the Council unsure of what my punishment should entail. I no longer thought anyone could reach in and take my soul. It was not something I was sure about, but for the first time I recognized a hint of fear from the Council. I now had powers they never thought I would obtain; something that I sensed frightened them.

"Caeles, let us speak the truth. This Council has tried to reason with you for decades now. I don't know how you were able to develop your new found skills, but now that you have them, you need to understand what it means. Restoring souls can have a devastating effect on our kind. They were stolen for a reason."

"You mean like grabbing the soul from a guitar player, who was pissed off at the world? Restoring his soul is going to have a devastating effect to our kind? This Council has kept all the souls for one reason and one reason only, to keep all the extra energy for our own survival. I recognize what is going on now, and you can't stop me from returning back to the original mission we were assigned from the heavens."

"You're correct, Caeles, this Council concedes the mission was altered. What you have failed to uncover is why it was done. Long before your existence or anyone on this Council, some souls, were injected with evil, while being stored and waiting restoration. Despite the best efforts to restore them with purity, once back in their given human bodies they continued to wreak havoc on society. They not only could not find beauty for themselves, they made sure others would not see it either. The Council decided it could no longer continue with the program of restoration. It's a practice that ended over one thousand calendar years ago."

I listened, but not with an open mind as Orcus continued.

"You will now argue with me that many have found redemption in the past thousand years, and you would be correct. But, they are people who never lost their souls, so it was not our responsibility to offer them redemption. They found peace on their own."

"Council members, how do you know that we cannot institute a system to prevent mistakes in the past from happening again? Why can't we try to find where the system broke down and try it again?"

Orcus raised his tone. "Because despite our best efforts, there will always be an element of evil in the world. It is time you accept this, Caeles. The Council will admit to erring on the side of eliminating evil too quickly at times, possibly even with your musician. But that does not alter the fact that evil does still exist. We have a much larger responsibility to society and our kind than you're willing to see. It's easy for you to think we keep all the souls only to grow our own powers. I will counter with the idea that our mission was to eliminate despair, greed and contempt from earth. We're not perfect, since our humble beginnings were of pure human form, but we do take our responsibility seriously. If you would open your mind to our side of the equation, possibly you will understand and not want to continue to restore broken souls."

"I beg the Council to reconsider. Look at Dylan James. Study him for a while. I am firmly convinced he will find his life again and harmony on earth. If he proves he can stay on the right path to redemption, will you reconsider my desire to restore souls?"

"The decision of this Council is final. You will not use your powers to restore souls any longer."

I refused to leave the large marble walled room. "There must be some form of compromise. I implore the Council not to make such a hasty decision. I still believe that restoring souls will improve our chances of survival not hinder them. However, I will offer you a deal and I will honor it. If you allow me to study why some souls came back laden with evil after restoration, I will continue to steal souls and not seek to restore any more souls. But you must allow me to restore two more souls before my research is complete. If you allow me to restore Kalani and Detective Nesstor's souls, with no further punishment to me or them, I will stop restoring souls until we find a cure for the system. In return, I will again become a loyal servant to our kind. You have my word. I will not use my powers behind your back or remove any souls."

The men all looked at each and nodded before Orcus spoke. "The Council will give this some consideration. You do of course understand that it is possible your own powers will be diminished should you attempt to restore souls not taken by others, like your wife?"

"I do."

"Then retire back to your home and await our decision. We will contact you once our decision has been rendered."

There were only three words I could say, "Yes, Elder Orcus."

I headed off to Tahiti to see my son and Kalani. I explained to her mother and father all I had been through and that I was attempting to get Kalani's soul returned to her. They weren't impressed.

"Cale, you spin many words from your mouth, but until she returns, they are only words," my mother in law said.

I held Kalani's frail frame against my chest. I had hoped for some improvement, but none was there. I wanted to believe she could understand I was trying to restore her soul, but there was no way of knowing. The vibrant green specs once in her eyes were now faded. Her rosy lips now chap from sitting alone in the sun. I didn't know what our future as husband and wife would be, but this would not be it. I made up my mind that no matter what the Council would decree, I would attempt to restore her soul. Whatever punishment the Council could hand down could never match the pain and suffering of allowing her to remain without a soul.

Spending a few days with my son was melancholy. I was so pleased to spend the time with him, but sad it was brief because of my job. I wanted so much for him and Kalani to be with me under one roof again, the way it was before her soul was ripped from her body. My emotions were racing between attempting to restore her soul alone, before the Council's decision, or forcing my way into their inner sanctum and testing my new found powers to eradicate the six Councilmen from the earth. Thankfully, the following day I was asked to return for their decision before I could anything foolish.

We were to meet in the library within the stone walls. The room was filled with mostly antique books, one computer, and a table you would find in your typical boardroom. The room wasn't large. The table filled over one third of the length of the room. The library had far more light than inside the Council room. The leather seats were far more inviting than the hard wooden chairs down the hallway. The entire atmosphere in the library was more relaxed. Once inside, the six Council members were sitting on one side of the table. I sat on the opposite side.

"Caeles, we have given this much consideration and debate. We have also again researched your bloodlines in an attempt to discover how you could have achieved all you have. It escapes us. We are an educated group. We have concluded that either some other powers are at work here, or someone has changed your records to hide your true identity. We don't doubt you are one of us, but we are perplexed as to how you have acquired powers only the few of us on the Council can claim. We must accept that you are indeed powerful as us now, and younger. With that in mind, we are offering you a truce or a compromise; you decide how you will see it. You will be given the right to restore Kalani's soul with no further punishment. You may restore Nesstor's as well if you still choose. However, in return you will do something for us. You will not restore any other soul under any conditions, unless we order it. There will be no further research on your part. You will continue to take souls at our behest with no questions asked. You will convince your wife to do the same should she return to full strength. You will be responsible for Kalani and Nesstor for as long as you have the power to do so. If either turns to evil, you will be responsible for them and should their souls need to be removed again, you will oblige. If you refuse, we will take your son's soul. There will be no discussion or debate. These are the terms of our agreement and are final. If you chose to accept these terms, it begins immediately. If you refuse, you will go back to stealing and stealing alone. If you try to restore even one soul, other than the two granted, we will fall back on our last decree and take the souls of everyone you love. Take your time to consider it."

I didn't need but one minute to know something more was at play here.

"I am somewhat surprised at your leniency. I must say it almost sounds too good to be true, but as you noted before, if I attempt to restore souls not originally taken by me, it could easily weaken my abilities."

"That's a risk this Council is willing to accept. Are you? One other item we have not discussed; should you prove you have the ability to restore souls and not lose your powers, you will be made a member of this Council when the next vacancy occurs. You will have proven your powers equal to ours. This has never occurred in our history. All of our previous members came from inside our own family bloodlines. It has never occurred outside of the six men sitting here. As you know it is all carefully documented."

I needed time to think. Was this all a set up? Did they already know I would lose my ability to steal and restore if I restored a soul not stolen by me in the first place? I was shaken when delivering Dylan's soul, but I didn't lose my powers. Would it take more than one before I would suffer? But then again, I took Dylan's soul and the other two would be ones I had not taken. I know how weak I was restoring a soul I had stolen. In the end, I knew Kalani had suffered long enough because of me.

"Council Members, I do accept your gracious offer and will honor my word."

What an idiot I was. I wanted to crush the members of this Council for what they had done and what they wanted to do to me or my loved ones. I was calling their offer gracious? What choice did I have? I was starting to understand why I suspected many of our kind really could steal, but chose not to expose their powers to the Council. Maybe they knew once you start, it was hard to walk away and live any type of life. Sure, I traveled the world, experienced things I never would have without my abilities, but at what cost? My life had become a marionette for six men I had come to despise and not much could be done about it.

"Since you have accepted our agreement, Caeles, your next assignment is Paulo Kopono. I believe you have crossed paths before in Hawaii. He has taken over the drug cartel and has ruined the lives of too many children. Take from him before he can destroy any more lives. We will await your report."

"This one will be my pleasure. However, I want to restore Kalani before I do anything else."

"You will take the soul of Paulo Kopono; then you may attempt to restore Kalani."

Again, the tired marionette had his task. I headed to Hawaii to settle the score with Paulo Kopono.

CHAPT3R TW3ИTY THR33

It disturbed me how Detective Paulo Kopono was heading up a drug cartel and still not be arrested by how own employers. Did Honolulu Police not know, or was it only speculation taht Kopono was in deep. If he really had taken over the cartel, he was not allowing it to be obvious. From a distance, his appearance hadn't changed. He was average height, slight build, tanned and fit in as a local. The hair around his temples were turning grey and new pudge around the belly, but nothing of any significant physical change since the last I had seen him. This time, I could see what others could not. I could see directly into his soul and it was as black as any soul I had ever seen.

I sat patiently all through the night outside his home. As Kopono was leaving for his morning shift, I approached him cautiously. He lived at the end of a secluded road with only two other homes in view. The one next to his was where Kalani had resided. Her old home had the venetian blinds closed. The other house didn't seem to have anyone stirring either. Two red-crowned parrots were sitting in the tree a few feet from his front door. All I could hear was the squawk from one of the parrots and the wind flapping through the nearby palm trees.

"Good morning, Detective. I think we have some unfinished business."

He let out a giant laugh then said, "Holy shit if it's not, Mr. Kalani. Never thought I would see your cowardly face on this island again. Either you have a death wish or you're plain stupid to get in my path. How's that sexy wife of yours? I ain't seen her in months. Did she send you to collect her money or something? You can tell her from me, she gets no money until she comes to collect up close and personal. I so love seeing that cute ass of hers."

"What are you talking about? How do you even know we were married?"

His laugh grew louder. "Okay, so we ruled out a death wish, and now moved to plain stupid. What you doing here? Hurry up and explain yourself before I either cuff you for good, or put a bullet in your skull. Then I can bury you with all the other stupid people who cross my path one too many times."

"First of all Detective, you won't be doing any shooting since there is a sniper in the nearby trees with his cross hairs squarely between your eyes. He will kill you if you reach for your weapon. See, I'm not so stupid after all. Now, tell me what money you're talking about and I will allow YOU to live."

"You think I believe you? Your wife, you know Kalani, the one you think you know so well, I know what she did to Kapena. See here on the islands, we believe in spirits. Since you don't seem to know so much about your own wife, the woman has powers. She put my old boss in that mental place with her voodoo. I pay her to use her voodoo powers for me now. It keeps my men from thinking they can muscle in on my side job. When anyone tries, she does her magic and they drop like swatted flies. But the beauty is; I don't have anyone looking for a dead body since they are still upright and walking. No cops looking up my ass, and I get to kill people in plain sight. I still don't know exactly what her voodoo does, but it sure is good shit. I love having my special voodoo lady working for me. Look at your face. What? You didn't know? Did you?"

I was stunned. I didn't know what to say. He had no reason to lie to me. He didn't seem to even give it a second thought that maybe I had the same power as Kalani. He was just so full of himself standing there, laughing in my face. I didn't know if I should thank him or rip out his soul. I decided to do both.

"Detective, you're right. I had no idea. However, I'm not here to collect any money. But I do want to thank you for opening my eyes. I just don't know why she would do it? We have plenty of money."

I stood there for a few moments listening to the parrot squawking incessantly in the tree above my head, as if the green and red bird was attempting to confirm all I had heard. I shook my head to clear my thoughts, realizing Kopono was not yet finished with his story.

"Who knows? Who cares why she does it? Maybe it has nothing to do with the money and only because she loves to please me. Oh, wait; if you didn't know about the cash then I'm dead sure she never told you she and I were more than friendly neighbors. You're downright blind to what goes on under your nose, aren't you? You think I didn't know she would take out Kapena for me? She told me about her witchcraft, so I wanted to see if it was all true. I got all scared when Kapena drugged her. I figured she didn't have any spiritual powers, so I was willing to cut her loose. Then you come charging in on your white horse and save my ass. I really should thank you. Maybe I'll let you leave here walking just because I owe you one. How's that, Mr. Kalani? You think I owe you one? Maybe I do. I can see you are in shock that you're married to a voodoo lady and don't even know it. I guess she hides all her magic potions from you. How's she doing?"

"She has been ill lately. I was hoping she would get better soon, but now I'm not so sure."

"I can tell all this news is not sitting well in your gut, eh, Mr. Kalani?"

He was right. I was second-guessing not only my marriage, but if I should risk my own life to restore her soul. However, I had to know the truth.

"One more thing before I leave, Detective. If you don't mind? When did it end with you and Kalani? It's important for her health. I need to know if you're telling me the truth."

"You want to know despite her secrets if she is a good wife? I woke up in a good mood, so all I am going to say is that she loves you. I don't know why, you being so stupid and all. Now, I'm going be late for work, so kindly move away from my car. I don't know what your true business was, and I don't believe you have a sniper pointing his rifle my way. But since I don't want my day to be ruined, just in case you are telling me the truth, I am going to let you walk away with no trouble. However, if you ever step foot on any of the Hawaiian Islands again, I'll know about it. I suggest you turn and move away quickly, before my good mood runs out."

It was time for me to complete the reason for my visit to Paulo Kopono and make sure he didn't harm anyone else in the future.

"Sure, Detective, but before I leave. I'd like to shake your hand and thank you for all you have shared here today. After all, I really only came here to shake your hand."

"You're one dumb asshole, but sure, if that's all you want, let's shake that you will never return here again. The next time send that sweet piece of ass you got at home to see me. Be sure to tell her to check in I might have more magic I need doing."

We firmly clasped right hands. I looked him square in the eyes and prayed that Mikael was right. I never required a camera. His grip started to weaken as he fell to his knees. He looked up at me in sheer horror, now understanding his fate. The shock in his eyes matched mine with what he had informed me about my wife. I felt no mercy, no pain for him, and no desire to offer redemption.

As I watched him struggle, falling at my feet, I said, "You will never touch or disrespect my wife again. Yes, you fool, I know all about my wife's magic. Here is another surprise for you, my magic is stronger than hers, and your soul is now mine."

As I let go of his hand, he completely fell to the ground. I turned, looked up at the morning sky in its full beauty, then staggered down the dirt road ignoring his snivel for mercy.

My report was sent to the Council and permission was granted to attempt to restore Kalani's soul. I headed off to Tahiti with the idea that I could do this alone. I decided not to go back to Jamaica and ask Mr. Duvalier for assistance.

I didn't want to believe what Kapono had told me was true, but why would he lie about it? She never told me about any trips to Hawaii after we were married. I knew there was no evidence of extra money. Could I have been wrong about my own wife? Maybe the Council had been telling me the truth about Kalani and I had it all wrong? I still felt obligated to restore her back to health and discover the truth.

After arriving in Tahiti, I was met with great skepticism from my in-laws. My mother in law was against allowing me to restore Kalani, but my father in law relented. After all, I was still her husband. I also believed he was starting to think if it was possible, any chance to restore his daughter was a risk worth taking. They both wanted to participate, but I knew the importance of having total peace during the process.

They told me of a secluded beach, where people were rarely seen. I told my father in law that he could stand guard off in the distance to make sure no one approached within screaming distance while I attempted to reclaim her soul.

I took my wife to the beach and propped myself against a sand dune several feet from the ocean's waves. The late afternoon wind was still. The only noise was the crash of the waves beating against the ancient sand. Off in the distant horizon, I could see a large ship heading towards my right. A few gulls nosedived for an early dinner to my left, but no other signs of life were evident. My father in law stationed himself many yards behind us to stop any curious onlookers.

I laid my wife across my lap so that her face was looking up at me. I ran my fingers through her hair, assuring her that things would be better. I revisited in my mind all the things that Mr. Duvalier had taught me the first time, and replayed all the actions I had taken the first time this was attempted. I was confident I could do this without the aid of others.

I relaxed my body, then my mind. I called upon the sprits to lift my soul to the Shadows of Souls and let me again communicate with the gatekeeper. The spirits heard my call and lifted my soul into another dimension. The light was dim. It all seemed similar to when I captured Dylan's soul, however this time the rays of light were orange.

It was hard to see the image of the gatekeeper but I could hear a man's voice ask, "You have returned to seek another of my protected souls?"

"I have."

"And for what reason do you believe this soul deserves redemption?"

"Because her soul was removed without justification and I'm sure she wants to reconnect with her family."

The light intensified sending a dazzling display of radiant orange beams of light dancing across the entire dimension.

"All of you, who come from earth to my gates, imagine you have the correct answers, but you do not. You dare to assume all my souls deserve restoration and return to earth. When they return, there is pain and destruction. Here there is none of that. Oh yes, many of the souls in my care added to the pain and misery of earth, but they are content here. Here we survive in peace. For some here, this is their redemption."

The intensity of the light subsided and the orange started to form a human body. I had learned the gatekeeper would always take the form of an object or person that made the intended soul think of good things on earth. As the image became clearer, I guess I shouldn't have been shocked, but I was. The gatekeeper formed in my image.

"You need to show me the way to the soul ," I said. "I seek gatekeeper. I seek the soul of Kalini Inoke Novo."

"I know who you seek. I also have told you not all souls deserve a second chance and should remain here. Why should I show you the way to her soul?"

"The Council removed her soul out of her love for me. She did it because she thought she was protecting me. This is not her time."

"You dare come before me and lie about your reasons? Do you think I don't know the truth about the souls I protect? Her soul is damaged, more than you tell me, and I think you know it. Now again, tell me why the soul you seek deserves to be reunited with its earthly body."

The light again intensified as if I had angered the gatekeeper.

"Gatekeeper, in truth, she is a loving wife, and caring mother. If everyone who made one horrible mistake was sent here, there might not be anyone left on earth. She deserves another chance at life in her earthly form."

Moments later, the lights were gone. Only a voice hearkened in the distance, "The soul you seek sends a message to you. She is not who you think she is, and you should return home and raise your son. Now leave, Caeles Novo. You have failed."

"Tell her that I know exactly who she is, my beautiful wife and the mother of our child. Nothing else matters. It is time to come home."

My mind raced with thoughts of failure. Our lives could not end this way. Time passed slower than a dripping Molasses tree.

I opened my earthly eyes and looked deeply into Kalani's brown eyes with the faded green specs. I used all the powers of my mind and begged her that if she ever felt connected to me in more than a physical presence to hear my plea to return. The green specs flickered as I again closed my eyes.

The spirits wrapped my soul around their tender arms, as one orange light penetrated through their protection, and attached an orange crystal to my soul. The crystal was not as vibrant as it had been the last time my soul was in this dimension, but it attached to mine. Within seconds, both souls returned to my earthly body, my mind noting the entire life of my wife. All her fears, joys, beliefs, and stories were tattooed to my brain.

As my body acclimated itself to being whole, I sensed something was wrong. Our kind was immune to most earthy diseases, but I felt like someone would when having the flu. I felt tired, run down, and my mind was blurred. The last thing I thought I saw before falling unconscious was Kalani's face looking up and smiling.

Kalani's father told me that I had slept for two days. I awoke in a hospital bed where my father in law worked. I made an effort to get out of the bed, but as I stood, I felt lightheaded and was helped back into bed. The nurse advised rest. All I could think about was restoring Kalani's soul, which now resided inside me. I needed to finish my task. I knew the strength I would need to restore her soul was evading me. After lying awake for an hour, my father in law came to visit.

"You gave us a scare, Cale. You had little signs of life for more than a day. I didn't know what to do for you other than lay you here and hope your body would heal itself. I couldn't find anything wrong with you specifically, that I could treat. All your reflexes were working, but there was little brain activity. How do you feel now?

"I feel like I was run over with a truck. How is Kalani?"

"She's the same. She's resting at home. You can see her in a day or so, but for now, you should rest. I really didn't think you were going to survive whatever it was you went through. You might think twice before trying that again."

"Thanks, Doc, but I'll be fine. I was warned that if I accepted a soul that I did not steal, this might happen. Once I regain my strength, I can restore your daughter's soul."

"You didn't do that already?"

"No. I brought her soul back to earth with me, but it remains with me."

Doc smiled. "That's a huge relief because we've not seen any change in her and assumed you failed."

"I refuse to fail."

"Get some rest. I'll check in on you again before I go home tonight."

Confined to a hospital bed far from home is not what I would call fun. Granted I was getting plenty of attention from the staff, but I had work to do. Much to my surprise, I had a visitor later that evening.

"Nice to see you are still with us, Caeles. The Council was concerned you wouldn't survive reclaiming Kalani's soul. I presume I don't need to tell you that some on the Council were even quietly rooting you wouldn't survive."

"Thank you for your visit, Elder Spia. And you, what were you quietly rooting as an outcome?"

"It's easy to presume that we stand united with every decision, but appearances are not always reality. As a Council, we're called on to make difficult decisions. Even the one to remove Kalani's soul in the first place was not an easy one. You would be unwise to assume we take our responsibilities lightly."

Elder James Spia was the oldest member of the Council. He rarely spoke anytime I was standing in front of our six elders. With him, you could tell his emotions by looking at his facial expressions or demeanor in his seat.

"Elder Spia, if you are not careful, I will confuse you with a politician running for the next election and not a member of our Council. You told me many words, yet did not answer my question, unless my brain is still not functioning.

With a soft chuckle he responded, "I was in favor of you succeeding. However, I am here to warn you of troubles in your future. Kalani had taken more than one unauthorized soul. She was reprimanded for it more than once. I know you believe we took her soul only because of the one incident, but you would be wrong."

"I know all about the others, Elder Spia, and I know why. Remember, her soul lives within me now, so I know all her secrets. She took those souls for money. Look around you. Although I do not agree with her choices, she donated all the money taken from the drug cartel to this hospital. It is why she did what she did."

"That does not excuse her, Caeles. I'm here to remind you of one simple idea. You cannot have good without evil. I know your intentions for wanting to restore souls is honorable and pure. I know you're not a perfect soul, but still one who wants good, not evil. But we cannot have good without evil. When you restore her soul, heed my words. You have accepted the responsibility of keeping Kalani from performing evil. It won't be a simple task. I will leave you to your healing now, but commit to memory my words. Without evil, goodness cannot exist."

CHAPT3R TW3NTY FOUR

Three days after waking, I returned to full strength. The time had come to restore my wife's soul. Unlike with Dylan, this time I had reservations. Not only because of what I had learned about Kalani's past, but how it might affect me physically. However, every time I considered my son, I realized he needed both parents. My love for her was strong. I needed to risk my survival for hers.

I took her back to the same beach, where I had reclaimed her soul within me. I wanted to savor a warm embrace, not knowing what would become of me after her soul was restored. We walked to the edge of the cracking waves. Standing together, we viewed a horizon ready to show the break of dawn to a new day. I pulled her tightly against me. I offered her a lasting passionate kiss.

We entwined with my realization this may be the last time. With our lips joined in a way they had not been since her soul was seized, I felt the thrust of her soul departing my body and restoring itself where it belonged. I pulled away just enough to see the radiance in her eyes appear as my body dropped to the salty water. The weakness now overtaking my flesh was overwhelming.

"Cale, please don't leave me."

Her words punctured me as my spirit ensnared in a frozen trance. It was as if my mind was fully aware of my surroundings, but my body was unable to act. Kalani dropped to her knees. She gently cradled my head under her arm as she too slumped to the sand. I felt helpless as tears flowed downs her cheeks. I couldn't reassure her or myself of my return.

Faint echoes and blurred images were all I discerned. My mind pushed my body to move. However, beyond having the power to control my eyes, my head, and being able to swallow, my physical abilities were no longer mine. I peered back at my wife's adoring eyes, until even my eyesight failed. Her cries for help on a vacant beach lanced my heart and soul.

It took hours before I had minimal use of my senses. I could hear more than one voice speaking. I knew I was back in the hospital, where I had left only a few days previous. I detested the idea that others had to care for me. I wanted nothing more than to embrace my wife and son, and catch the next flight back home to California. Maybe that was my wakeup call that my life was not as bad as I thought it was at times.

Maybe I too had become like others I had stolen from, not realizing life was worth living. It was all I thought about while lying in that hospital room having to hear others speak about me as if I was no longer a functioning being. It was horrid.

Several mornings later, I awoke to the faint sound and blurred sight of someone, who had visited with me the last time I was the hospital, Elder Spia. I did my best to focus my eyes and move my head to where I could see him.

"Caeles, it's time for you to leave this place. There are a few things that humans do to overcome certain illnesses. They're told to drink plenty of fluids, get rest and eat their mother's chicken soup. I know you've been resting longer than you would like. They've pumped you with fluids, so I have brought with me; my mother's cure all chicken soup."

Was he kidding me? I was lying not able to move and he was offering me chicken soup? Humans often have their strange ideas of remedies, but I was unwilling to think that chicken soup could cure my ills. He insisted.

"In a few hours, you will regain your strength and full body functions. This is a remedy from my mother, Madelyn, who said it was passed down through many generations. I've never seen it work, but I have all the confidence it will. She was always a very smart woman."

Elder Spia helped me sit up. He fed me a few mouthfuls of soup. I was still wasn't convinced of its presumed medical abilities but then again, I removed souls for a living. Who was I to judge?

"Caeles, I think it's best I give you this information while you are still debilitated. I have a feeling that your anger might over take you once you hear my news. This way, if the soup does work, you will still have a few hours to think about what I need to tell you, and not be able to rise up in anger. Then again, if you find it joyous news, you will have time to think of all the ways to show your appreciation."

I might not have been able to respond using my voice, but I assumed Elder Spia could notice the curiosity in my eyes, as I listened intently to his story.

"Blink if you remember your mother telling you about the earthquake and our records being altered."

I blinked.

"Mikael came to me as a young man, as he did you. He is an agent sent from the Lord of Life to ensure that redemption offered to broken souls once again becomes a reality. When he first appeared to me, I was as skeptical, as I assume you were. I knew by then, my training was so I could sit on the High Council. I never comprehended how hard my task would be. Once on the Council, the vote was always against me by the margin of five to one. Later, Mikael informed me that you would become my legacy. I was never about my voting record."

My eyes grew wider. Control of my vocal chords had begun to return. I attempted to speak, but only guttural sounds left my mouth.

"Do not speak. Let me finish, please. The plan was to restore my bloodlines to others, without the knowledge of the Council, or any of our recorded history. My blood flows within you, Caeles. I am your grandfather. Your mother is my daughter."

The turmoil that had grinded inside me for years was now being expressed in the tears streaming down my face. Knowing with confidence for the first time, all the internal battles that had raged through me had a purpose. His words offered me an instant sense of relief. I wasn't some crazy rouge creature on a mission sent to upset my Elders. Well, I was that, but at least I knew it had been planned for generations.

"I know your mother told you of her abilities. However, we could not risk her safety in allowing her to show any signs of being a soul stealer. If the Council knew of her skills, her life would have been terminated. The official records of her bloodlines indicate she should never be able to steal. However, she has all the same skills as you. She can steal, she can see into another soul, and she can restore them, the same as you. The last time you came before the Council and were to be punished, leniency was shown because the vote was always three to three. I know Orcus suspects secrets. Had the vote been six to zero, you would have lost your soul to the Council the last time you stood before us. However because of a tie, we all had to find a compromise."

My voice returned, weak but enough to speak. "Three to three, a vote, I asked."

"I'm the oldest on the Council. My time on this earth is waning. Of course, my vote was always going to be to protect you. Your wife's grandfather is also on the Council. She does not know. Mikael is a powerful spirit representing the Lord of Life. He convinced one other to join us in our mission to restore souls. It was at my suggestion, that if you showed your ability to restore souls, you would take a place on the Council. Elder Orcus is very suspicious. He's the one who speaks publically for the Council, but his vote holds no more weight than any other of the six who sit on the Council. My goal now is for you to take my position on the Council, as your son will take yours. Orcus won't make it easy for you, once on the Council. Remember, there cannot be good without evil."

"Why Elder Spia, err, grandfather, why did the Council take Kalani's soul and put us both through all this suffering?"

"It was a harder decision for Kalani's grandfather than it was for me to allow that to happen. Two reasons, first, Orcus and the others were questioning our loyalty. We had to show a sign of loyalty in agreeing to remove her soul or the others would have been convinced we were hiding something. For another, you needed the impetus to restore souls. Our choice was difficult to remove her soul, but we believed at the time, it was our best option."

The stunning news began to hit me hard. My newly discovered grandfather was right about one thing; I didn't know if I should hit him or hug him. Since I could barely wiggle my toes or fingers, he still had time to run.

My thoughts turned to my mother and father. Obviously my mother knew all of this, did my father? I grew up thinking my grandfather died before I was born and my grandmother soon after my birth. Feelings of betrayal were fighting feelings of joy, as I finally understood why I was so committed to believing redemption for lost souls was the right approach.

Maybe my grandfather deserved a second chance. He was only doing as asked. The room grew quiet for quite a long time. Funny thing was all the times I had stood before the Council, I barely took notice of the man who was my grandfather. I noticed a small resemblance, but his wrinkled skin and white thinning hair was far different from my full head of dark hair and boyish face.

"I'm at a loss for words, Granddad. Please tell me where this all goes from here?"

"Now that you have proven to have the powers any of us on the Council have, you will do what is asked of you. You will continue to take souls as ordered, and make sure Kalani not only steals souls, but only steals the ones requested. When a vacancy on the Council opens up, you will fill it. That is what you will do."

"We both know Orcus will find a way to reverse that offer. What will I do then?"

"You will listen to my words and understand there cannot be good without evil. When the time comes, not only will you know what to do, Mikael will be there to guide you."

I could now feel my ability to move my arms and legs. I felt reassured all was going to be ok.

"Caeles, there is one last thing you need to realize before you see Kalani. It is written that should you reclaim and restore a soul, not originally taken by you, while the soul rests with you, you have all the memories of that soul. However, once it exits your body, you lose the memories as well. Do you remember the memories that were Kalani's?"

I was confused. There were no recollections of past memories, or the knowledge that her memories were with me in the first place.

"I don't recall ever having that knowledge, Granddad."

He looked at me and nodded with a smile.

"Having never restored a soul not taken by me, it was only a question to verify what is written in our documents. Once again, the documents speak the truth. The last time I was here with you, you spoke about her stealing souls for money and offering the money to this particular hospital. Do you recall any of our talk?"

Scratching my head, there was nothing like that rattling around in my brain.

"No. If we had that discussion, it escapes me now." I stretched my arms for the first time in days as he continued.

"Well, confidentially, she has been in front of the Council more than you. I would suggest you pay her close attention. I don't think I would be able to even get a split vote if you fail to keep her from getting into more trouble. The Council will have no choice, but to make you suffer for her actions. To be honest, no one on the Council now knows if we could take your soul, even if it was warranted. It has never been attempted on anyone with your skills. But be warned, your son's or other family members would be at risk."

We sat and talked about my mother in her youth. My grandfather didn't see her as often as he would have preferred, only so he didn't draw attention to her. All the records were modified to look as though my mother's father passed away soon after her birth. My Grandmother raised my Mother. I barely remembered my Grandmother.

After several hours, I could stand on my own and no longer needed assistance of any kind. My thoughts now were with Kalani. My newly discovered grandfather took his leave, but assured me he would keep closer ties in the future. Even with all this new information, I never felt so alone. I no longer knew whom I could trust. How could I even really know if the man on the Council claiming to be my grandfather really was whom he said he was? I knew a visit to my assumed parents would be in my immediate future. Kalani soon joined me at my bedside.

"I was starting to have doubts you would ever return to me, Cale. I"ll never forget how you sacrificed yourself for me, my love. If the roles were reversed, I would like to believe I would have done the same thing for you. Let's hope I never have to be tested."

I wanted to believe she would. However, she wasn't the same person I knew before her soul had been lost. Kapena had told me stories. Wild stories. I wanted to know the truth about them before I could trust her again.

"Talk to me," I said. "While you were without your soul, I was given a mission to take Kapena's soul. Before I did, he told me some disturbing news.

"Whoa, stop right there. You were assigned to take Kapena's soul?"

"Yes, and I have no regrets taking it."

Kalani moved away from me. She took her hand from mine.

"Why would you do it, Cale? Don't you understand how important he was to me?"

"No, I suppose I don't. You never told me anything about your relationship and I'm starting to believe there is even more than he told me."

"Why, what did he tell you?"

"Among other things, that the two of you were more than neighbors and that he considers you his personal voodoo lady, who would turn even on me if he commanded."

Moments of silence ensued with each of us looking at each other, no longer knowing what to say or think.

"Cale, I had to do what I had to do. I had my missions too, but never once did I betray our vows with each other. If you don't believe anything else, believe that much."

"I do believe that, but why, why would you take the souls from others knowing it is forbidden so strongly?"

"You did it, Cale."

"I did, and I now regret it. I might even one day ask if I can restore it. I did it thinking I was protecting you. I never did it for the money."

"My father's hospital needed the money to survive. It still needs the money to help those who cannot afford good medical care. I won't say I did it easily, but it's important the money keeps coming from Kapena."

"Uhm, that might be difficult since by now he is likely a zombie somewhere on Oahu. I told you, I zapped that guy so frigging good, and was happy I did."

Kalani's face froze with an icy stare.

"You must restore him back the way he was, Cale, and quickly."

"That's never going to happen; and you're not going to interfere with whoever takes his position in the drug wars. I can't accept the idea that you take from drug dealers to pay for this place. It's going to stop."

"This place won't survive without the extra cash I supply. You can't stop me!"

"Maybe you didn't hear me clearly. I can and will. I have the full backing of the Council to punish you anyway I see fit, should you disobey me. If you take another soul without permission, our son will lose his soul. It's likely you will too. So, I would suggest you find another way to assist your father with his cash flow issues, but it won't be from stealing unauthorized souls."

The staring contest continued with neither of us flinching.

CHAPT3R TW3NTY F!V3

Several days passed. Our family unit was whole again. We decided to visit my parents in Florida. My mother had some explaining to do, and they had not seen our son in many months. Besides, Kalani and I needed time just being normal society creatures and heal some personal wounds.

"Ok Mom, spit it out. I would have preferred to know the truth long before an old man, who I have only known as someone I learned to despise, shows up with magical chicken soup from a recipe belonging to my grandmother Madelyn, who I barely knew."

"'It was all done for your protection and mine. I'm sure your grandfather explained it all to you. If you still have any doubts, yes he is your true grandfather. Your father knows. It wasn't easy for us either. I grew up not understanding many things, the same as you. Sometimes each of us is called on to do things larger than we might understand. It's now time for you to find your way and seek out what you know in your heart is the right path for you. I don't have any other secrets, nor does your father. I would caution you not to tell your wife. The Council has many eyes and ears in our community. I know you believe you're immune from any punishment, but I wouldn't tempt fate."

Secrets, soul stealing, offering redemption, raising a child from a distance, it was all taking a toll on me. Physically, I was never stronger once I recovered from restoring Kalani to full strength, but mentally, the stress exhausted me.

The next day while relaxing on the beach and listening to the radio, I heard an advertisement for a fundraiser for a local politician. There was to be a concert the next day with Dylan James and the Overture playing on behalf of a local Congressman. I dug out Carl Peterson's office number and gave him a call. After a few hours and a donation to the cause, Kalani and I had back stage passes to the event. I had asked about good seats, but apparently once Dylan caught wind that the tickets were for me, our seats were upgraded to back stage passes. We were even invited to the sound check the following day.

Kalani and I were ushered back stage the following afternoon. There was Dylan James and his band, his agent Carl Peterson and a few other people I didn't recognize.

Dylan was barking instructions. "Come on, we've played this song hundreds of times. We need to make this tight."

I stood in the shadows, something I was very adept at doing. After what appeared to me as a long rehearsal, well much longer than Johnny and his band ever bothered with, Dylan wiped his brow and strolled over to offer some choice words.

"It will be a miracle if we pull this off tonight. It has been a long time since we played as a band and it shows. We had a couple of rehearsals the past few days and there are a few people on stage we are not used to playing with, but hopefully we can rock this place later tonight."

"I'm sure you will be great Dylan, the band sounded terrific," I said. "You look great. How have you been feeling?"

Dylan offered a crooked smile and replied, "My drummer is never on time for sound checks, my youngest daughter thinks she can pick up her instrument and not have to work at it, my wife stuffs me with her cooking, my agent wants me to put out another recording and my back is aching. But I wouldn't trade a damn minute of it for the world. I don't know what happened back in London, Cale, but whatever you did, it saved my life. Thank you."

"I didn't do anything really. You had to want to see the good things in your life again and you did. That's really all that happened."

"We both know it was more than that. I wish you would tell me what really happened, because I was truly lost. Then whammo it was almost as if my soul was returned to me. I'll admit in my youth, I was a spiritual person, but after the accident, I don't know, my friend Gordy told me, I had lost my soul. I think maybe he was right, and somehow you returned it to me. Am I frigging crazy or what?"

The gates opened to the Amphitheatre and a few people straggled close to the stage. I knew it wasn't a conversation that should be done hastily on a performance stage, but then again, no time like the present. Who knew if I would ever meet Dylan again?

"Dylan my dear friend, if you really want to know, my job was always to take from people who could not appreciate life. Some were just bad people. Others like you, who lost their way. I helped them see life was not all bad. In truth, I restored your soul. You were my first. The fact that you seem so pleased to be living life again, has given me renewed faith that I did the right thing. So really I should be thanking you."

I could feel the presence of my wife and others listening in on our private conversation. I introduced Kalani to Dylan. In return, Dylan introduced us to the man for whom the benefit concert was being held.

"Yo, Cale and Kalani, meet George McAdams. The guy's a wiz banger with investments, but for some insane reason, he got himself all mixed up in politics. Personally, I think he's a crazy fool for wanting to work in Washington, but the guy helped to stock my bank account over the years, so it's the least I could do for the knucklehead. Really it gave me an excuse to jam with some old worn out players again like me, but George is a fine man, so it was payback time."

"Nice to meet you, George," I said. "Be careful of those politicians in Washington, some need a tune up on their souls."

George laughed, "Yeah, I didn't mean to pry in on your chat with Dylan, but it seems you're the man to talk with if anyone gives me a hard time. I've known Dylan since I was in college. I don't really know if you had something to do with his reversal of fortune or not, but if you did, one day you will have to tell me what you did. I might be able to put your talents to good use in Washington."

"I have worked for the same group all my life, but who knows, one day we may cross paths again. Good luck with your election."

Kalani grabbed my arm and yanked me off the performance stage. It seemed only the four of us were standing there as hundreds of people were filling the seats close to the stage. An hour later, the show began, and I enjoyed every minute of it. It was exactly what I needed to put my own life back into perspective.

After our quick visit to Florida, we traveled back home to California as a family unit. I was back to the grind of looting from others and taking commands from the Council. Every time I ripped out a soul, I put in my report how I thought I could offer each soul a chance at redemption. However, I would admit the thought of it at times was even distasteful to me. It was difficult at times for me to think some souls had a redeeming value.

After a few easy missions to get me back in a groove, the Council assigned me the daunting task of removing the soul from a dictator of a small African nation. Adai Amine was a ruthless man, who kidnapped young boys, then later use them as soldiers to protect drug smugglers working from his tiny empire. Amine

246

wasn't going to be an easy target, since he was constantly surrounded by his well-paid militia.

Amine declared himself President after taking over the country's small army. It was a country which was on the western border of Africa, with many small islands along the coastline. Amine would allow drug smugglers from Latin America to use the tiny islands as stopping points to smuggle cocaine into Europe. His soul was slated for theft for many years. Two of our men were killed attempting to get close enough to complete their assignment. I suspected this was a suicide mission and the Council knew it.

"Council members, with all due respect, why not allow government authorities through groups like the United Nations handle a case like Amine? I mean we have lost two of our family to his bloody regime. I do not like my odds of success."

"Shall I assume you're turning down our request and not living up to your agreement with this Council that if we allowed you to restore your wife's soul, you would take on any mission?"

"No Elder Orcus, but here again, if large nations with all their fire power cannot control this bastard, why should you believe I could?"

"Because, Caeles, you're the best we have. Unfortunately, most sovereign nations have ignored his wickedness. We're charged with eliminating evil, even when it's difficult. Would you not agree?"

"I would, but I could remove five or ten souls before I could take this one with far less risk to my safety. Or is this your ultimate goal? You want to eliminate me as a soldier on a mission because you know I cannot be silenced any other way?"

Members of the Council stared back at me for questioning their intent. I knew I had pushed the barrier too far, but I wanted them to understand I knew this mission was a no lose proposition for some of them. If I succeeded, another evil person would be without a soul. If I failed, one large thorn in their side would be eliminated. I looked at my grandfather. He did everything he could not to make eye contact. Once again, the puppet on the string was about to do another dance.

How do you get close to a well-guarded man, who uses body doubles and is rarely seen in public? I had to decide between posing as a drug trafficker looking for safe haven, or possibly a messenger from the United Nations offering a peace accord. Possibly, I could offer a truce that if he stopped kidnapping boys from neighboring lands; the United Nations would look the other way to his drug exploits. Either way, the odds of returning from his inner sanctum were not in my favor.

Being the resourceful soul stealer that I was, I called the one Congressman I had met, George McAdams. The newly minted Congressman was in a budget debate that was ruffling feathers in Washington. He seemed eager to be seen as more than someone with only one agenda.

McAdams jumped at the opportunity to introduce me to members of the State Department. After a few weeks of negotiating, the State Department allowed me to be a special envoy to meet with Adai Amine and explain to him that if he stopped kidnapping boys to act as military guards, the US Navy wouldn't block any ships from leaving his country's coast line. It should have been an easy sell to the State Department, since the United States wasn't blocking any ships anyway.

President Morrison was about to start his reelection efforts. Any foreign affairs victory would only be a benefit. However, since nothing moved quickly in Washington other than bureaucrats increasing their own wealth, it still took weeks to pull the trip together.

Since I was an unknown quantity to the international and the United States press corps, if I failed or worse was killed, no one would ever know I was in the country. The State Department wouldn't release any details of my trip, unless I succeeded. It was a winning hand for the United States. I now had an official reason to meet with a foreign leader with the backing of the President of the United States.

Before leaving, I met with the member of the State Department, who had been arranging the trip. William Hillary made sure I understood I was on my own.

"Mr. Novo, should you become detained against your wishes, the State Department will make no official statements on your behalf. Your visit will have been at your own risk. We have no way of protecting you. However, we do wish you success. Should Amine accept the terms set forth in this letter, there will be a press conference here at the Department and it will be touted that the President of the United States convinced Adai Amine to stop kidnapping boys, but there will be no mention of allowing any drug smuggling. Do you understand the terms of our agreement in allowing you to make this journey?"

"I do Mr. Hillary, but I would like Congressman McAdams to be mentioned as the one who had the idea, should it be a success."

He laughed. "Mr. McAdams will get the recognition of introducing you to the State Department, but it was of course the President's idea. The State Department will make sure Mr. Amine is well aware of your visit and we'll handle your travel arrangements. Good luck to you, sir."

Three long days later, I was on an airplane to Dakur, then another small plane, followed by a trip in the back of a supply truck, and a few miles on foot to get to my destination more than thirty hours later. Several average sized men with larger than average sized guns met me at the edge of the compound.

The frowns on their faces and the fact that they made me strip naked to check for weapons, or who knows what else, did not offer me an easy feeling before meeting Amine. After waiting another night, sleeping in a small room with the only breeze being a warm one, I was ready to end this charade as quickly as possible. My only fear was how I would get away from the armed guards before I needed my usual respite after taking a soul.

The next afternoon after enduring the sweltering heat of the midday in my tiny room with one window, I was shoved into a dirty jeep with no top. We drove along a muddy road until we reached a straw hut in the middle of a small fishing village. People scurried in every direction. Most were barefoot with little clothing, while a few were well dressed in army attire. The nose of a rifle nudged to get out of the jeep and directed inside the hut.

"Hallo, Mister Ambassador. I am Adia Amine. I am told you seek me. Yes? I am sorry for de long wait, but you see I am busy man. State your business then be on your way."

"Mr. Amine, I'm here by the request of the President of the United States of America. I was asked to speak with you about some young boys that you have possibly detained here in your camp. The President has given me the authority to tell you that should you release them back to their families and discontinue this practice in the future, the United States Navy will not set up a blockade for ships leaving your shores."

The large bellied man wearing army fatigues looked at me as if I had a third eye. He looked at his men, then at me again.

"You come to my home, my country, and think you tell Adai Amine what he do and do not do? Do you like your tongue, Mr. Ambassador?"

"I do, Sir."

"Then you tell your President that if he sends you to speak to Adia Amine again like I am his slave to dictate his stupid words, you will not return with your tongue. Do you think I live in fear of the paper lion across the sea?"

"I'm only the messenger, Mr. Amine. I don't dare offer you advice, but the Americans have a powerful army. If you offered the President more than a simple no, you might find a friendly face and army should you ever need one. It's something to consider, Mr. Amine. President Morrison doesn't have the love of his people like you do, and is facing an election. He was asking you, President Amine, for help. If you were to help him, I think he would look kindly on you should you need help from the United States in the future."

Amine rubbed his belly and laughed. "You take me for stupid man, don't you, Mr. Ambassador? Your President has sent men to kill Amine, why would he now offer favors?"

"President Amine, maybe he knows this is his way of making peace."

He again stared me in the eye and looked defiantly around the room. He grabbed a pistol from his belt and put the barrel to my skull.

"Your President does not want peace. He wants my head at the end of a gun, like this. Because Adia Amine is a peaceful man, you can go home to your gutless President. You may tell him that I do not take commands or make agreements with men who would rather shoot me, than offer your fake promise of peace. Do you think I care about the men on ships, who leave my country? I offer a resting place. They are not my people. Once they leave my home, I offer them nothing. If your President stops them, it is not Amine's problem. And, I do not take little boys from other places. They come here for work and money. Do I look like a cruel man to you?"

I didn't think honesty was my best choice at the moment considering the end of his pistol was pushing hard against my temple.

"I believe you to be a peaceful man, who was certainly misjudged, President Amine. I will tell President Morrison you are an honorable man, who only offers a safe harbor to passing ships."

He took three steps away removing the end of his gun from my skull.

"You are a liar and weak so I warn you. Do not return to my country, Ambassador, unless you bring joyful news and not commands from a man, who does not have the courage to find Adai Amine himself. He sends weak men like you to speak with Amine. I piss on him. If he was a real man, he would come himself. Now leave."

"I will Mr. President and thank you. May I shake your hand and thank you for you kindness in meeting with me?"

He moved closer and extended his hand. I took it and looked directly into his eyes. I felt the sensation I get every time I rip out a soul. I heard thunder in the distance and could hear the rain now pelting the roof of the hut. Amine let go of my hand and laughed at me. I knew I had succeeded in removing his soul, but I also became instantly aware at how little it affected him in losing it. Here was a true non-believer.

"Even your handshake is weak to Amine. Tell your President, Adia Amine hopes his shake is stronger. Now go weak man. My men are too busy. Find your own way to the border. I hope you find it before the lions find you."

The butt of a rifle shoved me to the door and out into the driving rain. I didn't understand it. I knew I had succeeded in taking his soul, yet he laughed at me. He seemed like he never felt a thing.

I found my way back to a quiet spot, where I could sit and recharge. After getting drenched from the rain, someone approached me in a jeep.

"Hurry, get in."

I jumped in not knowing what was going on, but I was lost in a small African nation, what did I have to lose?

"I'm Darin Weston. I was sent by the US Government to bring you back, well if alive, and if not, to bury you."

"Thanks for all the help when that monster had a gun to my head."

"Yeah well, sorry but I was told to keep a distance, because we aren't officially here. I can offer you safety back to Dakur; then you're on your own. By the way, if Amine didn't stick a gun in your ear, you'd be the first. He's not totally insane. He knows if he actually killed someone from the States, his head wouldn't hit the pillow later that night. We could eliminate him anytime the President gave the order, but he's no threat to the US. We would like to stop him from kidnapping those boys, but the bottom line is if we killed him, his successor would just continue the same nasty habits. It's the only reason why he still walks upright."

I really didn't care about the politics of it all. Amine was an evil man, who didn't deserve to be President of anything, but it wasn't my job to control him. Mr. Weston made sure I arrived safely in Dakur, where I made my way back in front of the Council.

"We are pleased with the job you did in Africa, Caeles. Amine is a strong willed man, who has evil in his veins. He will continue to wreak havoc, however our mission with him has concluded. It's time you leave that mission behind you now and focus on Kalani. She has ventured back to Hawaii when her assignment was in Arizona. So far, she hasn't taken any unauthorized souls. But I would suggest you get her out of Hawaii."

"Elders, how do you know she's not going back home for a visit or mini vacation? Why do you assume she will disobey?"

"Paulo Kapono is walking around with his soul restored. Tell me, Caeles, how that could happen? You stole his soul. We had our people keep an eye on your wife and she's been in contact with Kapono on several occasions. I would suggest you fix this problem of yours before we do."

I had no clue who restored Kapono's soul, but there was more than one way to put that rat out of business. Kalani would have to find another way to find cash and forget about Paulo Kapono.

CHAPT3R TW3NTY S!X

"**W**alking up the snow-covered driveway it was difficult to know what the reception would be. It was New Year's morning in a Chicago suburb.

"Hello Mrs. Nesstor, my name is, Cale Novo. I'm here to return your husband to you."

It took ten minutes standing on the frozen porch, before convincing Maria Nesstor to allow me inside their home. It took another hour before seeing Special Agent Nesstor.

"As you can see, Mr. Novo, my husband is now a vegetable. All he ever does is gaze at that television. I don't know what happened. One day he was working in California on a job and from what the police tell me. he dropped to his knees. He hasn't been the same since. He's seen every doctor I can find, from California to the best hospitals back east, but no one knows what happened. At first, they thought he had a brain seizure or maybe a heart attack, but there is no evidence of either. Our local church leader claims he has lost his spirituality. I think you have come here for nothing. You won't be able to help him."

"In a way, it is a spiritual thing, Mrs. Nesstor. However, it was nothing your husband did wrong. I knew your husband before his troubles and he's a good man. No matter what happens here today, realize he will always be a good man and loved his family.

"Thank you, Mr. Novo, but like I said, he's been seen by everyone the government could find to look at him. I don't think anything you will do here can help him."

I asked her to give me some space to work. Nesstor's soul was already with me since when I stopped back in Florida, I recaptured his soul from my parent's home. I had my mom create some of the chicken soup from the recipe my grandfather passed down. My recovery time was short because of the soup. Getting past the gatekeeper was an easy chore since this time the gatekeeper took on the aura of J. Edgar Hoover. It was easy to convince Hoover the facts were on my side in Nesstor's case. The last step was to restore the soul of Elliot Nesstor.

Despite my efforts to communicate with him, Nesstor sat in his favorite armchair, his eyes barely following me. He would speak, but the sounds he made were that of a child attempting their first sounds. It was difficult for me to know if he could understand what I was about to do. I took my fingers and gently closed his eyelids, then focused on returning his soul. I could see his wife standing in the doorway making sure I wouldn't harm him any further.

My breathing picked up. My heart pounded. Sweat seeped from my forehead. I could feel his soul lift from my body and find its way home. I opened my eyes to see him staring back at me. My body relaxed to the point where I wasn't sure I could stand easily. I was sitting on the footrest in front of Nesstor.

My hands joined with his. Elliot shook his head and blinked several times. He let go of my hands. He tried to speak, but his wife rushed back into the room to put a wet cloth against his cheeks. She slowly padded his face, as I moved to another chair on the other side of the room.

All my sensations were working at less than capacity. His wife glanced at me to ask if all was ok. "Yes, thank you. I need a moment", I responded. She kept padding her husband's face and forehead, as I watched her husband slowly recognize that he was himself again.

Elliot reached for his wife's hand and told her, "I love you baby. What the hell happened, can you tell me?"

He looked closer at me and mashed his eyes. "Baby, get me my gun, that man over there, he's my prisoner and is dangerous."

I looked back at her and shook my head. I smiled at her and him. "Once a cop always a cop, Mrs. Nesstor. I can assure you I am harmless, to you and your husband. Think about it, I didn't need to come here and do this, so please no reason for panic on anyone's part."

Nesstor sat up in his chair. "Really, Honey, you can't trust that son of a bitch. Get me my gun."

She looked back at me again, then him, "Elliot, the man just brought you back to life, there will be no guns being swung around in my house. You know I don't like guns, plus the kids will be home soon. I can't allow you to shoot a man, who just created a miracle right before my own eyes."

Tears were now streaming down her face as she finally realized what happened. Her husband was again speaking normally. Elliot Nesstor reached around and pulled his wife into his lap. They sat and cried for several minutes. I could have left for my own safety, but my mission was only half-complete.

I watched as the two of them exchanged tender moments, which only made me miss my wife. I hadn't seen her in several weeks. As I sat there watching them, I knew Elliot Nesstor was a good man and ultimately I would be able to trust him with the task I would soon ask of him. I don't think either of them even noticed me for over an hour. Their kids came home and the celebration continued. It wasn't until his oldest boy questioned who I was, did Elliot ask for the room to be cleared so he and I could speak.

"Ok, come clean, who the hell are you and what did you have to do with me being incapacitated? Then I will decide if I call the local Bureau office and have you arrested. Only this time you won't get away."

I decided to do as he asked. I told him the truth. I told him about me, my wife and what happened when his soul was taken. I told him about why he spotted me at crime scenes. I told him everything. When I finished, he looked at me and with a snicker said, "No really tell me the truth. If you don't, I will have you arrested."

"Agent Nesstor, it is all the truth. I could zap you again right now, if you reach for your weapon. Please understand; you will never arrest me. You will never find me again. Our people have hidden in the shadows for centuries. You're a very good cop, but I'm even better at disappearing. Do your wife and children a favor, don't call your local office, don't reach for your gun, and do not think you can ever arrest me. Even if you did arrest me, we have so many connections; I would be released within hours and gone forever."

He stared at me. I wondered if he was starting to believe all I told him was accurate.

"Agent Nesstor, after the FBI reinstates you and let's hope they do, I have a case that could make your career. I can give you many of the sordid details surrounding the drug kingpin in Hawaii. However, I am sorry to report to you, he's another cop. I have photos, names, and locations of stash houses. I have almost everything you would need to crush his network right now."

"And why would I believe you, Mr. Soul person. What's your name again?"

"Cale, and all you have to do is have someone follow up on some of the small potato guys, I will give to you. I want the number one man behind bars. His name is Paulo Kapono. He works for the local police. I feel like I owe you. Consider this my apology for what happened to you and your family. I promise you that this case has enough clout to get you promoted."

"Where'd you get all the intel, Soul Man?"

"All I will tell you is that I robbed the man of his soul, somehow he got it back no sooner than I stole it. He's a bad guy, Agent Nesstor. I am really trying to help you here. You must believe me."

We talked it over well into the evening, until he claimed a football game was about to begin and he wanted to watch it. He offered to speak with me more in the morning, but I wanted to go home. I also needed more soup that was in a canister in my car, before I was too weak to get to the car. We agreed to talk again later in the week, after he had time to reach out to his boss in Washington. He wasn't sure he would be able to get his job back. No one was going to believe the truth. He had to think about what to say.

It seemed like years since I was in California with my wife and son. Kalani was there when I arrived. She claimed to have just arrived home from an assignment in Arizona. I wanted to believe her, but I had to admit I now had my suspicions of her. I was home for a couple of days before I brought up the topic of her going to Hawaii and seeing Kapono.

"I need the truth. Tell me what you were doing in Hawaii."

"What makes you think I was in Hawaii, my love?" Kalani said.

"Were you back in Hawaii, when your assignment was in Arizona? The Council tells me you were in Hawaii. And did you see Paulo Kapono?"

"Cale, I have no idea why you're asking me these questions, and I really don't appreciate your tone. I can assure you, I haven't been anywhere near Hawaii since my soul was restored. You asked me to stay away and I have. Now can we move on from this topic?"

What was I to think? Why would the Council lie to me or why would Kalani? It was clear, someone was. I was torn in not knowing whom I could trust any longer. I searched my own mind to ask for guidance from Mikael , but none was forthcoming. I sat with my thoughts for days not knowing what was up and what was down any longer.

Later in the week, I spoke with Agent Nesstor. He was given his job back, but it would be behind a desk until the medical people would clear him to return to full duties. He informed me that he did pass along some of the information I had given to him about Kapono, and his network.

All my information was true. Nesstor's boss asked to meet with me personally, but I declined. I had no way of knowing if I would be able to walk out of the meeting without being arrested, despite being innocent. I offered more information with the agreement that I would send along a photo of my wife. If anyone saw her in the area, I wanted to be contacted immediately.

Nesstor and his boss balked about me not meeting with them in person.

"We will search you out, Novo," Nesstor said.

"I live in the shadows," Detective. I will see you long before you see me. And you don't want me to find you first. Besides, I can be a great asset to your agency."

They agreed to see it my way as long as my evidence continued to be credible.

After another week at home, both Kalani and I were given new assignments. Hers was close to home, but mine was back east in New York City. I packed my bags and caught the red eye that evening. It seemed like a quick assignment and I assured Kalani I'd be home within the week. I was assigned to remove the soul of a man, who owned a title company and had been arrested for stealing hundreds of thousands of dollars in escrow funds for large real estate deals.

Ryan Jaxson was arrested at the airport, while trying to flee to South America. My problem was I couldn't get a photo or touch him. A judge declared him a flight risk and was denied bail. I would have to steal it from behind prison bars.

Mr. Jaxson denied my request to see him several times. This was going to be more difficult than I had predicted. One day while scheming on how to get inside the prison to see him, I received a call from Agent Nesstor.

"Hello, Cale. I wanted to let you know that the FBI busted the case wide open and arrested Paulo Kapono. I wanted to call you and personally thank you. However, we did run into one small problem. When the boys went in and raided the main stash house, they scooped up your wife. We have her in custody. The Director wants to meet with you in person before we release her. We can't charge her with much and the Director is willing to look the other way since you helped us, but you must meet him in Hawaii. I can't be there because they still won't let me get on a darn airplane."

"Please don't BS me, Elliot. Do you really have her in custody and why can't a lawyer handle this? Why does he have to meet with me personally before releasing her? Are you trying to get us both in custody?"

"It's not a set up. The Director wants to do something to repay you for giving us one of the biggest cases we had all year. Drug Enforcement is trying to take credit since they'd been sitting on Kapono for months, but the information you gave us really led to his arrest. He wants you in Honolulu as soon as you can. If you do as he asks, he won't process your wife."

I had to think. Why did he really want to meet me? Kalani should be out on bail in a day. I was tempted to let her suffer for disobeying me, but I didn't want her photo or identification in the judicial system. I would assume they ran her prints and found nothing, but I knew I had to risk meeting with the FBI director in person. We negotiated the meeting to take place in an open area, in the Sheraton Hotel on Waikiki Beach.

Two days later, I met with the Director of the FBI, Ken Richards. He wasn't the only one from his agency in the hotel, but I was assured I wouldn't be arrested. They really had nothing to charge me with, other than Nesstor finding me suspicious. Other than that, they could try to say I evaded arrest months earlier, but I had a feeling they wanted more from me.

"Mr. Novo, I have no clue who you really are, or what your story is, other than what Agent Nesstor has told me," Richards said. "I suspect there is so much more to know. We've run a background check on you using data from around the world, and we have nothing on you or your wife. We don't even have a birth record. Why is that, Sir?"

I gave the tall thin man a long look. "Director Richards, I have told my story one too many times now. I am a disciple of a group, who removes souls from the undeserving. It has been going on for centuries and I suspect will go on for centuries more. I have committed no crimes in your land or any other. I will be pleased to help your agency in the future, like I have this time. However, if you continue to dig into my background or my wife's, you will never see either of us again. We are very good at disappearing into thin air. I suggest you accept my terms which are, release my wife and I will continue to provide Agent Nesstor with valuable information in the future."

"That's just it, Mr. Novo. Where do you get your information?"

"If I told you, you would never believe me."

"Try me. I'm an open minded man."

I was losing my patience. I didn't see Kalani anywhere in plain sight, but I did see enough dark suits to know it wouldn't be easy to leave without giving the man something.

"Director, if you really want the truth, I can see into your soul. I can see into the man over there, the woman with her kids, and the man with the dark glasses, who likely works for you by the door. Him. I would do another background check on if I were you." I laughed but he didn't seem amused.

"Oh? And why should I review Agent Tanner's background?"

"Well, there is black, there is white in a soul and then there are shades of grey like I see in Agent Tanner. I am not saying he has committed any crimes, maybe he is depressed, or cheats on his wife, or has lost faith that the world is a beautiful place. I really don't know. But I can tell you with certainty that he has a soul in need of repair, but not bad enough yet to remove."

The man looked at Tanner than back at me. "I'm a very logical man, Mr. Novo, and what you're telling me, quite frankly, I don't believe a word of it. If you want your wife released, you will tell me the truth about how you knew about Kapono and how you made Nesstor come out of that coma he was in for weeks."

His frown annoyed me. Honest was supposed to be the best policy, this time I was willing to stretch it.

"Director Richards, my wife had followed the drug cartel here for months. I read her journal and I gave Nesstor the information contained in it. I work for a highly skilled network of people and we at times run into criminals. We have no authority to arrest them, and I never carry a weapon. I assure you, I can see into your soul. I also believe that you deep down believe me to some degree, because you are a spiritual man. You have a clean soul. I suspect even though you deal in crime on a daily basis you believe in the goodness of the world and the goodness in people. I suspect you are a family man and have a strong faith. That's why you are going to release my wife and accept my offer, because part of you wants to believe me. As far as Elliot Nesstor, he is a good man, who was caught in a bad spot. I made sure he got his life and soul restored. I cannot prove it beyond that. I am forbidden to take souls without permission, and if I did take one now, only to prove to you that I can, my family would suffer. You can trust me enough to release my wife, or I will find another way to have my wife released. It's now your call."

He remained reluctant to release her, until I thought of a better plan. It was highly risky since I wouldn't know how it would affect the man, but Director Richards agreed with my idea. I think he was more curious than eager to make a trip back east.

The next day, he arranged for me to meet with Ryan Jaxson in federal prison. He and Elliot Nesstor were watching from behind a glass wall. I finished my mission. Jaxson slumped in his chair. I felt woozy as several men rushed in. I think they were stunned at what they saw, and were afraid to do anything more than release me back into the streets with my wife. Both Richards and Nesstor escorted us to a cab with Richards offering a parting shot.

"Keep your wife away from Hawaii for at least a year. I still think that was done with hypnosis but then again, I'm afraid to have you try it on me. Besides, I'm not releasing you because of that. I am because Elliot Nesstor is a fine man and his wife is a fine woman. She believes you saved him and she personally asked me to help you. Consider it your one time get out of jail free card. Now take your wife and get lost."

Kalani and I vanished into the shadows.

CHAPT3R TW3NTY $3V3N

My anger boiled over with my wife. The taxi driver taking us to the airport had to ask the two of us to keep the noise down, or he would stop the car. I couldn't understand why Kalani would have any reason to return to Hawaii and see Paulo Kapono.

"Cale, you need to stop your yelling and let me explain. Paulo insisted I return or he would hurt Nic. Besides, I wanted to see if I could find out how he got his soul returned, since you told me that you stole it from him. It was important for me to see him in person to let him know that if he didn't stop with his threats, that either you or I would remove his soul again."

"I want to believe you, Kalani. I really do, but you kept this all to yourself and let's face it; had you told me about Kapono's threats, he never would have found Nic or you, nor would that embarrassment of a cop still own his soul."

"I thought I could handle it. You had enough going on without him burdening you."

It was a silent trip back to California after our initial argument. I was starting to learn that as strong as your body can be physically, if your mind is confused, it is hard to function properly. I had enough of all the lies, and not knowing, who was telling the truth. My body couldn't sustain the pace it had been running at for weeks. I collapsed into a deep sleep on the flight home.

As I slept on the flight, Mikael came to me in a dream. It was hard to remember all of it, but when I awoke, I could remember the words he stated many times, "There cannot be good where there is no evil. Your test will be to control the evil that lurks inside you."

When we arrived home, I attempted to relax. There was an uneasiness that I never felt before around Kalani. I wanted to believe her, but I wasn't a fool. I didn't believe her story. She had changed. She tried a few times to defend her actions about being in Hawaii, but I was having none of it. She tried to play it off on me that I was somehow the bad husband, since I no longer trusted her every word. My heart wanted to believe her, my mind did not.

The next day, we were both summoned to meet with the Council. I was confused as to why, since I knew I'd been doing everything expected of me. Kalani swore to me despite being in Hawaii, she had done nothing wrong. She was as perplexed as I was as to why we had were requested to stand in front of the Council. I made a quick phone call to Agent Nesstor and asked him to have someone interrogate Kapono about Kalani.

"Ask him if he had her do any of her voodoo magic."

He got back to me the following day. Kapono swore she had done nothing for him in months. However, we were both asked to once again return to the compound and appear before the High Council.

I had become far too familiar with the coldness of the Council room. The walls that I would assume were once white were now turning a depressing soft grey. The dark wood dais, where the Council sat was raised on a platform several feet off the ground. This way they could look down upon whoever came before them. The floor was made of marble and no matter the time of year, it was cold as ice. It made me ill every time I walked into the room.

"Caeles and Kalani Novo, you've been called here because once again the two of you have broken our laws. Do either of you have anything to say before we hand down our punishment?"

We looked at each other. I had no idea what Elder Orcus was implying. Kalani shrugged at me.

"Council, please explain what laws were broken."

"For you, Caeles, it was because you did not watch over your wife as promised to this Council. For your wife, she has yet again taken a soul without permission."

Kalani pointed her finger at Orcus and moved towards him. "That's a damn lie. I have done no such thing!"

I believed my wife. I wrapped her in my arms as if to shield her from the Council.

"Council, I demand proof of such an accusation! She has taken no forbidden soul."

"The man's name is Danny Kapu and was a drug enforcement officer investigating Paulo Kapono. He worked undercover. When it was discovered he was a cop, Kapono had your wife remove his soul."

Kalani denied the accusation. "I have never met the man, nor did I remove his soul. It's a damn lie."

"Council, before traveling to meet you, I had an officer interrogate Paulo Kapono and he was asked specifically if Kalani had done any work for him in recent months. He said no."

Orcus rose from his seat and pointed back, "You would believe a murdering soulless drug dealer over this Council?"

"I believe in the truth, and the truth is, I believe in my wife. Since you brought up the subject, Kapono had his soul returned to him. Why would that be and who did it?"

The room went quiet. The six members all peered at each other, before leaving the room. Kalani and I stood alone in the cold room for several minutes. I begged her to tell me the truth, but she reiterated that she had not taken any unauthorized souls.

I knew I had to stand with her. I didn't want to believe she could lie to me any longer.

I pulled her close enough for our heartbeats to join in perfect rhythm. As our hearts pounded away, I could for the first time since I knew her, feel her body shake because of the unknown. I gently ran my hand through her hair. I stared into her eyes, assuring her no harm would come from any decision handed down from the Council.

The six men reappeared through an ancient wooden door and again took their seats at the dais. The stern look on each of their faces did not bode well for our future. Five men took their seats, one moved toward Kalani and me. Elder Orcus looked back again towards the door and with a wave of his hand; my son emerged into the Council room. Orcus had him stand to my right with Kalani already to my left. Disgust was in Orcus's dark eyes.

"Our decision is final, Caeles Novo. You were warned of dire consequences if you failed to meet the obligations in our previous agreement. You failed and must now suffer your punishment. You must choose between your wife and your child. One will be lost to you forever. This is the penalty for your wife disobeying the Council and you not being responsible for her actions. You have failed in being responsible for Kalani, and you Kalani have failed in not obeying our laws."

This could not be happening to us. I believed Kalani. She hadn't disobeyed any laws and I had lived up to my responsibilities. I refused to accept the penalty.

"I reject your thoughts of what he have and have not done and I refuse to accept your outrageous punishment. I will not choose because we are leaving."

Orcus moved close. I was doing all I could not to show fear, yet I failed.

"You're weak, Caeles," Orcus said. "I see fear in you. Leaders may fear, but do not show it in the face of danger. You'll never be on this Council because your fear has been exposed. We as a Council must face difficult choices in order to lead our disciples. However, you, Caeles, you have failed on so many levels and don't even know it. Again, I offer you the choice of punishment, your son or wife."

I looked at my son. He was unaware of all that was taking place. Kalani held her hands to her face, her eyes streaming with tears. I could see her knees begin to bend as if she was ready to fall to the floor. I tried to keep my wits about me and find a way out of this pending disaster.

"Caeles, you had the power all along to delve into Kalani's soul and see the truth. It's what we do on the Council every day. Instead, you only searched into your heart, never investigating her soul. The truth was always there for you to see. You were too weak to observe the truth. You will never be the leader we need on this Council. You have failed us. You failed your family, and now yourself. Had you faced your fear and used your power to probe deep into her soul, you would have known the truth. One last time, your son or your wife, make your decision."

Orcus was right. I was fearful of what I would see. I never used my own abilities to see the truth. I didn't trust the one person who deserved my trust. This time when looking at my son and wife, I did dig into their souls. My son's was beaming with goodness. I spied Kalani's as well. It was as pure as it had been the day it was redeemed. It was impossible for her to have taken any souls not authorized by the Council. Why would the Council want to ruin us? We had done nothing wrong. I stood motionless desperately trying to defend my family.

Orcus stretched his long wretched fingers out and placed them on the shoulders of both my wife and son. Their bodies became like statues, only still in the flesh. The sorrow and frustration that poured from Kalani went silent. My son's face now had a sign of hopelessness frozen across it. I had to turn away.

I wanted to refuse the thought that Orcus had stolen their souls because my body had no reaction. Had he taken their souls, I would have had an instant reaction. Confusion filled my thoughts. What had he done to my family?

Orcus scowled at me and announced, "Leave this Council chamber now. Do not return until we call for you, my mindless pawn. Forget your family. They are dead to you now. We on the Council were worried that one day you would be a true rival, one that could force us to alter our ways. Instead, you're nothing. I pity ones like you, who come here to disobey and mock our laws. Cowards, who when it is time to fight, leave in a puddle of tears. Maybe you're correct. Some do deserve redemption, but as long as I am on this Council, our laws remain. Now leave and wait for your next assignment."

Shock consumed me. How could anyone be so cruel, yet declare himself to be the leader of anyone? Was this man worthy to be my leader? My family was frozen and I had no idea what to do. I wanted to fight, but I had lost everything. I died from the inside out. I turned to leave, feeling like the coward.

A few steps from the door a vision of Mikael appeared before me. For the first time his vision was one of defiance. "Caeles, you cannot experience goodness until you face evil. There is evil in all of us." The vision vanished.

I circled back in the direction of the Council. The fear of the unknown was evident among the five Council members, as I stared at them now standing at their seats on the dais. I couldn't not tell if they were more fearful of Orcus or me. Orcus stood between my wife and son as if he had claimed the rights to my family.

My beautiful wife and child were motionless. My desire to destroy the monster, who took my family quickened with every second. However as young and powerful as I was, I still wasn't sure I could out maneuver six men, with the combined power far more than me.

Orcus did make the comment that the Council feared I would be a rival. Maybe the Council did not fear me as a rival, only Orcus. Was it Orcus, who feared me more than I did him? Since I had grown stronger than any one member of the Council, including Orcus, maybe I wasn't up against six men. I only knew I could no longer be their puppet on a string.

I marched back towards Orcus, my disdain for him growing with every footstep. His bitterness towards me was evident as he gnashed his teeth. Orcus raised his chin in defiance as I grabbed his arm. All the evil that was locked in all the souls I had stolen over the years was now pulsating through my veins. Evil consumed me. Yet, I felt alive like never before.

Peering into his dark eyes, I witnessed the fear in Charon Orcus. I reached inside the repulsive creature, who I once respected, and ripped out his darkened soul. Our once exalted leader collapsed to one knee begging for my forgiveness and redemption. I hovered over his body that looked insignificant to me. Anger pierced my soul. I understood evil like never before.

The five remaining Council members huddled. I stood in silence with Orcus at my feet. The beat of my heart slowed as my body slowly lowered itself to rest on the cold marble floor. The body of Charon Orcus twitched beside me. I hated the feeling of evil flowing through me, but I realized at least for this moment in time, it was necessary. I suddenly recognized what Mikael meant when he declared that you cannot know true goodness until you understand and defeat evil.

My thoughts turned to a conversation I had with my grandfather the last time he had seen me. He informed me that he controlled three votes on the Council. Was it possible that Orcus acted outside his boundaries as leader of the Council and not just with me? Had the Council grown weary of his abuse of others? Were they terrified to remove him as leader? Did the remaining Council members use me to eliminate their problem? Could my own grandfather have used me in such a way to jeopardize my own health and the security of my family? What was his purpose in making sure I knew he could control three of the six votes on the Council?

Now facing the Council, I noticed my grandfather waving me towards the seat previously occupied by Charon Orcus. I lifted my head but could not move.

"Council Members, this is my grandson. He is of pure blood dating back to our founding. The documents were manipulated to conceal his identity. He matches all the criteria demanded in our laws for him to sit on this High Council. In our agreement with him, should he obey, he was promised a seat beside us when the next opening occurred. I submit to you, there is an opening."

I was too busy attempting to understand all that happened to care about their chattering back and forth. I gazed at my wife and son. I wept. No seat on any council could replace my wife and child. My first mission would be to find an antidote for whatever spell Orcus had cast upon them. I stood slowly and approached my beloved Kalani and Nic. I caressed the tenderness in my wife's skin. I could see in her eyes she was captive and needed my help. My son, so pure, so docile, how could any being want to hurt such a child? I fell to my knees and wrapped my arms around each of them. I wept until I felt the hand of my grandfather on my shoulder.

"I know you are in pain, Cale. I can assure you, we will have every scholar on our staff scour our books to determine what Orcus did to your family. There is a remedy, and we will find it. Once we do, Kalani will again be your trusted partner and your son will find himself on this Council when he comes of age. However, for now, it has been determined it is time for you to take your rightful place among us. There is a majority vote for you to replace Charon Orcus and lead this Council. It is our highest honor."

"Grandfather, how can you ask or expect me to accept the responsibility of being among our disciples leaders when moments ago, I was running in fear?"

"It is precisely because you overcame your fear. Not only did you overcame your fear, you now fully understand our most basic principle. It has always been your destiny, Caeles. Do not fear it any longer, embrace it."

My belief in our most basic principle was why I restored Dylan's soul years ago. I did it because I believed almost all souls deserve a second chance.

Everyone has the capacity to be good or evil. Humans at times lose sight of what is important in life, because they don't know how to control the evil that sits in all of us. At times humans become mired up in acquiring assets or power and become blinded by things that in the end don't seem so important. Evil creeps into our souls, and many cannot find a way to get it back under control. I pray that should the day come that I lose sight of all that is good and seek redemption, it will be granted. After all, I am human. Well sort of.

Buddha stated, "There has to be evil so that good can prove its purity above it."

Possibly Charon Orcus fell to being human with human faults. Over time, the power of being a leader allowed evil to sink into his soul. The best leaders understand how to control the temptations of using their power for personal gains. When not, that is when evil can find its way into your soul. You do not have to be a leader of others to be a leader. Everyone is the leader of their own destiny. It's why you've been given the power to know the difference between good and evil.

When evil wins the internal battle for your soul, you are lost. You might think you're alone and the only one who feels that way. You are not. It's been the mission of this Council to identify those of you who feel that way. We will cleanse your soul and offer you a second chance. A third chance is forbidden, so make your choices wisely.

My next mission will be to find a cure for my family. Once I succeed, I will make sure the Council regains its focus and restore the ability to offer redemption for those who seek it. Should you ever fall; the Council will be lurking in the shadows. Should you ever need and obtain a second chance in warding off evil in your soul, don't abuse it. Redemption was a promise sent down from the heavens long before you or I existed. It is a promise that will exist long after you and I have vanished from this earth. I have found my destiny. I have peace in my soul. Seek and you shall find yours.

FINAL WORDS

A friend of mine would tease years ago about how he didn't believe that computers were here to stay. He still uses film in his camera. The digital age has changed publishing. Readers and authors can debate if the change is for the good or bad.

Soul Intentions was originally released in 2012. In late 2016, I began to make more of an effort to market my work. One of the changes was to develop a new website. The first version of this book had the old website noted in the front, now it's the new one.

Soul Intentions was my third release. As I write this in early 2017, my ninth book, True Justice is being readied for publication. My tenth book, the next of my Presidential series is being written.

My writing style has changed over the years. Some readers claim they don't see much of a difference, but I know it's changed. For example in my first book, A Beautiful Song, I didn't use as much dialog as I do in later works. There are other style differences as well, but I'll let you read the others and see if you can spot a change.

To all my readers, thank you. Please send me a note and say hello. I answer all my email and appreciate hearing from you.

www.ingramcontent.com/pod-product-compliance
Lightning Source LLC
Chambersburg PA
CBHW070322260626
47160CB00003B/914